The opening sentence of "I Had Sex with a Martian" warns its readers, "If you are at all shocked by startling unconventionality and descriptions of male sexual members, do not read my story."

Here are 24 previously unpublished stories from the noir master, Gil Brewer. Beyond the fact that Brewer wrote outstanding short stories, an important reason to read his shorter works is artistic freedom. Brewer's obsessive theme was the destructive power of human sexuality, and he had greater freedom to explore this literary terrain in magazines than books.

But the stories in this collection exist for more than their sexual content (nor do they all have explicit content). They represent a range of noirish responses to the literary marketplace of the 1970s, when Brewer was casting about and targeting publications ranging from *Boys' Life* to *Hustler*. These 24 stories are by turns artistic and vulgar, enjoyable and off putting, accessible and challenging. Together, they form a fascinating final chapter in Gil Brewer's career as a story writer.

DIE ONCE—DIE TWICE

More Unpublished Stories of
Gil Brewer

Edited by
David Rachels

Stark House Press • Eureka California
www.starkhousepress.com

DIE ONCE—DIE TWICE

Published by Stark House Press
1315 H Street
Eureka, CA 95501
griffinskye3@sbcglobal.net
www.starkhousepress.com

PHOTO CREDITS:
Back cover and pages 8 (right), 10, 12, and 14 (bottom): Courtesy of Gil Brewer Papers, American
    Heritage Center, University of Wyoming.
Pages 7 and 14 (top): Courtesy of Marvin N. and Dorrie Lee.
Page 8 (left): Courtesy of Julia M. Rhodes.

ISBN: 978-1-944520-88-5

Book design by Jeff Vorzimmer *¡caliente!Design*, Austin, Texas
Cover Illustration by Angel Badia Camps

First Stark House Press Edition: January 2020

Table of Contents

Introduction

I.

I have always done the wrong thing.
Gil Brewer
October 7, 1974

Noir writer Gilbert John Brewer first appears in the St. Petersburg (Florida) City Directory in 1948. He is living with his parents, and his name is listed, erroneously, as Gilbert T. Brewer, Jr. He is two years away from selling his first short story, and his occupation is listed, optimistically, as "author."

The St. Petersburg city directories were compiled by R. L. Polk & Co. from a door-to-door canvassing of the city. Presumably, the Polk canvasser found the aspiring writer working at his typewriter and eager to proclaim his career.

Brewer was not a native Floridian. His hometown was Canandaigua, New York, and on March 8, 1943, he had enlisted in the army in nearby Rochester. While he was away serving in World War II, his parents, Gilbert Thomas and Ruth, moved to Florida, a growing haven for retirees. When their son returned from Europe, he joined them in St. Petersburg to live rent-free while pursuing his literary dreams.

Brewer in France during World War II.

In the 1949 city directory, Brewer is still living with his parents, and he is now listed, still optimistically, as "writer." Soon, his mother would kick him out of the house because he refused to get a paying job.

There was no city directory in 1950.

By 1951, much had changed for Brewer. He appears at his own address in the city directory—160 21st Avenue South—and he is listed with his wife, "B. Verlaine." Again he is listed as "author," but now this isn't just wishful thinking—or at least it wouldn't be for much longer. 1951 would be the first and most successful year of his professional career, as he would publish his first three short stories and his first three novels, including his million-seller, *13 French Street.* By the end of 1951, "author" was his actual occupation.

Gil waiting for a check.

Author portrait, October 1951.

Brewer's 1952 appearance in the city directory adds a small wrinkle. Gil and Verlaine are now at 1016 24th Avenue North, and in addition to their names, the listing identifies Joseph T. Shaw as Brewer's literary agent. It is difficult to imagine that users of the directory would have found this information useful, but that may not have been the point. Just as Brewer proclaimed himself a professional "author" and "writer" before that was really the case, he now took the visit from the Polk canvasser as an occasion to brag that he had an agent. The name of his agent would not appear in the city directory again.

Now things settle down for the Brewers, at least as far as the city directory is concerned. They move in 1954 and again in 1956, when they first appear at 344 20th Avenue South. They would live at this address, and also in the back at 344½, until 1974.

In 1974, Gil Brewer's career was circling the drain. He had already published the last novels that would bear his name, three spin-offs from the TV series *It Takes a Thief*. The TV series ran from 1968 to 1970, and Brewer's novels appeared in 1969 and 1970. Brewer's name no longer meant anything to readers. For years he had been billed as AUTHOR OF *13 FRENCH STREET*, but that wasn't going to sell books anymore. He never stopped working on novels that he hoped would appear under his own name, but the novels that he managed to publish after 1970 appeared as by Harry Arvay, Mark Bailey, Al Conroy, Hal Ellson, Elaine Evans, Luke Morgann, and Ellery Queen. His nearest miss at financial stability came in 1974 when he failed an audition to ghostwrite for Don Pendleton's Executioner series. Brewer completed a full manuscript, *Firebase Seattle*, which he sent to his agent on August 23, 1974. It was returned to him less than a month later, and the following year, a different *Firebase Seattle* was published as *The Executioner #21*.

On October 6 or 7, 1974, Brewer scrawled his state of mind on a legal pad. His handwriting suggests drunkenness:

> Back in 1949 I wrote a story called "It's Always Too Late." It sold. This is true, isn't it? The title. It's 1974 now.
>
> I had it.
>
> I've got to get it back. I'm nearly 52. You think you'll always be young.
>
> All I wanted was $25 a week, a wife who loved me, and a place to work.
>
> I got them.
>
> Now I <u>need</u> more. And want more!
>
> --
>
> No mail.
>
> No understanding of me.
>
> The promise I knew I had—gone?
>
> Bickering.
>
> Nerves.
>
> I am dead alive.
>
> My tooth that was pulled is not healing correctly.
>
> At the typewriter I get pains in the chest and moreso in the left side of the chest, under the arm.
>
> Fear fills me.
>
> The medications are wrong.
>
> Spirit. Where are you?
>
> I sometimes feel spirit, in small tokens.
>
> I have so much in my head, but it lies dormant.
>
> I don't know what to do anymore.

On an undated sheet of paper, Brewer typed, perhaps more soberly:

It's sometimes difficult to come up with the right kind of situation for the proposed new book. Often, the mind is contaminated with situations which, while not actually trite, are obviously trite when viewed in comparison with what has been published during the past eight years in the pocketbook field. The idea itself may be very good, and quite entertaining, but to my mind this is all a lot of shit, so why trouble yourself with it? It won't change anything.

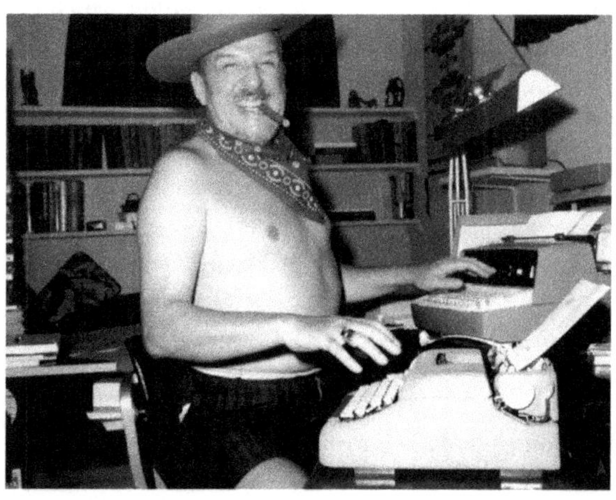

And yet, despite the drunkenness and the self-pity, Brewer kept writing. At some point during the final years of his career, he wrote an odd tribute to his own indefatigability, a poem he titled "Ode to the Slow Establishment of a Disconcerting Personality":

Turds
       come
and

Turds
     go

BUT

Brewer
      goes on
Forever.

In the 1975 city directory, the Brewers lose their first names. The tenants of Apartment 404 in the Whitehall Convertible Apartments, 3301 58th Avenue South, are listed simply as "Brewer." If Gil or Verlaine answered the door, they may not have felt chatty, though it seems more likely that the canvasser talked to no one and found "Brewer" on the apartment's mailbox. That year, Brewer published four of his last five novels, thrillers ghostwritten from raw manuscripts by an Israeli soldier named Harry Arvay. In 1976, Brewer published his last novel, *Togo Commando*, the fifth Arvay thriller, and that was it. After 25 years, Gil Brewer's career as a novelist was over.

Brewer's first published novel, ghostwritten for Day Keene.

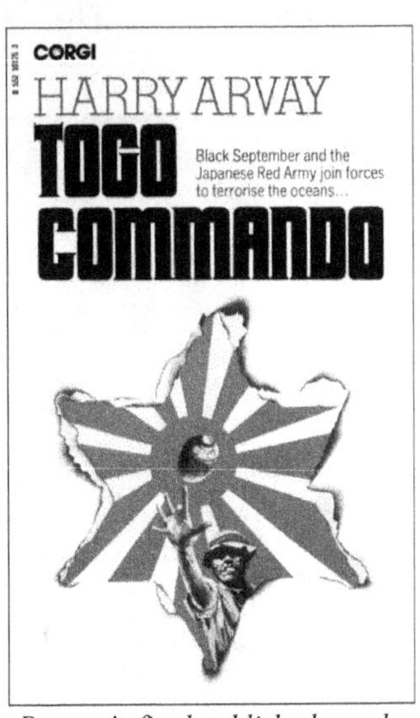

Brewer's final published novel, ghostwritten for Harry Arvay.

Now in the city directory, things get strange. In 1976, Gil and Verlaine are no longer living together (which may also have been the case in 1975, but if so, the city directory did not capture it). Gil is in Apartment 107 of Southgate Towers at 5790 34th Street South. Verlaine remains in Apartment 404 of the Whitehall Convertible Apartments at 3301 58th Avenue South, which sounds far away but is actually next door. Gil was a night owl who liked his apartment freezing cold. He loved his jazz records and his cornet, and Verlaine wanted to sleep. So they separated. But each morning, Verlaine would leave her apartment and cross two small parking lots to Gil's building. There she would make Gil breakfast and spend her day. When night came, she would cross the parking lots back to her own apartment for warmth and quiet.

"Gil Brewer," however, is gone from the 1976 city directory. While Verlaine appears in her apartment, unremarkably, as "Mrs. Verlaine Brewer," Gil appears, bizarrely, as "Galio R. Brewer."

Galio R. Brewer? Is this a mistake? An alias? A drunken joke? A poetic suggestion of Galileo? Galahad? Ernest and Julio Gallo wine? And what of the middle initial? Gil's middle name was John.

However "Galio" originated, it kept going: Gil appears as Galio in the city directory seven times, every year from 1976 to 1982, the year before he died. It would be surprising to learn that the Polk canvasser actually spoke to Gil each year. At this point in his life, Brewer was not much inclined to answer the door. His apartment had two entrances: a front door to an inner hallway of the apartment building and a sliding glass door to a tiny patio that was just a few steps from the parking lot. Gil preferred to use the patio door.

When Brewer was asked to ghostwrite a series of novels for Israeli soldier Harry Arvay, he turned to dictation.

In Verlaine's brief memoir of Gil, she writes, "The last seven years of his life were miserable. . . . The bottle was his only solace." Sometimes late at night, when Verlaine was ensconced in her own apartment, Gil would sit at his typewriter and pour out his heart to her. On April 16, 1982, he wrote,

Dearest Verlaine:—

I just want you to know that I appreciate everything you try so hard to do for me: all that you do do. I'm conscious of your every effort, even when it seems I'm not. I think of you always, and love you very much. I know you go out of your way to do things for me, when you don't very much want to do them, hate them, in fact. I wish I could remedy this, and it's what I'm trying to work toward. . . .

You mean so much to me, Verlaine. You know this, but I like to tell you, anyway. I wish we could somehow live together, perhaps even in adjoining efficiency apartments, if nothing more. It would help so much. . . .

This isn't much of a letter, but it's something; it's an attempt to tell you how much I love you and appreciate you and all you do. Please try to understand my position. I'm working with all my volition to attain some success again. Please bear with me, and forgive me for [my] mistakes. I'm trying, and I love you deeply. . . .

Love,
THE TOOTHLESS, BACK-ACHEY, GELPLESS GALLANT

Gil Brewer died with a mountain of empty gin bottles under his bed, along with one empty bottle of Aqua Velva aftershave. He may have learned to drink Aqua Velva in France, back when it was a mouthwash. Desperate soldiers would imbibe it when no other alcohol was available.

Gil's body was cremated. His ashes were scattered in the woods behind Southgate Towers, where he lived his last years and wrote many of the stories in this collection.

II.

"It's a squall!" Chuck shouted.

Wind and rain lashed at the small
outboard.

"We should never've come out into the
Gulf," Billy Martin said. "This boat won't
stand it."

> —opening of Gil Brewer,
>   "The Ghost of Hermit Key"
>   early 1970s, intended for *Boys' Life*

I was in Florida that July, licensed,
bonded, with a palm-frond hat business
on the side. I lived on the Gulf, and
Valerie Dedrickson sucked my cock every
night; drunk all the time and with a coral-
rock fireplace and a polar bear rug. We
fucked on the rug and smashed bottles in
the fireplace. It was fine.

> —opening of Gil Brewer,
>   "Death with a Ten Foot Pole"
>   later 1970s, intended for *Hustler*

In the years after Gil Brewer's death, as he crept into the canon of classic noir, he was decidedly middle tier. If you were a fan of the genre, chances are that you would want to read his half-dozen best novels, and maybe even a few beyond that, but writers of this stature do not often have their stories collected. That distinction is usually reserved for the giants—Hammett, Chandler, Woolrich, McBain, Block, and the like. So why are Gil Brewer's stories worth collecting and reading?

Brewer in his 1957 Porsche 356A Coupe.

After crashing his Porsche, Brewer had a typing desk specially made so that he could write in bed.

Beyond the fact that Brewer wrote outstanding short stories, an important reason to read his shorter works is artistic freedom. Brewer's obsessive theme was the destructive power of human sexuality, and he had greater freedom to explore this literary terrain in magazines than books. His great noir stories of the 1950s appeared in digest-sized magazines with names like *Accused, Guilty, Pursuit,* and *Manhunt.* These magazines did not aim for the same respectability as the era's leading publisher of noir novels, Gold Medal Books. As a result, story writers had considerably more freedom than did novelists. As well, there is a natural shift in judgment when an editor is deciding whether to publish something short: What might seem an unhealthy subject for detailed exploration over the course of 200 pages may be acceptable at one-twentieth that length. Or, to put it another way, whereas *Manhunt* was willing to publish a 4000-word Brewer story about a panty-snatcher, a Gold Medal novel with the same protagonist would have been unthinkable.

Indeed, when Gold Medal rejected Brewer's work, it was often because his writing was too sexual. For example, they rejected *Gun the Man Down* for having "too much sex, and most of it . . . of a filthy kind," and they rejected *Shadow on the Dust* because the novel "[depended] entirely upon sex to carry it through." Brewer would have seen these rejections as a kind of denial: As much as Gold Medal might protest that his novels were too sexual, Brewer felt that he was telling the truth about human nature. In a 1967 interview, he went so far as to suggest that sex drive and human nature *were the same thing:* "sex, of course, is the big element we deal with in life every day—the push and pull of human nature." Thus, when Brewer was not free to portray sex as freely as he wished, he was not free to portray his understanding of the human condition.

Of course, Brewer's primary goal as a writer was *not* to help his readers understand the human condition. More than anything, he was trying to make a living. He had abandoned art for art's sake circa 1949 when he quit writing overtly literary novels in favor of selling to Gold Medal. But in the 1970s, two decades after his Gold Medal heyday, Brewer was having difficulty selling both novels and stories. In searching for new markets, he was willing to try anything as long as it was fiction. Given his thematic predilections, an easy market for him to exploit was pornographic novels, and he published five of them, all in 1972: *Mouth Magic* (as Mark Bailey), and *More Than a Handful!*, *Ladies in Heat*, *Gamecock*, and *Tongue Tricks!* (all by Luke Morgann). As well, Brewer found a market for a few of his stories in men's magazines such as *Swank*, *Cavalier*, and *Stag*.

Much had changed since the days when Gold Medal had balked at Brewer's rampant (and by today's standards, mild) sexuality. Now there were publishers able and willing to publish content that would have resulted in obscenity trials in the 1950s. (In fact, *Manhunt*'s April 1957 issue *did* lead to an obscenity charge, but Brewer did not have a story in that issue.) In this new era of artistic freedom, Brewer did his best to provide permissive publishers with what they wanted. Though he did not publish in the Greenleaf Reader series, Brewer studied their requirements, which contained two paragraphs of such importance that they were entirely in capital letters:

THE APPEAL OF THESE BOOKS SHOULD LIE IN PROVIDING THE READER WITH VICARIOUS SEXUAL EXPERIENCES OF A PLEASURE/GRATIFICATION NATURE BY PRESENTING CHARACTERS WITH WHOM HE CAN IDENTIFY TO SOME EXTENT, EVEN THOUGH THEY INDULGE IN PRACTICES OUTSIDE THE "SOCIALLY ACCEPTABLE NORM". . . .

THE GIRL MAY SECRETLY OR OPENLY ENJOY SEX WITH THE PROTAGONIST AND/OR ANTAGONIST BUT, A LOUSE REMAINS A LOUSE AND A HERO A HERO. A DOG VILLIAN *[sic]* DOES NOT BECOME A NICE GUY JUST BECAUSE HE'S GOT A 9-INCH PENIS.

Another sex publisher attached a note to its guidelines that further emphasized,

No super-studism allowed[,] i.e. men can only make love for so long a time then they must rest. If they go at it more than once, it must be logical and reasonable. They do not keep it up . . . or the action either . . . all night long. Likewise, females can't be totally insatiable . . . and both sexes must sleep now and then. The men are hung like men, not like characters in books, and the women aren't necessarily always ready and willing. There is some definite concern for contraception and pregnancy to the extent that it actually occurs. [ellipses in original]

But the most important characteristic of these novels was "flip appeal," which meant that "sex scenes, or at least sexual thoughts, must appear on virtually every page, so that the potential buyer flipping through the paperback on the newsstand constantly has his eye caught by a sexual reference, and therefore buys."

These principles would have been intuitive to Brewer. Many, if not most, of his novels and stories from the 1950s and '60s featured protagonists designed for male reader identification, and these works often teased sexual content before relationships were consummated. Brewer's challenge, then, was to take what he had done many times in the past and ratchet up the sex. Ironically, he now had to do the opposite of what Gold Medal Books had urged him to do.

But Brewer still had to exercise restraint. The guidelines from one sex publisher warned, "The novel MUST have a story line that is interesting, that would carry the reader's interest along even if there were no sex. . . . The sex is never just thrown in. It results from and is an integral part of the story." And the dangers of overwhelming a short story with sex were even greater. With this danger in mind, Brewer wrote to his agent regarding "Mantis 36" (included in this collection), "I went over the story carefully, Dave, and interjected as much sex as I felt the story could stand."

Some of the stories collected here begin with explicit content. In its short opening paragraph, "Mantis 36" includes references to both male and female genitalia. In the opening paragraph of "Hung Up," Sheriff Reb Klayville has "a big hard-on." The opening sentence of "I Had Sex with a Martian" warns its readers, *If you are at all shocked by startling unconventionality and descriptions of male sexual members, do not read my story.* These are short-story manifestations of "flip appeal."

But the stories in this collection exist for more than their sexual content (and not all of them have explicit content). They represent a range of noirish responses to the literary marketplace of the 1970s, when Brewer was casting about and targeting publications ranging from *Boys' Life* to *Hustler*. These 24 stories are by turns artistic and vulgar, enjoyable and off putting, accessible and challenging. Together, they form a fascinating final chapter in Gil Brewer's career as a story writer.

Sources

"I have always done the wrong thing": loose page in Box 9, Collection 8187, Gil Brewer Papers, American Heritage Center, University of Wyoming.

St. Petersburg city directories: St. Petersburg city directories were consulted at the St. Petersburg Public Library, with the exceptions of 1955 and 1956, for which information was provided by the USF Tampa Library.

Firebase Seattle: correspondence to and from Jack Scovil, 23 August and 16 September 1974, Box 5, Gil Brewer Papers.

"Back in 1949": loose page in Box 9, Gil Brewer Papers. At the top of the page, Brewer has written, "6/7 Oct 74 (cont'd)" with the 6 and 7 superimposed.

"It's sometimes difficult": loose page in Box 6, Gil Brewer Papers.

"Ode to the Slow Establishment of a Disconcerting Personality": loose page in Box 3, Gil Brewer Papers.

"The last seven years of his life": Verlaine Brewer, "Notes on Gil Brewer," in Gil Brewer, *Wild to Possess/A Taste for Sin* (1959/1961; Eureka, CA: Stark House Press, 2006), 12.

"Dearest Verlaine": Box 3, Gil Brewer Papers.

"The Ghost of Hermit Key": Box 7, Gil Brewer Papers.

"Death with a Ten Foot Pole": Box 8, Gil Brewer Papers.

Brewer's obsessive theme: the rest of this paragraph is adapted from my essay "Gil Brewer's Sexual Obsession; Or, Why You Should Read Noir

Short Stories," which first appeared in the blog *Paul D. Brazill: Brit Grit & International Noir* in 2012.

"too much sex": Quoted in Joseph T. Shaw to Gil Brewer, 31 January 1951, Box 4, Gil Brewer Papers.

"[depended] entirely upon sex": Richard Carroll to Max Wilkinson, 5 February 1953, Box 3, Gil Brewer Papers.

"sex, of course": Gil Brewer quoted in "Writing Is His Work and His Hobby (Gil Brewer—Profile of an Author)," *St. Petersburg Independent*, 14 August 1967, 6B.

"THE APPEAL OF THESE BOOKS": Brewer's guidelines from sex publishers are in Box 6, Gil Brewer Papers. Of these, only the guidelines for the Greenleaf Reader series are labeled with the name of a series or publisher.

"I went over the story": Brewer to David Harris, 14 January 1977, Box 4, Gil Brewer Papers.

A Note on the Editing and Dating of Stories

The stories in this collection are reprinted as they appear in Gil Brewer's original typewritten manuscripts, which are held at the American Heritage Center at the University of Wyoming. Typographical errors have been silently corrected. Idiosyncrasies of punctuation have been altered when necessary to clarify confusing sentences.

A few of the stories in this collection can be dated with precision based on Brewer's correspondence with his literary agency. Most of the stories, however, can be dated only generally to the early or late 1970s based on the addresses of his literary agency during that decade and the fact that, at some point after 1969, he appears to have purged his files of nearly all unpublished story manuscripts. This evidence, however, is not sufficient to rule out the possibility that some of the stories dated here to the early 1970s might, in fact, be earlier.

Nepenthe

Megs said, "No. We can't. And we can't see each other again, because he knows. He even knows your name. He told me. I don't know how. He said he'd as soon ram your head out your ass. It's that bad. He's mad. When he gets mad and jealous, and everything . . ."

"But we can't quit seeing each other."

She just stood there and looked at me.

"Timothy," she said. "I mean it. You've got to understand. Oh, God, I want you, just like always—"

"No, you don't."

"Yes, I do."

"You don't, or you wouldn't let him get away with it like this."

"Get away with it! Christ, Timothy. He'll kill me. He'll kill you. He actually will ram your head out your ass, and he can do it. He said he may not be any good; he may not be a streak, but he can kick ass, that's the one thing he can do."

We were in this motel room. We had used it off and on.

She just stood there, looking all sexy, and full blown, and I was as hot as ever, and she didn't want it anymore. I called it "love" to myself and I knew it was sex, but that didn't change things. All I had to do was think of her, see something she owned, that's all.

"And you believe I'd just stand still?" I asked her.

She laughed and drew her hand down her beautiful face, the face I could never escape; the eyes, the nose, that mouth.

"I *know* him," she said. "After all, he's my husband. He'd smear you like paste."

"You can say that."

"But I mean it," she said. "He would. He will. It's ended, that's all. Finished. Get it through your head. Please!"

I went over by the nightstand and got a cigarette. We hadn't done anything this afternoon. We'd just come into the room. I'd put the cigarettes on the table, and she'd come on with the put on.

"Then—just this once," I said, looking at her.

"No. We can't. I've got to run. He's probably following me."

"Oh, you're cool," I said. "Cool."

"Timothy."

"Megs," I said. "Are you forgetting what we've got? What we've had together."

She went all soft in the mouth, but it was a pose, I could tell. I knew everything about her.

"I'll never forget," she said.

I lit the cigarette. I couldn't believe it. She was blonde, tall, Nordic looking, with high cheekbones, and slanting eyes. The eyes were a kind of cerulean blue, something you just don't see, very big and very clear, the whites like milk. Her body sent me to hell. Just thinking of her. Any time. Anywhere.

"Megs," I said. "Megs."

"I've got to go, Timothy."

She turned and put her hand on the doorknob, then glanced back at me over her shoulder.

"Believe me, Tim—I'll never forget."

Then she was gone and I was staring at the closed door.

I sat down on the edge of the bed. I couldn't believe it. Her perfume still lingered in the room, mingling with the cigarette smoke.

There is a static interim when they pull the curtain. You don't believe, you can't believe—but you know it's true. Only nothing was happening inside me. I was as cold as ice.

Then I heard the crunch of the Jag wheels on the gravel outside as she gunned off. She was gone. Out of my life. Forever.

He would ram my head out my ass. I had seen him. He could do it. Then I thought, No more thighs, no more breasts, no more mouth, no more hair, no more hands, no more of those fine hips, no more of the squealing when I squeezed her ankle.

I dropped the cigarette on the rug and ground it out with my heel. It left a filthy mark. It was squashed, just like I was squashed.

Maybe he'd grown ridges on his cock, or something, because she'd been so quick about it, and so cool.

After all we'd been through . . .

And now it got to me. It got to me hard. I couldn't explain it to myself. We'd known each other for ever and a year, and it had been one incessant hot-box, furious, steaming, the real body heat. Sometimes we'd enter a room and she'd simply leap on me with her legs spread apart, biting my neck, squealing. Once she'd worn a pantsuit, and we hadn't been able to wait; wild with it, driving. I tore the seam on her pants, and rammed it in. We were like that: gnawing on each other, and it never abated.

Until this afternoon, the phone call at the office. Cool and contained. I'd known something was up, but not what.

Well, when she'd been here, I had put up *some* argument. I was outstanding.

I left the motel room, bought a bottle, and returned. I took two or three drinks, waiting. Then I called her.

The maid answered.

I said, "It's about Mrs. Nester's insurance. Is she there?"

"Just a minute."

I was sweating. I imagined all sorts of things. I didn't want to lose her, not ever. I'd always told her that, too.

Then she was on the phone.

"You can't do it," I said. "You can't do it. Is he there?"

"No, but he will be any second. Now, don't start it again, Timothy. What d'you think I'm going through? You think it's easy for me?"

"But what am I going to do?"

I heard myself say those words and they sickened me. I took a drink, waiting for her to answer. I heard her sigh.

"Timothy?"

"Yes?"

"Find somebody else. Find somebody else." She said it twice with the same intonation each time.

"But, Megs!"

"Timothy, I don't want you all broken up. I don't want you in the hospital. I don't want you hurt. I don't want you on me. We had it, and it's over with. It's just a fine cut, that's all. He's coming in, I've got to go. I just heard the door."

"Megs!"

"Don't call me again, because I can't talk with you. I won't talk with you."

"Then you still . . . ?"

"No, Timothy. No. No." She hung up.

I sat there with the phone receiver dangling between my knees. Finally, I hung up, too.

Find somebody else, she'd said. I'd been around enough to know they could turn it off and on easily, but I'd never thought this would happen. I recalled the many times I had mentioned divorce, and I recalled her laughter. Those were the good times, the times when it would last forever.

Lust is a funny thing. But when the same lust goes on for over a year, what is it? What is it? What would you call it? Do you still call it lust?

Every way. In chairs. Under tables. On the edge of the sink. In bed. Beside the bed on the floor. On many floors. In the car. Mine. Hers. She'd even sat on my lap in this middle-aged couple's apartment in the Village, and I'd worked her skirt up and screwed her, right there, while she was discussing the way Mailer's hair bushed out with a dim-eyed economics professor. It was hard to believe. In a rocking chair, at that.

The first time we'd met, in a dark bar, we hadn't known each other more than ten minutes before she said, "Fuck me, or I'll go crazy."

We were both the same. Walking down the street, she would put her hand in my pants pocket, and grab. You don't let those things go. It hadn't worn out in over a year. It was worse, if anything—stronger. She sucked me on a bus going to the Catskills, with her head under a road map.

And all the time, she was taking care of him, too. I'd asked her about that. She'd said, "Every day, every day."

"How come you've got it for me like this," I said.

"I can't help myself."

We were together every minute he wasn't around. He wasn't around a lot. She let me in the kitchen door of the apartment once, and he was in the living room. We did it up against the electric range, and I left. Things like that happened all the time.

It was trite to think about it, but she was a part of me. Without her, I couldn't go on. I couldn't do anything, and I knew it.

For the next three days, I fooled around the office, doing nothing, and going mad. And it was then that I began seeing her. On the street, in bars, everywhere. She would be walking along, and I would run up to her and say, "Megs." But it was always somebody else.

I tried to call her, but always got the same answer.

"Mrs. Nester is out."

She wasn't "out." She just wasn't going to speak to me again. It was all true, and I couldn't stomach it. I couldn't work, I couldn't sleep, I couldn't do anything.

My vacation wasn't due for three months. So I talked Armbruster into letting me have a couple of weeks right then. I told him I was going stale. He could see my nervousness; it was plain enough, and he said, "All right. Two weeks, but you'll have to forfeit."

"So, I'll forfeit," I said, and when I left the building and headed for Chase Manhattan to draw out the money, I knew I wasn't coming back.

Get the picture. I was psychotic. Even the teller had high cheekbones, and blue eyes, and blonde hair.

I had no idea where I was going. South. East. North. West. I took the car and went to the apartment, and packed fast. It was all done in a daze. Time and again, I would be standing there, staring at the phone. I kept hitting the bottle. I kept remembering. And it was now that something came to me I'd never thought about before; the velvet feeling of her skin, the smooth velvet feeling, silken, her thighs, her arms, her cheeks. I remembered the down on her belly. I could hear her talking.

Armbruster wouldn't see me again. I wanted to lose myself, because I knew it was all up. It was done.

I drove south through rain.

The farther away from her I got, the worse it became. There were all the thousands of little memories, the tiny, insignificant things that were no longer significant. Lust, lust—they called it lust.

In my book . . . but it didn't matter now.

I stopped at motels and I drank. I still kept seeing her. Every tall girl was Megs from the back. I thought of how she might have dyed her hair. I was living in a dreamworld. I thought of maybe driving to Key West and straight off into the Caribbean. Because she would be everywhere, and I knew it. She would haunt me, as she was doing at this very instant.

Expensive motels were out. She was expensive. I wanted no reminders. I stopped at joints. I kept drinking. I didn't want to eat. I ran out of sleeping pills, and sleep became a problem. I would drink myself into insensibility each night. I traveled from motel to motel with only an hour or so in between.

It was six days later, in Atlanta, when it happened.

Oh, I knew I was running. I should have faced him. I should've let him tear my guts out, if that's what he wanted. I thought how maybe he could have been sensible. But he wasn't. She attested to that. And the many things I'd heard about him proved it out.

The place was called The Vista. They were red brick cabins, set up on a hill, with winding drives, and poplar trees. The poplars made me sad. Poplars always did that. I wanted to weep and yell, all at the same time. And the hell of it was, I kept thinking about her sexually, and I kept asking myself, Define it. Define it. You couldn't define it. So far as I was concerned nobody could define anything in this world.

Her name was Margaret. But I'd always called her "Megs" from the very beginning.

I sat in the brick cabin and drank. Atlanta was supposed to be a busy town. I thought of staying. I thought of going. I paced the floor. I smoked like a fiend, inhaling like it was nineteen-sixty. I even quit filter tips and went back to straight Camels. What did it matter? What did anything matter?

It was dark outside, and I went over to close the blinds. I looked across to the next cabin and saw Megs standing there in the window, taking off her blouse. I just stared.

The girl turned toward me, and she *was* Megs; Megs in every detail. The long blonde hair, the high cheekbones, the slanting eyes, the pouting lips, the fine hips and waist. Bright light was on over there, and the blinds were open. She didn't give a damn. I was shaking all over, and ash fell from the cigarette in my hand.

It was right then that I was gripped by compulsion. It hadn't really happened until now. I had seen Megs hundreds of times, thousands, on the streets of New York. I had seen her everywhere. But there had never been anything like this moment, right now.

She closed the blinds. She was getting ready for bed. Had she seen me looking? It was Megs. Megs. I had to know her tonight. I had to speak with her, at least. I had to touch her.

Compulsion can act like a bulldozer. And I was in the grip. That girl over there was Megs, and she was my bag.

You've got to understand. I knew it wasn't Megs. *But it was, see?* It was. Right now I was a stallion. Young Lochinvar rode out of the West, and in all the wide world, his steed was the best.

I was that steed. To hell with Lochinvar.

I was also drunk.

It was now I heard a door slam. I looked out the window and saw her in front of the cabin. She was moving slowly toward a pick-up truck, which stood in the parking area, silver gray under arc lights.

I did not think. I went to the door, outside, and walked across toward the girl.

She had removed the blouse I'd seen through the window, and replaced it with a man's white shirt, the tails hanging down over tight jeans.

But it was Megs, all right. It was Megs.

"Hello," I said.

She barely gave me a glance, and stepped to the hood of the truck. She opened the hood, propped it up. She leaned high, looking inside. I heard her mutter something.

"Can I help?" I asked.

She turned her head slowly and looked at me. It was those eyes, under the arc lights, cerulean blue. Megs' eyes. Megs.

"Maybe," she said. "You know anything about trucks?"

"Not much. But I catch on fast."

"I just got rid of one that was loaded with flak, like that," she said. She looked back inside the truck, and reached toward the carburetor. I knew it was a carb, I knew that much. Then she walked around the truck and came back with a tool-kit. She opened the kit by the front bumper and brought out a screwdriver. Then she began prodding around the carburetor again. She took off the air-cleaner, looked at it beneath the arc lights.

"Really," I said. "Maybe I can do something."

"You're all sloshed up," she said. "Just like that flak I left down the road. It's a piece of shit, anyways." She threw the air-cleaner across the parking area and it clanked and clattered and rolled over against the curbing.

Now she knelt on the front bumper and examined the carburetor again. She stuck her finger in it, looking at it. Then she eyed me.

"You coulda offered me a drink," she said.

I was still in a state of shock. It was Megs, kneeling there on the bumper, looking at the carburetor, then looking at me. The only thing that wasn't Megs was the girl's voice. I had never heard Megs say "shit."

"Right away," I told her.

I went back to the cabin and got the jug, and returned to the truck. "I forgot glasses," I said. "You want ice?"

"Just gimme the bottle," she said. She reached for it, grabbed it from my hand, shoved it into her mouth, and gurgled. She finally took it out of her mouth, and some ran down her chin, shining. She eyed me.

"I'll leave you some!" she said and laughed. After that she drank some more.

The jeans she wore were very tight and pale-washed and patched, ragged at the seams and cuffs. I wanted her and there was nothing I could do about it.

I went by the bumper of the truck and leaned close and looked at the carburetor. As I looked, I heard the bottle gurgle. She was drinking again. Then she was laughing again.

"You sure are a one," she said. "You seen me through the window, didn't ya?"

I looked at her. "Yes."

"Get a good look?"

I didn't say anything.

"That flak I left down the road, he always wanted a good look, too. Ain't you going to take a drink?"

She offered me the bottle.

I took it and knocked off a short one, then handed it back to her. Desperately, I wanted her as drunk as I could get her. She poured more of it down, watching me all the while under the arc lights. The blonde hair. The blue eyes. The thrust of her breasts perking beneath that white shirt. And the tight curves of her thighs.

"What you doing, anyways?" she asked.

"Nothing. Nothing. I'm doing nothing."

"Just scouting around, right?"

"You could call it that." I paused, then said, "Why don't we go into your cabin and have a drink together?"

She eyed me over the tipped bottle.

"I could get another bottle," I told her.

"You do that, whyn't ya! This one's almost gone!"

I stood there for a moment, caught in inertia, an interim of despair. Here she was. If I left her, she might vanish before I got back.

"Go," she said, "go! I got to fix this fucking carburetor. It don't blow gas right."

I was running. Then I was behind the wheel of my car. I gunned it out of the area, looking back at her. She was still tilting the bottle. I made it to the liquor store fast, bought two quarts of bourbon, and drove back to The Vista cabins.

She was seated on the fender of the truck as I walked toward her. She grinned, held the bottle up and dropped it. It shattered on the macadam.

"I brought two of them," I said.

"Good for you. You know where it's at. You sure know what a girl likes, don't ya? Is it panther piss?"

"My name's Timothy," I said. "Timothy Montrock."

She began to laugh, uncapping the bottle. She got it uncapped and put it to her lips, still laughing and sputtering. Some of the bourbon ran down her chin and she wiped it with the back of her hand. She took the bottle away from her mouth, and looked at me.

"Montrock, Montrock? What a hell of a handle."

"What's yours?" I asked.

"I'm Verna."

"Where you from?"

"Around."

"I mean originally."

"Idaho. 'Way out there in Idaho. They grow 'em big out there."

"I'm pretty big," I said.

"I know it to look at you."

She was getting drunk. I wanted her drunker. I didn't care about anything now. The lust was up in me hard and fine. Megs. Megs. The girl drank some more, a lot, and I watched her throat work. She slid down off the fender of the truck and her skirt hitched up, showing her bare belly.

"Are you just a bunch of flak?" she asked.

"No."

"I didn't think so. You're the serious type, ain't ya?"

"Well," I said.

She gave me a long slow look from the sides of her eyes, and said, "Bring along that other jug. We'll go into the cabin now. We can discuss the carburetor later. Ain't a hell of a lot we can do with it, anyhow. But I got a carb in there, needs fixin'."

My loins went hot. There was a brutal stirring.

She walked ahead of me, toward her cabin. The shirt was still hitched up in back, and there was a big patch on the left bun. She opened the door and stood aside as I entered. As I walked past, she swatted my ass.

"Ever seen a carb in a cabin that needed fixin'?" she asked.

I turned and looked at her. She slammed the door and tipped the bottle to her mouth again. Her throat worked, and her eyes were glazed. She snapped the bottle down and some of the liquid splashed on the floor.

"That goddamned flak," she said. "Give me a bunch of shit, that's what. They grow 'em big in Idaho."

I was still holding the other bottle. I went over and put it on the nightstand beside the bed. The cabin was exactly the same inside as mine, excepting that clothes were strewn all over the floor. A suitcase was partially unpacked on the rack. A bottle of gin lay unopened in the exact center of the bed.

"Got any grass?" she wanted to know.

"No."

Even as I answered she was speaking, "No, you wouldn't have. You're a juicer, same as me. I just like grass sometimes. The weed stirs it up." She laughed. "Stirs the carb up, y'know? Gets it to blowin' right."

I walked over to her. She watched me closely, the eyes never blinking. The eyes were large and round and cerulean blue. The cheekbones were high and I knew the feel of her skin would be velvet.

She screwed the cap back on the bottle of bourbon and tossed it into the suitcase. Then she took off the shirt. She wore a black bra, and it was too tight for her breasts—they squinched up.

The next thing I knew, she was peeling off the jeans. She had nothing on under them. She'd been wearing mocs, and now she kicked them aside.

"You say you're big like they are in Idaho," she said. "You fix this carburetor."

She was very drunk now. She lurched toward me. I caught her. I'd been right. The feel of her skin was silk and velvet. Her mouth opened, and I felt her tongue lashing.

We sprawled back across the bed and she began to curse. "Goddamn fuckin'!" She wriggled around and brought out the bottle of gin from beneath her back, and hurled it. It shattered against the wall, and I immediately smelled it.

I was trying to get out of my pants. She lay back, laughing up into my face. Her eyes were dizzy. They were beginning to look hazel now. There was a pinkness to the cerulean blue.

"You're a big cock from nowhere," she said loudly.

"Megs," I said.

"Nowhere at all," she said. "I tol' you they grow 'em big in Idaho. Bet you ain't that big. That fuckin' flak was a penny pencil. Oh, baby! Oh, baby!"

I started to lie down beside her, but she rolled around and scrambled off the bed. She went over to the suitcase and began heaving clothes across the room. She came up with a small, black transistor radio, and flicked it on. Immediately blasting scratchy rock filled the room.

I was lying on the bed, with my pants down to my knees. It was a dream. All I could think was, Megs, Megs.

Verna said, "I'll take it on top," and dove spraddle-legged across me, still holding the radio.

The damned radio was beside my left ear, blatting the horrible rock, and some guy was screaming.

She sat up on me and fumbled with her bra. Then her breasts were free. She flung the black bra across the room. She moved her hips a lot. She began to curse; she sprawled down on me, and I heard her gag as I entered her. She was cursing and gagging.

Then she threw up.

She coughed and threw up some more. It went down my neck, and over my shoulder, and into my ear, and over the transistor radio. The music was muted but still loud.

The stench was bad.

"Put it on!" she gasped. "Put it on!"

Then she puked again. She lay with her face in it. Her hips were moving rhythmically. I grabbed her by the shoulders, and rolled her over, and squeezed out from under her, and tumbled off the bed onto the floor.

She lay back, coughing and gagging, with her legs spread apart. There was puke all over the bed, and in her hair, and down her face, and on me, and the radio rocked.

I got up, and peeled off my shirt. It didn't help.

I could smell the gin and the puke.

"C'mon!" she wailed. "They grow 'em big in Idaho. You said you was a big one. Don't be no penny pencil. Look at ya, you're like a wet rag. You just hang there."

I yanked my pants up and buckled my belt. I kept looking at her under the bed light, the overhead ceiling light, the arc lights that glared in the front windows.

She was mewling and drooling and rubbing her hands between her legs.

I dropped my shirt to the floor and walked to the door. Christ, she had eaten oysters, or something. The stench was wild and the music crashed, scratching, blatting.

"Fix my carburetor, fix it!" she yelled.

I just looked at her from there by the door. She was still working one hand between her legs.

I opened the door and went outside and closed it.

The truck stood there with the hood up, under the arc lights. The shattered glass from the broken bourbon bottle twinkled.

I went back to my cabin. I could still faintly hear the music, and her calling. I went inside and closed the door, then locked it. I took a long shower.

After that, I packed everything up, went outside and slipped under the wheel of my car.

The lights were off in her cabin. Everything was black. The hood was closed on the truck.

I drove to the office and paid my bill.

On the highway, headed back north, I thought, Megs—Megs. Nothing happened. I had taken the cure. I could still smell it and hear it and see it, lying there on the bed.

Armbruster would be surprised to see me back from vacation so early.

I knew I would never go to Idaho.

Clean Sweep

March 1976

Farnol stood in the darkened room of the shack and watched the man through the smeared window. The man was carrying something over his shoulder; it resembled a rolled rug, but Farnol couldn't be certain because the desert moonlight left the man mostly as a dark shadow. Farnol had heard the crunch of the man's feet on the sand, and immediately looked out the window. He did not have a light on in the shack and there was a gnarled piece of scrub on the lip of the wash, partially shielding the meager building, so he felt reasonably sure the man hadn't noticed any signs of habitat. Farnol hoped this were true. He had long ago shied from civilization and he wanted no intruders. Only hours ago he walked the considerable distance to the town trading post, bought some bacon, salt, flour, two boxes of noodles and a newspaper with his last money. It had been a hurried trip, full of fear because people stared at him, pointed, and said things.

Farnol was extremely tired, but the man being out there energized him somewhat.

The man leaned and dropped the rolled rug in the desert moonlight and Farnol saw that he also carried a shovel.

He was quite attentive now.

"Damn son of a bitch."

He said it out of fear. Fear was ingrained in him. He was an old man and frightened of everything, but especially of any intruder. Not that he'd had any intruders before now.

He watched the man out there. The man began to dig. Farnol could hear the hollow scrape of the shovel carrying in the still night. For Christ's sake, the son of a bitch was going to bury the goddamn rug out there.

The man was digging on a small desert rise. He stood on the top of the rise, outlined against the paler sky, digging furiously. Farnol had never observed such activity; the man was obviously bent on digging a hole as fast as possible. Sand and rock flew, spattering the ground. The man would place the shovel, ram it with his foot, then hurl it and its contents wildly.

Farnol could hear the man breathe in sharp gusts.

He did not move from the window. He did not move at all. He stood there in the cramped position he had assumed when he'd first looked out at the sound.

"Son of a bitch," he whispered.

But the man kept digging. Then, after a time, the man hurled the shovel to the ground, swiped his brow with a shadowed forearm, and leaned.

"Now the rug."

Farnol watched as the man tugged at the rolled rug and tumbled it into the hole he had dug. Then the man began kicking sand and rocks into the hole. He grabbed the shovel and dug and scraped and worked very hard until probably the hole was filled again. Then, without any hesitation, without even seeming to take a breath, he whirled and stomped down the rise carrying the shovel. He vanished from sight.

Still Farnol did not move.

He even held his breath for a long moment.

Then he just stood there, looking out the window. He stood that way for just under an hour, waiting. The man did not return.

Farnol moved. It was painful because he'd been in the cramped position for so long. He tip-toed to the door of the shack, opened it and went outside. He breathed shallowly, walked steadily across the flat patch of sand, then on up the rise until he stood by the place where the man had buried the rug.

He'd forgotten the shovel. He sighed, went, and got the shovel, long-handled, cumbersome, and, laying it across his shoulder, he came back up the rise to where the rug was buried.

He immediately commenced digging. He thought fearfully of how the man had dug, the vitality.

Steel scraped against something.

Farnol quickly knelt in the cavity and scrabbled at the loose rocks and sand with his hands.

It wasn't a rug. It was a stiff tarpaulin, wrapped around something bulky. He dug and brushed, hurling rocks and sand out of the cavity, and turned up a flap on the tarpaulin. He yanked the flap back and the diamond-colored moonlight palmed a pale girl's face, eyes open, mouth open.

Farnol knelt there. For a moment he could not move.

The dead girl stared directly up at the round moon with blank, glazed eyes. Farnol shivered and gave a short sob.

He touched the pale face. It was stiff and chill.

"Dead."

She had long, snarled, dark hair and was perhaps fifteen years old.

He knew what he had to do right away, and a sort of electricity was all through him, along with new fear on old fear.

Invaded . . .

The agonies of memory made a hermit of him and he could never forget, even with age. The fear he lived with never dulled. And now this . . . three counts of child-molesting, it had been, years behind bars, and when he was free he could find no freedom, only taunts and slanted looks, until he sought his place, long ago, here in the desert. The trauma never died, only grew as time passed. *And now this . . .*

He looked up at the sky and his mind was utterly empty for a long moment, as if he were stunned. He could not think. Then he came around again. He leaned and began digging savagely with both hands. He dug that way until he had completely freed the tarpaulin, then he dragged it out of the cavity. There was a waxed rope threaded through eyelets on the tarpaulin. He fastened it around the body as best he could, with a handle of rope hanging out by the head.

• • •

Thirty miles to the north-west lay a range of mountains. This was where he could take the body of the girl.

He ran down the rise, stumbling, and over to the shack. An Indian lived here long ago and there was a well. Farnol managed to bring up some dark-looking water from where the bucket scraped and dragged at the bottom. He drank thirstily, ignoring the grit. He wanted coffee, but there was none. Usually he made coffee from burnt beans, but there were no beans, and anyway there wasn't time. He went inside the shack.

Taking a knife, he cut a chunk of raw bacon from the two-pound slab and stood there, chewing it, trying to think. His mind felt thick. He was tired. He had walked the twenty miles to the trading post, spent all his money, and walked back and now he had to drag the body of the girl thirty miles to the mountains.

He wanted to chew the bacon and sit and read the newspaper by candlelight. He hadn't seen a newspaper in four months. He had read the last one till it fell apart like ancient cloth in his hands.

He suddenly realized he was standing here, doing nothing, with the body of the girl out there. Fear shot through his veins, his muscles. Time was passing. They would find the body, ruin everything.

He ran out of the shack, across the sand patch and up the rise. He grabbed the loop of rope and began dragging the tarpaulin-wrapped body of the girl. He dragged it down the rise, around the shack, and immediately set off across the desert in the direction of the mountains.

• • •

The body, wrapped in the stiff winding sheet, was much heavier than he'd figured. Even dragging it like a sled was a problem. He kept thinking of the man, and the vigor he'd revealed when he dug on the rise. Once

Farnol had been like that. But now he was an old man. He shouldn't be called upon to do things like this.

He had to. He had to carry the body of the girl to the mountains. He could not leave her anywhere near the shack. Things could happen.

He breathed rapidly, staggering slightly as he pulled on the rope, sliding the tarpaulin across the sand, scraping along small rocks. They would find her. He knew they would. Fear was so strong, his head throbbed and troublesome matters swam at the corners of his vision.

He knew it was murder. He did not want to look at the body more than he already had. He didn't want to know anything about it. He knew too much already. He was involved and it was a terrible feeling.

For a long time he hurried, staggering along, yanking at the tarpaulin, hauling it, wheeling to scurry backwards, then pulling it with hands behind his back, trying to run.

He moved blindly along in this manner for some twenty minutes. At the end of this time he was breathing in burning gusts and knew he'd have to move more slowly.

Then he remembered the shovel.

He didn't even pause. He took one hasty look at the moon, dropped the rope loop, and began running back over the terrain he'd just covered. A sob broke from his throat, and he wiped his nose. There was only the sound of his feet scraping the earth. Then he fell, tripping over his own feet. He slid forward on his elbows, skinning both of them through his shirt, tearing his shirt. His elbows began to burn as he stood and started running again.

As he stumbled and trotted along, he couldn't get thoughts out of his head about how the man had killed the girl. Why? They were in a room and the girl said, "No, no!" and the man drew a knife and plunged it into her breast. Blood.

"No, I'd never do that, Uncle John. Never."

"You promised. You don't want to go back on your promise, do you? You know what things is all about—don't try to pretend. Now I'll be nice and you be nice."

"Don't say that, Uncle John."

"I'll show you what I got, then. See this white packet? And this needle? I know you. You're all alike. You always wanted it, baby—you always kept asking. Now you got your chance."

Farnol kept running. He could not control his mind. It was alive with pictures and words. His chest hurt. He had to slow down. He couldn't slow down. He had thirty miles to cover. Thirty? My God. Sixty miles. To the mountains, and back.

Suppose they came when he was away. He couldn't defend himself.

"Where you been, old timer?"

"No place. No place at all."

"You're all fagged out."

"No, I ain't."

He saw the shack in the moonlight. He halted and stood still. There was absolutely no sound. Just his breathing. There was no wind, nothing. Just the long, cool, desert tent with the moon up there, shedding its diamond-blue light on everything.

He hurried to the shack, paused at the well. The bucket lay in the sand. He dropped it into the well, scraped around at the bottom, and brought it up. He drank the gritty, tepid water, shivering, his hands trembling.

Hurling the bucket down, he ran into the shack.

Then he remembered he'd left the shovel up on the rise. Hastily, he cut another chunk of bacon, poked it into his mouth, and hurried stumbling across the sand patch and up the rise.

He found the shovel.

Dragging the shovel, he ran down the rise and out across the desert floor, chewing the raw fatty bacon, trying to breathe.

His nose was running. This was probably because of the chill desert night and his exertions. He snuffled, trying to breathe, chewing the raw bacon.

The shovel scraped and sang against sand and small rocks.

He went on like this for some time. Then it suddenly seemed to him that he hadn't come this far. Had he missed seeing the tarpaulin?

Fear drenched him. He stopped, whirled around, searching the desert floor in the moonlight. He saw the tarpaulin-wrapped bundle. He gave a little cry in his throat, stumbled to where the bundle was and knelt down, feeling of it, groping. It was all right.

For a moment, he stood there, regaining his breath and trying to find new strength. The bacon had helped a little, but now he wished he had more water. He should have brought water with him. He could not return to the shack now.

Fastening the shovel to the bundle by threading the handle in and out of the rope, he felt easier.

• • •

Pulling and hauling on the rope, he tugged the tarpaulin across the midnight desert. He walked now, steadily with his hands behind him, twined in the rope loop. He moved for over an hour this way, his mind inert. Then he began to notice that the weight seemed sloppy, somehow. He had covered some distance. He turned and looked and the moonlight revealed loosened ropes, an open tarpaulin, with the body lying on its back, both arms outspread, dragging in the sand.

The girl's body was naked in the moonlight.

Farnol moaned, and knelt quickly, covering the body with the tarpaulin. He began threading the rope through the eyelets again, sewing the package up tightly.

Where was the shovel?

He sprang up, looking wildly around. He lifted the bundle. No shovel. Immediately he ran back along the desert floor, pounding, and he saw the glint of the shovel.

"Ah."

He ran to the shovel, grabbed it up, and ran back to the tarpaulin-wrapped bundle.

"Oh."

This time he fastened the shovel so it couldn't possibly break loose, and the bundle wouldn't come open, either.

"There—there."

He started out again, pulling on the rope loop. He had worked up a sweat and now he was cold. But gradually he warmed and soon he was sweating again. He was also beginning to feel very tired and it was difficult keeping his hands behind him, twined in the rope loop. When he walked backward, it was even harder. The girl was heavy, the tarpaulin bulky— dead weight. The rope cut into his hands now and he had to keep changing them around.

Finally, he ceased walking. He was breathing quite hard, and he had a pain in his left side. He stepped to the tarpaulin, found the rope end, and managed to tug it out until he had about four feet. He knotted the end of the rope, then turned and laid it across his shoulder and stepped out.

This was a little better. Not much.

"Damn it, Lisa—hold your arm still."

"I feel funny from all that wine, Uncle John. Now you want to stick my arm with that needle. I'm dizzy. No, no!"

"Hold still!"

"No!"

"Get on that bed. You got my blood up, child. I'm gonna strip you naked."

"Please—please!"

"Get down there."

"It's heroin. That needle's full of heroin."

Uncle John laughed.

Farnol struggled on, his mind swarming. He could hear the voices of Uncle John and Lisa. He knew what they were like; he'd read the stories in the magazines.

She struggled and kicked, naked on the bed as he fought to jab her arm with the needleful of heroin. She kicked again and the needle flipped from his hand, shattering on the floor. She saw a steak knife on a shelf by the bed, made a wild grab for it, got it and cursed him.

"Damn you, Uncle John."

But Uncle John was quicker, snatching the knife with a wild, maddened look. He'd already taken some of the heroin and he was crazy. He'd had some coke, too. He mixed them. He didn't know what he was doing, kill-crazy, as he sprang at the bed with the knife in his hand . . .

Then Farnol remembered. There hadn't been a mark on the girl's body, lying in the moonlight.

"If I had a knife, I'd kill you for smashing that needle. That's precious stuff."

The pain in Farnol's side was bad.

He stopped in a moment of bright agony, and just stood there, dazed, with the pain steady and cramping. His nose was running and he could hardly get his breath.

"What's your name?"

"Lisa. What's yours?"

"John."

Farnol leaned over abruptly, gagging, but nothing came up and his mouth was as dry as the sand beneath his feet.

"How's about getting a bottle, Lisa, baby. We'll go up to my room."

"Well—I don't know."

"What's the matter with my room?"

"Who the hell d'you think you are, anyways?"

Farnol gave a small tug at the rope. The tarpaulin did not move. He continued to stand there. Then he realized he was staring directly at the range of mountains. He could see them. They seemed quite near. He knew distance was deceptive, but still they couldn't be too far.

Farnol said, "C'mon, Lisa," and pulled the rope over his shoulder. The bulky tarpaulin slid across the desert floor and the moonlight was icy blue now.

• • •

Farnol reached a dry riverbed in the foothills of the mountains some time during the morning. The sun was a white blast, the sky white, the sand shimmering.

He dropped the rope, which had cut into his shoulder, and stumbled in a running fall to the riverbed. He sprawled on the sand, digging with both hands. He had to have water. The riverbed was quite dry. There was no water, even after he had clawed a fairly deep hole. Not even mud.

His shoulder was bleeding and caked, the back of his shirt black with blood. He breathed almost like a dog, fighting for some kind of relief. Then he came to his feet and rushed staggering to the tarpaulin, grabbed the rope, and dragged the whole thing up the first slope of the foothills.

He tripped and fell, opening the skinned places on his elbows. He lay there for a moment. He knew he could go no farther. This was it; he had reached the foothills, at least.

He was exhausted. His skull was on fire.

He trembled all over. But he managed to regain his feet, head swimming, and started digging with the shovel.

It was hard going.

• • •

He scraped sand and loose rock over the hole and the tarpaulin was completely covered. He was reeling, now. He had to rest. He slumped down.

"Lisa."

"John."

"Lisa—I'm going to kill you."

Finally, Farnol came to his feet again, leaning against the shovel. He could not carry the shovel back to the shack. It was too much. He'd leave it out here, someplace—bury it.

He buried the shovel. He surveyed his work. It was neat. He felt some relief now.

He started back across the desert, heading for the shack. Not having to pull the bulky, weighted tarpaulin was like being re-born. He walked rapidly at first, and it was high noon before he began to slow down. He immediately wanted to lie down and never move again. But he kept moving. Thoughts of water at the well, and bacon, and tobacco, kept him moving. He reeled and sagged and the pain in his side started up again, but he kept moving steadily.

. . . desert rat, that's what I am.

He could think that now. He had disposed of the body completely. Nobody would ever find it, and nobody would ever attach him to that body, that tarpaulin, that murder.

Where was the man now? Gone. Probably flying to Europe, or something. Mexico. They always went to Mexico, didn't they? Well, they used to.

Farnol half wished he were in Mexico.

He would have to get another shovel somehow. He never knew when he might need a shovel.

The man's name was John.

"There, by God! Quit your yelling!"

"No, no!"

"Lisa, child—Lisa. What's the matter with you? Good Lord—must've been an overdose."

Farnol stopped walking sharply, shocked. He whirled and looked back where he had come. He moaned and ran to one side, staggering, reeling. Then he just stood there, looking off toward the range of mountains, the foothills and the trail he'd been following. It was *his* trail. He turned the other way, looking off toward the shack. His trail. The trail the tarpaulin had left. It was a stark cut in the desert floor, stretching from one horizon to the other, like an arrow. Mostly like an arrow, that is: just curving in and out a little here and there. And footprints where his shoes had scraped.

A trail in the sand, the desert. They would follow it and find her.

He immediately came to life, began running back and forth, kicking at the sand, scraping with his feet.

It did no good. It only made it worse. He'd never seen anything like it.

He looked at the sky. A white blaze, and not a single cloud. And there was no wind to cover that trail.

. . . broom.

He glimpsed a scrubby-looking bush, ran to it, tried to yank it free of the soil. It was tough, rooted deeply. He fought with it, wrenching and gasping. Finally he tore it loose, hurried back to the trail marks and began brushing at them. Pieces of the bush came loose and shed everywhere. It was worse than before. It only made the trail look tampered with. He kicked at the trail, scraping with his feet again. No good. He hurled the bush down, and turned, running wildly, reeling, dragging his feet.

He would have to get the old broom from the shack and go back thirty miles to the mountains, and obliterate the trail carefully.

The thought of it was monstrous. The pain in his side was like a sherd of glass now, probing, cutting.

"John!"

"Lisa—Lisa!"

"John, don't."

"I'm going to kill you. This is raw stuff and nobody'll ever know. Uncut. You'll be dead in seconds and you can never tell."

Farnol had not known that he was this old. It was only now that he knew. He had always imagined himself as much younger, even though he considered himself an old man.

• • •

The last mile to the shack was the most difficult he had ever walked. He fell all the time. His elbows were bleeding, and his chin and forehead scraped raw. His nose seemed to be a pulp. His shoulder pained where the rope from the tarpaulin had sawed through his shirt. The pain in his side was like another person attached to his person, all cutting edges, wanting to kill him. His mouth was a dry, gaping wound; his tongue a piece of wood. His throat was a hot metal tunnel, leading to burning lungs. His pants were torn, his knees bloody. His feet were clubs that moved in directions of their own.

• • •

He crept that final few feet on hands and knees and collapsed by the Indian well beside the shack. He tossed in the bucket with a last effort of will and lay there.

Finally he worked his way to the very edge of the well and scraped the bucket around at the bottom and somehow managed to pull it up. He drank of the gritty water, sloshed some over his head and lay there thinking about the broom.

He lay there for a good half an hour. Then he knew he had to get up and get the broom. It was past mid-afternoon and he would be out there again tonight. But he'd made good time. Yes.

He struggled to his feet and entered the shack. He fell down and got up and located the broom and immediately gave a tiny sob, staring at it. It was nothing but a stub of bristle. He had been imagining it as he had bought it two years before at the trading post.

He hurled it from him and it struck the newspaper which was lying on the edge of the wooden crate he used as a seat sometimes. The paper fell to the floor, opening.

He crouched on his painful knees, staring at the newspaper and the broom, each in turn, as if they were alive.

Then he saw the headline. It was like a searchlight in his skull.

LOCAL GIRL BELIEVED KIDNAPPED

. . . Moira Standish, daughter of well-known retiree George Standish, one-time publisher and financial genius, was apparently abducted from her home some time during the night. When last seen, the seventeen-year-old girl wore blue jeans and a white sweater, and jewelry she never took off; a turquoise bracelet in a heavy silver setting on her left arm . . .

Farnol *knew* there had been no bracelet. He had seen the girl naked, lying on the tarpaulin, and she had been stark naked—not a thing. Then he recalled that her arms had probably dragged for a long time outside the tarpaulin, brushing on the desert floor. *That* could have pulled off any bracelet she wore.

He stared at the photo of the young girl, head and shoulders. It was her, all right—Lisa. No, no—Moira . . .

But she'd been naked in the moonlight. She'd worn nothing at all.

He rose, stumbled and lurched toward the door of the shack. She'd worn nothing. Nothing.

He wanted to yell it. *Nothing . . .*

He was filled with it. He had to somehow get to the trading post and get a broom—maybe two brooms. He had to sweep away the evidence. Twenty miles to the trading post and twenty miles back, and he'd have to somehow steal the brooms.

Turquoise bracelet, he thought. He was filled with it. He ran in a blind stagger from the shack and began following the trail he had made toward the mountains. His heart was hammering now, cracking against his ribs, and it, too, was painful. His side was agonizing. He hurt all over and he could hardly see. But he knew he had to hurry, because the day would die and moonlight wouldn't be enough. Moonlight would be all right to sweep the trail with, but not to find the bracelet.

If he didn't find it, somebody would. He knew this.

But I've got to get to the trading post . . .

I've got to have a broom . . .

He fell. He was going to come instantly to his feet, but it didn't work. He tried to stand, but he couldn't; not for a long time. It took perhaps a half an hour before he regained his feet and began running along the trail again, watching the ground eagerly, eating it up with his gaze.

His eyes streamed, his nose ran. His mouth was dry.

He thought he was running, but actually he was just shuffling along now, staggering from one side to the other, nearly falling at every other step.

He kept this up for an hour.

Then he saw the sun glint on something, and it was a heavy silver bracelet, with turquoise stones. He fell on it, cupping it to his chest, his hammering heart, and lay there, panting, snuffling the dust.

The broom . . .

He jerked around, clawed the desert, got one knee under him, blazing with pain, came wildly to his feet, and fell again. The bracelet slipped from his fingers. He went after it crazily, scrabbling on hands and knees, and grabbed it, and got his feet under him, and began running back toward the shack. The pain was in his stomach, now, too . . . he was all pain, a fist of pain.

"Lisa."

"Uncle John."

"How you feel, now, honey?"

"Whoozy."

Uncle John laughed.

• • •

Farnol stood at the door of the shack with the bracelet in his hand, clutched tightly. He reeled dizzily to the wooden crate, slumped down, staring at the newspaper spread out at his feet. The words swam in his squinted vision, bleared by tears of fury.

. . . turquoise bracelet in a heavy silver setting on her left arm, and a still heavier black jade bracelet in a filigreed silver setting on her right arm . . .

Something inside Farnol screamed. *A black jade bracelet.* But he had to get to the trading post for the two brooms.

Looking up at the doorway, Farnol made a sly face and winked to himself. He would leave the black jade bracelet out there until he got back from the trading post with the two brooms. Then he would work at brushing out the trail—no! He would get the two brooms and go along the trail until he found the black jade bracelet, carrying the turquoise bracelet with him, and he'd take the two bracelets to the foothills of the mountains, and bury them with the shovel. Then he would return to the shack, brushing out the trail as he came. Simple.

He felt the shadow in the doorway, two shadows, really, but they didn't mean anything.

"Hello, old timer—how's things?"

He stared. It took him a long time to make out the fact that two men stood there.

"Didn't mean to jar you," the tall man said. He took off his hat and banged it against his leg. "I'm Sheriff Bennett. This here's my new deputy—Max Stelsky. Say hello, Max."

"Hello, there," Max said.

They did not move from the doorway.

"We come to ask you, mebbe you seen something about the kidnapping? I mean, anything unusual, out here? Car was seen coming down the highway out there. Going to explain about the kidnapping, but I see you're reading it. What happened to you, old timer? You look all beat up, or something."

Farnol did not answer. He just sat there on the crate.

"He's all over blood," the deputy said. "He's covered with blood. Listen how he breathes. Look at his eyes, for God's sake."

"Say, old timer. What's that you got there in your hand?"

Farnol thought he put the hand with the bracelet in it behind him, but it did not move from between his ragged, bleeding knees.

"Nothing," Farnol said, croaking it. "It's nothing."

. . . he had to get the brooms. Then . . .

"Hell," the deputy said. "It's her turquoise bracelet, can't you see, Jim?"

"I see," the sheriff said. Then he said, "What you been doing, old timer?"

Farnol's skull screamed awake. He came to his feet in a crazed rush and ran at the door, clutching the bracelet to his chest. He had to get the brooms at the trading post . . .

The sheriff stepped aside. Farnol ran through the door and dove at the ground. He rolled over once, close to the well, and lay there. He still held the bracelet against his chest.

"I'm going to have a look around," the deputy said.

"Wait. Say, old timer!" The sheriff knelt beside Farnol and shook him with a large hand. Then he took hold of Farnol's shoulder and rolled the old man over.

"Christ," the deputy said. "He's dead."

"Yes," the sheriff said. "He's dead, all right." The sheriff slowly shook his head, still kneeling. He pried stiff fingers, took the turquoise bracelet.

The deputy said, "God. You think he done it?"

"No. He didn't do it. He's too old for that kind of thing."

"How old you guess he was?"

"I know how old. He's ninety-nine years old. It was out he told somebody he would make a hundred. Lived here over forty years, now. Don't know where he come from. Don't know much about him. He come to town, everybody'd point him out—a real, genuine old timer." Sheriff Bennett shook his head again. "Sad."

"How'd he get the bracelet, then?" the deputy wanted to know.

"Oh, get along, Max."

"I been noticing something, standing here," the deputy said. "There's a kind of trail like that comes down over that little rise, and it comes to the shack, here, and then it swings out across the desert. What could that be."

The sheriff sighed. "Indian, most likely, dragging something. They do that in these parts." He paused, then slowly stood up, scratched his head, replaced his hat. "Listen," he said. "I'll put in a call for an ambulance. Then we'll follow the trail. All right? I know you won't rest till we do that much."

"Well, the bracelet and all. The way he looked. Anybody'd be—"

"Yeah," the sheriff said. His tone was dry. "Ninety-nine years old an' looking like he tangled with a wolf pack."

"Makes me itchy," the deputy said, peering off across the desert toward the dim outline of a range of mountains, shadowy in the dying sunlight.

I Had Sex with a Martian

May 1976

If you are at all shocked by startling unconventionality and descriptions of male sexual members, do not read my story.

My name is Ann Randall and I live in South Carlin with my husband of one year, Des. We love each other very much. I teach elementary school, third and fourth grades, in Allendale, twenty miles away.

It was Tuesday, July 13th, and the day had been hectic. It seemed the children were overly obstreperous, and quite negligent in their attitudes toward learning anything at all.

To top this off, I had been in no way able to concentrate on teaching them anything. I simply did not care and couldn't get with it. Des and I had just learned from our doctor that he was sterile and we could never have any children, unless induced by artificial insemination.

We desperately wanted a child . . .

I knew how Des felt. He must have been absolutely out of his mind, traveling around as a paint salesman. I fully expected him to go off somewhere and get drunk. I didn't know what I'd find when I reached home. I had only just left the Greenlawn school at Allendale some five minutes before, and was now on the well-traveled highway leading to South Carlin.

It wasn't a particularly warm day for July, and a cool wind dusted my face through the open window. I drove in a kind of awful dream, on the verge of tears, carrying a load of fear and trepidation I couldn't control. How could I ever face Mother and Dad with this terrible news? How could I face anyone? It seemed that everybody had been asking when we would have our first baby.

Des and I had so wanted a child. We'd worked at it, and we'd been puzzled, even this early in the game, so we were brutally shocked when we learned about Des's condition. It had only been a laughable matter, seemingly, when Des went to enquire.

"Now your mother'll be satisfied," he said bitterly.

"Oh, Des, darling—don't say that."

"You know what she thinks of me."

"Please, Des. We were never going to talk about that again."

"She's even changing your father's opinion of me. And what did I ever do to them? Or to you?"

"Nothing, Des. Nothing—please. We've got to think . . ."

"Think! Jesus. Is there a God? What's happened? I'm sterile, Ann—sterile. I'm not even a man anymore."

"Des—Des—"

And I'd had to leave him that way this morning, wondering what he would do—what I would do in a schoolroom full of frolicsome children, watching them, yearning for them, wondering for the child we could never have. All those eager young faces with the marvelous wide eyes; the things they said, bright and original, unhampered by the traumas of adulthood. I wanted to love them all, each and every one. I could only stifle my tears.

And Mother. The way she acted toward Des. But not in his presence, no, never that—she was a hypocrite about that. She would come to me after a stiff and formal act toward Des. She would ask if he were still a "paint seller." That's what she called him.

"It's so demeaning," she said just the other day. "And you're making more money than he is, Ann. I'd think you'd wonder what will happen later on. He's lazy, Ann—I can tell. He doesn't want to become anything. He's satisfied, content to just travel around in that old Ford and sell paint. How do you stand it?"

"Please, Mother. I don't want to discuss this."

She worried her mouth, tightening her lips, and her eyes were full of hypocritical concern. I knew her so well. I tried to love her, but there was this problem I couldn't handle.

"I've spoken with your father again," she said, shaking her finger in my face. "It won't be long and you'll start having children. I know how Des is, he's like all the rest of that loafer type. He'll just saddle you with kids, and you'll be worn out at thirty, a tired old woman, with kids pulling at your skirts, crying and yelling—wet diapers on the lines, washing and cooking— you won't even be able to carry on with your teaching, wait and see." She took a deep breath.

"I told you, I don't wish to discuss it. We want children and we're going to have them and they won't interfere with anything. You had me, didn't you? Was I such a terrible problem? You're a mother. I want to be a mother to Des's children."

"Hush, now, Ann. You mustn't talk like that." She patted my arm, squeezing with her fingers, clinging. It was getting so I was discovering hate for my own mother. "Ann, you were different. You were an exceptionally bright child—I worshipped you, Ann. I think the very world of you, you must know that. And that's why I'm so concerned. I know Des. He's not right for you. I've told you that and your father agrees. Why, he should be a day laborer. He'd make more money. And at least, it would be honest work!"

"Shut up! I won't listen!"

"Why, Ann, dear," she said in that awful calm tone she had when I disturbed her. "I love you, don't you see? Would you go against the wishes of your own mother?"

"Yes! Yes, I would—in a case like this."

And I'd run out of the house. Father was on the lawn, tending the roses he grew so preciously, and he waved to me. I did not wave back. I got out of there, running, running for the protection of Des's arms.

And now look—now we couldn't have our own children. We would have to adopt, or the other way. And we both hated the idea of adoption.

Driving along the highway, it was then that I began to weep. I couldn't help it. I gripped the wheel tensely, till the white stood out on my knuckles, knowing nothing was going right. Here I was, a healthy, sexually demanding female and there could never, never be any real culmination, and my own mother didn't even understand.

It was just then that I spotted the Detour sign. A man stood there with a red flag, waving cars off the highway onto a mountainous dirt road. I thought it was rather peculiar because this was a main artery, a State Highway, and nothing looked wrong up ahead.

But I turned off onto the rutted, bumpy shadowed road, wondering when I would be able to get back on the main highway.

After going some distance, I was surprised not to see any further cars in the rearview mirror, and there were none up ahead, either. It was as if I were alone on this old mountain road. Weird winds rustled in the trees, moaning in tall pines, and I heard the shriek of a wild bird.

Then, without any previous sign of him being there, a tall man stood in the road, the exact middle. There was no way of going around him, and he had one gloved hand up, staring my way.

I stopped the car and called out the window:

"What's wrong—please get out of the way!"

I was angry, and still in tears; I knew my face was blotched and I didn't want anybody to see it. And I was a bit afraid, being stopped by a man in this country.

His small, close-lipped mouth did not move, but I distinctly heard his voice. It was a frightening sensation. The nape of my neck tingled, and I had to swallow.

"What—what?" I cried. "Please, move it!"

"You must get out of your automobile and come with me."

I sat there, wanting to speak, but suddenly unable, unable to find words. And it was then that I began to feel a peculiar numbness all through my body, and I didn't wonder anymore about not seeing his lips move.

He was a very tall man. He must have stood seven feet, easily, and he was very thin, almost like a reed. And for the first time I saw that he wore strange, tight-fitting, silver-colored clothing, a sort of jump-suit, it was, but without any signs of zipper or buttons or pockets. There was a belt, and a long rod was fastened to the left side, a golden rod.

His face was beautiful; that was the only way to describe it; the most beautiful face I had ever seen, with large, liquid dark eyes. And he had no hair, but this did not seem unnatural. It was, on the other hand, terribly endearing, that smooth, white skull. His face was very white and as he strode toward me, I saw that he had six fingers on each hand.

But there was no surprise in me.

"Who are you?" I asked.

"Please—" I heard the lovely tones of his voice in my head, like musical notes, almost, watery and warm. "Please, just *think* what you wish to speak, do not speak aloud. Do as I do."

And I laughed at myself, because I went along with it so easily. I felt terribly happy. There was no longer any thought of Des, or babies, of Mother or Dad or tears. Just awesome happiness.

"I'm Ann Randall," I thought, and the man came back with those delicious tones in my head; I could almost savor them on my tongue.

"I know, Ann Randall. And you've been chosen because you have such a problem. Don't imagine there are any other cars on this road, and don't imagine you'll be harmed. You won't. But we have a special surprise for you, to solve your problem and to help us solve ours. To introduce myself, I am Morg Thorn, and I am from Mars, the place you people call Mars. We have another name for it."

"Mars," I thought. "But I didn't think it was inhabited."

"It is inhabited for a short time, before we return to our galaxy. It, and for a time, Earth, can become habitable to us."

"I don't understand." I shook my head.

"There isn't really time for explanation. You must not be held up here for longer than it takes. You must return to your husband. People might become suspicious, and we don't want that."

"But—"

"You're very pretty, Ann Randall—I am happy that you are mine."

I just stood there watching him, feeling new sensations in my body, centering in my abdomen now, and the tips of my breasts, and in my throat and along my shoulders, like tiny orgasms. I was breathless. I could not control my thoughts.

"Come with me," Morg Thorn said.

And I walked naturally with him, off the road, and through some trees, and down an incline and up the other side.

"I know how you feel, Ann," he said, holding my arm with those peculiar six fingers. "And I wish there were time to tell you everything. There isn't. Suffice to say that at this precise moment, this very act is taking place all over your known world, in every country. It has been planned for many Earth years. You see, our civilization is rapidly dying away and our females can no longer bear fruit, produce offspring. We have androids, but that is not what we want. We must truly populate to certify the continued growth of our advanced intelligence, so the Universe will not decrease. This is inherent and awake even in our newly birthed children, and this now is the only way we know. Your planet Earth is the closest to us genetically and in substance and degree, so we have chosen you. You will know me for a time, then I shall be gone forever."

"But—should I call you Morg?"

It was only later that I wondered how I had spoken so easily, felt so secure with this being. He was a man to me, a friend.

"Yes, you may. As I call you Ann."

"I still don't understand," I said in our new thought language, and again felt and heard those silvery liquid tones and experienced the fine electricity in the centers of my very brain.

"You will understand, soon. And you will remember all. Now, we are here."

There was a blue haze, a heavy vapor that suddenly vanished, clearing, and an enormous round thing, a huge sphere was revealed, directly in front of us. At that moment a whining sound rose into the air and a slit appeared in the side of the sphere nearest us, and a strip of some white metal projected smoothly down to us. Morg Thorn took my hand and led me to the strip. We stood on it and were whisked upward into the sphere, like on an escalator. It was a marvelous feeling.

I was still numb and the sensations were wonderful.

Then we were inside the sphere and the slit closed.

There was subdued pinkish lighting, coming from nowhere; a soft suffusion, a glow. More of these curious people, all men, and all wearing silver, all tall and handsome, but not quite so handsome as Morg Thorn, stood about the large silvery room. There was no furniture, nothing at all in the room, save for a golden couchlike mattress in the center of the shining warm floor.

"You must excuse me," he said, or thought in my head. "No one but me will think to you, and they all will be present. There will be no humiliation, I promise. Come to the couch, the time is precious."

"But—Morg—?"

"Come, please—I must be insistent. We have very little time on Earth."

He led me to the couch, and with what must have been a smile, began to undress me. He did this with rapidity and ease. Then I stood naked and unashamed before him.

"Lie on the couch, Ann."

I did as he asked, looking up at him as he suddenly shed the silvery skin as a snake might. It slipped from his beautiful body and he stood up there, looking down at me with a curious expression.

"Oh, Morg," I thought. "You are gorgeously handsome!"

"I'm glad I make you happy," he told me. "Now, we must get on with it. I am going to penetrate you, Ann—you will like it. And you will have a child in exactly three months from this time. He will look and behave normally, but he will have a super-intelligence. This is happening, as I said, all over the world, to other women we contact—women, I might add, who are in need of solace. You and your husband will be happy, very happy and our race will survive, here, though we standing in this ship will not survive—"

"Oh, Morg!"

He waved the thought aside and immediately, as he knelt beside me, I saw his manhood rise and become erect. It was much longer than the kind I knew and the testicles were enormous. The penis was curved more than man's, and there were fleshy blue ridges all along the shank, and a circle of knobs on the red glans.

"I cannot speak, as you know it," Morg said. "But I have two tongues, as you will see and feel. I will give you forepleasure, as you call it—then the act, itself, which you will enjoy."

"Oh, Morg—"

"Just remember, you must talk with your husband, and make the proper explanation for the three months' appearance of your child."

With that he kissed my abdomen, then between my thighs, which spread without hesitation, and I felt his twin tongues and the excruciating pleasure. I climaxed twice this way.

"Now," Morg thought in my brain, and he knelt between my thighs and penetrated me. When he was inside me, I thought I would leave my senses with the exquisite joy, the crazed pleasure. The orgasm itself was continuous, and I was in a state of pure epilepsy, of wonder and blind, terrifying enjoyment.

He filled me with his substance.

In moments we were outside and I was dressed and in the car. He was gone, and though gone, his thought reached me.

"Now you are normal again, Ann. Good-by. And thank you."

I wept as I drove away, shuddering and shaking.

I drove as rapidly as possible and soon was back on the main highway. I was dizzy with wonder, still betraying in my body some sense of that furious enjoyment Morg Thorn had given me. And I could recall everything.

I spoke aloud to hear the sound of my own voice.

I thought, "Morg—Morg!"

There was no return thought. There never was again.

When I told Des about it, it was as simple as telling him school had been fine that day. He took it easily, and we planned the excuses for the three months, wondering what our child would be like.

And we wondered, too, about the rest of the women in the world. And how would the child be? What would he be like to us, to us who were implanted with the Martian seed?

Nethra

late 1960s

Gregg Hanson hesitated warily by the apartment door, looked at the luscious body of his wife. She stood nearby. He tried to remain calm. It was difficult, knowing what he planned. Nethra Karne was waiting for him, and Virginia seemed suddenly utterly absurd. He stifled nervous laughter that worked in his chest. Absurd. But there would be an end to the absurdities, the false love.

"You don't really love me, do you, Gregg." It was a statement, not a question. Small, well rounded, with firm breasts, she stood there squinting at him with those deep blue eyes that had once appealed, wearing a too-tight minimal dress. Now he saw errors in her make-up; the knees were too dimpled, the brows too quizzical, always frowning. "You don't really have to leave tonight. You could wait till morning," she said. The sly smile she gave him, scraped against his mental wound. "You can't see anybody in Baytown tonight, Gregg. You know that. It's some woman, isn't it?"

"Sure, sure. A bevy of redheads, didn't you know?"

"Don't try to cover, Gregg. I know you." She hesitated, then suddenly rushed to him, threw her arms about him, thrust her plump body against him.

He felt sharp repugnance. After Nethra, he would never be the same. He was spoiled for everything. Especially, he was spoiled for Virginia.

"Please," she whispered. "I love you. I don't want you ever to leave me—ever!"

"Virginia. Baby. Nobody's leaving anybody."

"Something's wrong, I can tell." She pressed tightly against him, breathing into his neck. Her wet lips drew across the skin, and he shriveled inside.

All he could think was Nethra—Nethra. All he could see in his mind was the shadowy, darkened room, the candlelight, the ultra-comfortable scene. Nethra might be a kook, but what a kook.

"Say you love me," Virginia muttered.

"For Christ's sake, baby."

"Say it—please . . ."

"I—love you. There. Happy, now?"

"I'll never let you go," Virginia said. "That's why I'd never give you a divorce. You're my crazy, mixed-up bike rider, Gregg. It's not just because of religion—it's because I couldn't bear it without you. Can't you see?" She thrust partially away from him, looking up, her eyes stricken, lips twisted.

"I love you, Gregg. Don't slip away from me. I need you right now. Can't you wait till tomorrow?"

"It's important," he said. "I'm taking a hotel room, and I'm going to work all night, get up early to approach those guys. They want to buy bikes for this insane festival, and I sell 'em. It'll mean a bunch of loot. Don't you see?"

She still clung to him. "All right, Gregg."

He forced a smile. "Go to bed," he said. "Read a good book—"

"I thought I'd go to the movies."

"You know I can't stand thinking of you on the streets, Virginia. Anything might happen."

If she went out, it would louse up everything.

"Well," she said. She smiled tremulously, and subtly worked her hips against him. "You could make me stay."

He knew what he had to do. He knew any other guy would jump at the chance. To him, it was a tired old haul.

But he did it, anyway. He kissed her, and she came to life. He backed her into the bedroom, and lifted her skirt, teasing between her thighs. She wore no panties, never had. She began breathing hard and fast right away. It was almost as if she were different, somehow. Then she seemed to go wild with it. Her hands tore at his pants, and she fell back on the bed, yanking her skirt up to her waist, never releasing him. With her other hand, she ripped the dress across her breasts, and they puffed out, full and rosy-nippled. She leered at him, and lifted her knees, opening her thighs. "Hurry," she gasped. "I'm all nerves from worry!"

He plunged into her, and did her like a machine. His mind swarmed with Nethra. It was Nethra under him, not Virginia. Everything was wild, all mixed up. And abruptly, his mind went blank. Then he was standing by the bed, looking down at her. She laughed up at him.

"You can go, if you must," she said. "I'll read that damned book. You're bigger than ever, wildman."

"That's my girl."

Helping alibi what he planned, he said, "Evening," to Jake, the doorman of the apartment house, and as he rode away on the big black Kawasaki, Jake waved again. His mind swarmed with thoughts of Nethra. She would be waiting for him, in that place, that dark, shadowy place, with the candles burning. They would drink, and make love on the scattered vari-colored pillows, with the yellow candlelight flickering over them. He could see, in his mind's eye, Nethra's long, willowy body, probably encased in tight silk, black silk. Her wild, jetty hair would be down to her shoulders. Her darkly crimson lips would be his. Those swimming black eyes would stare at him, filled with love, with urgent giving. Then Nethra would read to him, poetry. She even said she conversed with the Devil. He didn't care. Every cell in his body yearned for Nethra, for her beauty, her dark, evil ways. The candlelight was a symbol of Nethra. She studied the occult. She was learned in the mysteries of Isis. She was going to teach him.

And—most of all, Nethra loved him with an all-enveloping love that surpassed anything he had even in his most far-reaching moments, thought existed. He drowned in Nethra. She was many loves, all in one. She sought only to please—to please him, Gregg Hanson. *"I'll never let you go!"* she said, so different from *Virginia*. *"We'll be together always. I've found you, among all the others. You're mine, Gregg—you're mine!"*

Nethra was weird, and he loved it. The black and crimson walls of her apartment. The books, the esoteric music, the ubiquitous candlelight, the fuming incense.

To think Virginia had introduced him to Nethra, at that garden-club get-together. Nethra had looked almost plain, then. "Somebody new," Virginia told him. "Meet Nethra Karne, Gregg. A new member." Virginia had never known what Nethra was truly like. And from that moment on . . .

"I spoke with Him again, Gregg. He approves of you. Satan approves of you, Gregg. He says I must devour you with love, weave you into the scarlet pattern of dark desire."

Gregg's hands were sweating on the bars, thinking back. Nethra was like some outré drink, smoking green, bubbling in the tall, slim glass, promising untold ecstasies. He knew she was a heady potion, but he knew, too, that he was caught in her devotion. She was completely different, young, and very real. She waited for him in that dark room.

After tonight, she would be able to teach him her ways. He had never experienced such complete love from a woman. It erased all other existence.

Riding along, he forced himself to consider what he must do.

He had it planned quite well . . .

He parked the bike a block from his apartment. The house was at the end of the block. There were tall trees that darkened the sidewalk. He slipped through shadows, down an alley, scaled two walls, approached the apartment house from the rear.

He climbed the fire escape, stood before their bedroom window. He had unlatched the window, so there was no problem. The bedlight was lit. He could tell through the blinds. Nine chances out of ten, Virginia would be asleep, book in hand. It was her way.

It had finally come to this—to murder. But, for some curious reason, he felt no fear. Mental snaps of Nethra drove him on, seething inside him.

Everything else was a gray fog. There was only Nethra, the pot of furious gold at the end of the tunnel. The living gold.

He flung up the window, brushed the blinds and curtains aside, and entered the room.

Virginia stared at him from the bed, her eyes sleepy.

"Gregg!"

He said nothing, only drew the knife. It had to be a knife, because it must look maniacal. He stepped to the bed, holding the knife.

"Gregg—what's that? What are you doing?" She sat half up in bed, gripping the book with white-knuckled fingers, eyes wide now, lips parted, breast heaving.

"So long, Virginia—so long, for good."

He did his work, then stepped back and viewed the results. He was satisfied. She was dead. He left the knife on the bed. Crimson blood was everywhere. Her book was saturated. He glanced at the book. A sexy love story, a picture of a pale-faced young girl, with seeking eyes, on the dust jacket. There was blood on the girl's face.

Systematically, Gregg tore the room apart. He yanked out the drawers, flung them on the floor, tore up Virginia's clothes, made a complete havoc of everything.

Then he took lipstick and scrawled on the broad dressing mirror:

"LOVE WINS!"
"DEATH TO PHONIES!"
"WE ARE THE CHILDREN OF LOVE! DEATH CUTS DOWN THE FLOWERS OF SATISFACTION! SHE WAS A SATISFIED PIG. DEATH BELONGS TO HER!"

He read the blunt words, smiled grimly, tossed the lipstick on the floor, and went to the window. He climbed through, hurried down the fire escape, and headed for his bike up the block.

Crazed dope heads were doing these things. He'd read about it in the papers. And he had a perfect alibi. He'd told several people he was going to Baytown tonight. There actually was a motorcycle meet, and a wealthy man was purchasing bikes for the rodders to burn up. He would be at the hotel all day tomorrow, waiting for notification of Virginia's death.

But tonight—tonight he would be with Nethra.

Strangely, the murdering of his wife seemed to leave no impression on Gregg Hanson. It was a job he'd had to do, and that was all. And, remembering, he had performed it in a strange kind of dream. He had considered it from every angle. But he had to be free. Nethra was the true answer. She was strong inside him. He could think of nothing else. He wondered if he would eventually tell Nethra of what he'd done? Or would she guess, when she learned of Virginia's death?

It had been so diabolically simple, really.

In Baytown, an hour later, he checked into the hotel, went to his room, dressed, and immediately rode back through the night to Nethra's apartment. He drifted smoothly up in the elevator, overwhelmed with what was to come. He had hidden the Kawasaki in an alley, behind stacks of garbage crates.

. . . it had been like sticking a knife into butter.

She opened the door, and he knew it had all been worth it. They would have endless years together. She would teach him the things she knew.

"Hi," she said.

But she wasn't smiling. She had always smiled when she greeted him before. Her face was even paler than usual, and her dark eyes glittered. Her lips were very red and damp. She wore the tight black silk, sheathing her slimly voluptuous body like filmy paint. Her breasts thrust at him. Her black hair gleamed and shone, falling about her shoulders.

"I came, exactly as I promised," he said. "Aren't you going to ask me in?"

"Yes. Come in, Gregg."

Her voice was soft, very low, almost a whisper.

The foyer was quite dark, the odor of incense strong, much stronger than ever before. They stepped down the three stairs and moved into the big room. Shadows seemed to writhe on the scarlet walls. Music purled in the room, red music, with lines of black. It was Saint-Saens' *Danse Macabre.* She often played it, and he had come to realize some sort of thrill from it himself. Candles burned, tall, slim black ones, smoking thinly toward the high, dark ceiling. There was no other light.

Suddenly her arm slipped around him, and she was against him, kissing him with burning lips, her tongue lashing in his mouth, her hips snaky and urgent. He seemed to fall straight through her, into the abyss of love, sex, pulsating evil.

"God," he said, running his hand over her curved bottom, along her thigh. "You're lovely."

"Don't say that. I just finished speaking with Him."

"Ah?"

"Yes. He says we must be together forever. We must never be apart."

"I think that can be arranged, Nethra."

"I *know* it can," she whispered. "I love you. You are a thing apart, Gregg. I've found you, and I recognize the evil in you. Nothing escapes me, Gregg."

"The evil in me?"

"Yes." She breathed it, eyes glistening. "It's exactly the way I like. We are both evil, and we must remain together. Sit down."

He lowered himself onto one of the huge cushions that littered the heavily rugged floor.

"A drink?" he said.

"I was about to suggest it." As she moved past him, her finger trailed along the back of his neck. He experienced overpowering lust, revelling in it. Moments later, she returned with two tall, slim glasses, filled with green liquid. "Absinthe," she said. "Just for us." She knelt on the floor, then half rolled over and reclined on a cushion. Her lips were solemn as she sipped.

He sampled the absinthe. He'd heard a great deal about this drink, and was prepared to like it. The music was a ghostly sibilance. He took another larger swallow.

For the first time that night, Nethra smiled at him.

"You like the incense, darling? It's something new. A devotional incense—just for us."

He thought it rather over-sweet, but he said, "Yes. It's wonderful. I like it."

"We love each other," Nethra said.

He stared at that body, knowing her evil ways. "Yes," he said, swallowing. "I couldn't wait to get here." He had a passing thought of Virginia. When would they find her? He hated to think he must remain at the hotel all day tomorrow, until authorities reached him. He would carry on with the sale of the bikes, of course. Business as usual.

He took another drink, eyeing Nethra.

God, she was so beautiful in the candlelight. The big cushion was so soft. The music—

"Gregg?"

"Yeah?"

"We're going to be together now."

He smiled, touched her ankle. "I know," he said. If *she* only knew. He had killed for her. He had a long life ahead, and every moment would be spent with Nethra.

"I can do anything," she said. "I have learned everything there is to know about the mysteries. I was taught by my grandmother. She was a witch. I know these things, and can perform miracles."

He could no longer stand it, the way she looked at him, those lips, those eyes, that marvelous body, waiting. He slowly ran his hand up under her long black silken skirt, feeling her thigh. She watched him and breathed tightly. Then she said, "Yes," in a whisper, and with a single motion the encasing silk fell apart, and she lay nude before him—wearing only silky black stockings, gartered blackly high on her white thighs. She flung her hands overhead, and lifted her knees, opening her legs for him. "Come," she whispered.

He crawled to her. She reached down and fondled him, then unfastened his pants. He could hear dark, obscene curses emanating from those red lips. Abruptly, she leaned forward, open-mouthed, and kissed his belly, then lower, till he felt her hot lips working. He crushed his fingers into her hair, arching his back. She drew away, said, "Oh, my darling!" and sprawled legs apart. "Now, now—" she said fiercely.

Once in her, she was like fire and light and tunneled darkness, all at once. She was savage, like an animal. She raked teeth along his shoulder, drawing blood. She was viciously strong and wildly urgent. And all the time she muttered imprecations in a language he did not understand. But he understood the intonation well enough. Her head was flung back. Her jet eyes stared like an animal's. Then she shrieked, and at the same moment she seemed to draw fire down his backbone, and out, into her. It was a streaming shock. He thought it would never end, the excruciating wonder, the violent thrill, the endless pumping—a human succubus. She took the last drop, and he fell back exhausted.

"Ah," she said. "You are one of a kind, my love."

He felt rather giddy, now. Of course, it was the drink, the absinthe.

"I read your mind, my love. But you do not really know—not really." Her voice was frilled with laughter.

"What—what did you say?"

"It's the drink, Gregg." She lay there, propped on one elbow, watching him, her long, pale fingers holding her own glass again. "He told me to do it, you see."

"What?"

She set down the glass and rose slowly, and moved like a cloud behind a scarlet curtain. He watched the silken and uncertain rustling of the curtain, and then she emerged again. But—*what!* Who was that?

It was Virginia.

He reeled halfway up, the room spinning. It was his wife, Virginia. She was naked, standing there before him. The knife wounds were purple on her body. But her eyes were on him with love. She stood perfectly still.

The two of them. Nude. Together.

"He told me," Nethra said. "So we can all cross to the other side, my love. And really be with Him. Virginia is mine, too—you see? I love her, the same as I love you—and she loves me. It was all arranged. Virginia has been under a spell for weeks, my love. She's deep under now. She will retain this present form until we all go. You see? It was in the absinthe, love. We've both taken it, and Virginia waits. Just a little more time—it works very fast, darling—"

He stared at the glass of absinthe.

The room was spinning weirdly. The music rose and fell among the scarlet shadows and candlelight. He fought to his knees, refusing this—refusing all with sudden deadly fear. The glass fell from his hand. He came staggering to his feet, wild with fiery panic.

"It doesn't matter where you go, we'll be together," Nethra said. "I love you, we love you, my darling."

He lurched violently across the room, and found the door. He ran reeling down the hall, and into the elevator. Then he was on the street, in the alley. He found the big black Kawasaki, swung on, and started it up, shot out of the alley. The inhuman whining roar beat against the darkened streets.

He could hear her laughing all around, the wild sounds echoing from vaulted buildings.

He was doing one hundred and forty miles an hour when he struck the stone wall.

Friendly Persuasion

late 1960s

Love Me Too walked up to the middle-aged man who was seated on the green bench by the railing overlooking the river. For a long moment, Love Me Too just stood there in his dirty jeans and droopy black sweater, watching the man, as he sucked on the last half inch of his last roach. It had been good grass, though, and admiring the butt lovingly, he abruptly popped it into his mouth, chewed twice, and swallowed.

"Say," Love Me Too said. "You don't look so happy. You strung out, something?"

The man looked up slowly, apparently seeing Love Me Too for the first time. He was a stubby, round fellow, with a face like an overgrown apple, red-cheeked, and twinkly eyed, but he looked sad. To Love Me Too, he looked very sad, but just the same . . .

"This time of night," Love Me Too said, "you shouldn't sit in the shadows, like this. It's dangerous. Muggings, all that. Don't you realize?"

"I just don't care," the man said.

"Well, man, you *got* to care. That's the one thing about everything, man. You got to care! You don't care, where would things get? That's just the trouble, in fact, dig? People don't care. They've forgot how to care."

"Maybe you're right," the man said, staring down into his lap. "But I cared too much. I think that's the trouble."

Love Me Too hitched at his belt, then fiddled with the brass necklace around his neck. "You can't care too much. You see," he said, moving closer, then sitting down beside the man, looking at him closely. "That's my bag. I mean, it's my *real* bag. Caring, I mean. I really care. You've *got* to." He paused. "Say, you got any grass?"

"What?"

"Hell, man," Love Me Too said. "Don't subtract me. *I* know you're a real swinger, you're carrying a sign. I can tell, true. Sitting here in the shadows, caring the way you do. I can tell, all right. Dig, you should see Blue Lips."

"Blue Lips? What's that?"

"My chick, man. I care about her. She's got a heart condition, but a true swinger, man. Sock it to me, I say. She takes me literal. She really does. Any time. Of course, that's the way I live, and that's the way it should be. You need a real swinging chick to groove, man. That old rocker don't bother her." Love Me Too suddenly ceased talking, and touched the man's arm, leaning very close, peering into his face. "Say, what's your name?"

"Dickerman. Albert Dickerman."

"Say, Al. I need some grass, some speed, acid, something. You tried acid?"

"What's acid. What d'you mean?"

"Ah, forget it, Al. Just let it slide by. Say, Al—it's a damn good thing I found you, y'know? I just banged Blue Lips, and I wandered out, and I come along the river, like, and here you are. It's tragic."

"How do you mean?"

"I mean, like, it's marve, simply marve." Love Me Too laughed heartily, slapping Mr. Dickerman on the arm. Then he ceased laughing. "You believe in love, don't you?"

"I don't know anymore," Albert Dickerman said.

"What you mean you don't know!" Love Me Too said loudly. "You got to believe in love, man." He lowered his voice. "Man, look, y'know. Love is the BIG bag. Love, generosity, kindness, looking out for the other guy, *thinking* of the other guy. Thinking *all the time* of the other guy. It's got to be that way. Love. Goodness. That's what I live by, Al. That's my code, you might say. If you love out far enough, it all comes back to you, a hundredfold. Don't you know that?"

"My wife just left me."

Love Me Too licked his lips, peering closely at the other.

"Say, Al," Love Me Too said. "How much money you got?"

"Not much. I'm not sure if I have any money at all. Why?"

"I just wondered's all. Dig, love, Al. That's the WORD. If you have the WORD, you have everything. Love. Jesus. It makes me ache, I get goose-pimples, Al, just thinking about it. And all the love-starved people in this world. I could give them love. You know it. Christ, I—why I got enough love to feed the world."

The round man glanced at Love Me Too. He started to rise from the bench, but Love Me Too pressed him back with a flap and a push of his arm. The man sat there, staring at Love Me Too.

"Kindness," Love Me Too said. "Sweet everlasting love." He gave a little sob and his voice cracked. "It's hate you got to fight, man. Dig?"

"Yes, I suppose you're right. But I didn't hate Alice, and I'll never believe she really hates me. She just said she was 'fed up,' and she left. She took a suitcase, and packed it, and left. I don't know what to do."

"That's a toughie, man. I dig you. Say, Al?"

"Yes."

"You positive you haven't any bread?"

"Yes."

"Take a good look in your pockets, man. Don't hang me up like this."

"I'm not doing anything."

"You're hanging me up. You're putting me down. You're a regular old sticky-finger, Al. Christ, Al, I got to have something. I need, man. Dig? I love you, Al. I mean I like you to pieces. I could just cream, with the love that's inside me for everybody. But I got to have some bread. Don't be a freak."

"I'm not a freak." Al was trying to rise from the bench again, now, but Love Me Too held him back with his arm. Love Me Too scraped dank hair out of his eyes with his other hand, and smiled at Al.

"Say, man," Love Me Too said. "You don't want me to take flight, do you?"

"I—I—"

"Of course, you don't. Now, Goddamnit! Come up with some bread, man. Hurry up. I can't wait all night. Jesus Christ, He's watching."

"Who's watching?"

"The Great Watcher In The Sky, that's who. You want Him to think you got no love, something ratty like that?"

"I've got to go, really, I—"

"We've all got to go, man. That's just the ass-crimping trouble. We've got to GO, man! Now, look," Love Me Too lowered his voice almost to a whisper. "You've simply got to brace yourself and dig this, Al. I've *got* to have some bread."

"You mean money. I don't have any money."

Love Me Too jammed his chin down and stared at Al.

"You're putting me on," Love Me Too said. "I'm all loaded with love, and you come along and put me on. I don't dig that kind of crap, Al."

"Really, I've got to—"

Love Me Too grabbed Al by the front of his jacket and screamed at him. "I've got to make it, see? I've got to really swing, dig?" He screamed it. "You give me some bread, Al—give me some. It's love—all the way!"

"I got no bread—I got no—"

Love Me Too raged and flung his head around, his mouth open wide as he screamed. "Sock it to me!"

"I'm telling you," Al said, gasping for breath.

"You lie!" Love Me Too said.

"I wouldn't lie," Al said.

Love Me Too shouted something and dug in his pocket. He was shaking all over, his head bobbing up and down, his eyes shot with a strange glaze. A knife was in his hand, and the silver blade glinted.

"Don't!" Al said.

"Dig it, man—just dig it, that's all I can say," Love Me Too shouted as he slit Al's throat. Blood pulsed out and Love Me Too leaped to his feet, standing away, holding the knife. "Christ, almost splashed me."

Al crumpled forward and folded into a pile in front of the bench. Blood gushed out, forming a gleaming puddle on the cement.

Love Me Too leaned down and wiped the knife blade on Al's jacket. Then he straightened. He folded the knife and put it away. Then he cleared his throat and spat into the night.

"Ah, God," he said, looking up at the sky. "It's a drag, I tell you. It's a drag. Look what I done." He paused, turned, started walking away. "They don't understand. They'll *never* understand. It's enough to make you weep."

Hung Up

Sheriff Reb Klayville had it strong on his mind all the time he was talking with Deputy Cliff Waters this morning. He shifted his enormous bulk in the swivel-chair, and leather creaked as he rubbed his round, freckled face with a banana-fingered hand. He had a big hard-on, tight in his crimped khaki pants, well hidden under the edge of his cluttered desk, wishing it would work with his wife, Annie Mae. But he knew it wouldn't work this way. It had to be the other way, like how he was thinking about Hollis Younger, Black Creek's chief cocksmith.

"Well, what'd you like me to do?" Deputy Waters wanted to know. "No telling who the kid is. Could be anybody."

"Use your melon, you sumbitch. Get out there to the high school, and keep an eye skinned like a onion. This here's a small town, Cliff, boy. We got to know damn well who the stink he is, handing out that speed an' grass. He's one of them kids, sure as I sit here. Get your ass out there, an' report back to me no matter what you find out. I'll be somewheres. You know how to find me. I'll kick that sumbitch's ass. You know it. Getting them fine little girlies all high an' hot on that shitty dope. Worse than New York."

Deputy Waters was long and lanky, with a reddish scale on his lantern jaw, from too much sun and a bad razor blade. He blinked solemnly. "Well, I'll sure as heck do what I can."

"You do better than that, you sumbitch."

"I can't wear a mask, Reb."

"I ain't asking you to play phantom of the opera. Just get what you can get. Now, stretch it, and come back with his scalp."

Deputy Waters grinned a half grin, turned, and left the office.

The sheriff, still and all, had much more than high school paint sniffers on his mind. His hard-on was as rigid as ever and it felt good, tight in his pants. He thought of how sweet and nice his wife was, how downright smart-pretty, and of how she would love this hard-on, if she could have it. But every time he got close to her it wilted. He was no good. But that wasn't because he didn't have the answer. The answer was Hollis Younger, and he knew damned well how Annie Mae felt about Hollis.

They'd discussed Younger and his probable prick, how he serviced all the tail in town, and how he maybe likely had snaggles on his cock, so as to make them squeal.

"You think that's actually true, Reb?" Annie Mae sometimes asked.

"You bet your fancy ass."

"I wish you had snaggles."

And he would want to cry, because he didn't even have a stiff cock around his own wife.

But he had discovered something. Every time he thought of Hollis Younger and Annie Mae doing it together, he got hard and stiff and rompy. He had tried just the thinking about it, but that didn't work either. What he had to do was get Younger over to the house and have him fuck Annie Mae right smack dandy in the mouth and cunt, and all. Then he, Reb, could take over properly.

He knew it would be stiff as a poker, just the seeing of them doing it together, and it would stay stiff, and he could ride her down the way it was meant to be. If it came to that, by hellfire, he would pay Hollis Younger. But he didn't think it would come to that, because Hollis Younger was a cocksmith, and cocksmiths did not take pay for their work, not according to the Bible, leastways.

God, how he had prayed for it to be big and stiff; he prayed to God it would stand up like a fence post for darling Annie Mae. But it wouldn't. And he would cry and say he was sorry and it would get better.

"I only hope so, Reb, honey. I hate doing it with my hand. It's nasty, like it ain't right, somehow."

"I know, Annie Mae. I swear it. It'll cure."

She would leave him if he didn't do something. He was certain of it. Annie Mae was the hottest-looking piece in town, and she was his wife. And it had been over a whole year since he began wilting when he got close to her round, luscious body. He'd tried everything; having her wear net stockings and sneakers and leather pants, or a raincoat, but nothing helped. He wasn't a fetish man. He found that out. But when he thought about Hollis Younger and Annie Mae together, why his cock simply surprised him. It got like a crow-bar.

He had the answer. Now to approach Hollis. It would be a damn' ticklish proposition and he wasn't even sure he could carry it off. He felt so crazied nervous. But he *had* to do it. He had to get them together. And he didn't *half* worry about telling Annie Mae. Her being church-going and knitting-minded, and all.

Well, he might just as well get at it. It had to be today. He had made his mind up to that. And Deputy Cliff was out to the high school, snooping on them dopers.

Jesus H. Christ on a mountain, what if Annie Mae wouldn't agree?

But Reb figured the snaggles would get to her.

. . . whacking off his wilted little weenie in the bathroom, like some scaredy-cat ten-year-old . . .

God! Hear me, now! Make it big an' stiff an' fat!

An', God—pleasure me—make Annie Mae want Hollis Younger.

Amen.

• • •

He found Hollis Younger at *The Low and Wet*, a tavern where bikers and them that was on the make hung out, just at the edge of town; a low-ceilinged smoky room, rocking with Thin Lizzy, with a horseshoe bar and lots of teen pussy lollygagging on the red-cushioned, chrome-tubed stools.

"Hollis, boy—ain't seen you for a chunk. Lemme buy you one. What you drinking?"

"Why, Reb Klayville, Sheruff! With your big gun hanging out at the ready, and your badge polished like a righteous flatback's bottom. You really want to know, I'm drinking Jack Daniel. Got 'im by the curlies, too."

Reb ordered two drinks, paid for them, and lounged, feeling horsey with his nickel-plated, bone-handled revolver and spacious with his star and Stetson.

Hollis Younger, a handsome, jack-jawed, black-maned, backdoor folly, in a yellow shirt with crimson flowers embroidered across the shoulders, and super bell blue jeans, hauled at a female wrist, which brought around a white face framed with flame-colored hair and a mouth cut like a watermelon.

"This here's Honey Lee Merry, Sheriff. Meet the Big Gun of Black Creek, ol' Reb, the sheriff, Honey."

Honey Lee Merry showed two inches of gum and a bulging thrust of pale breast, valleyed pink, and encased in tight shimmering green.

"We're passing the time of day," Hollis said.

He's damn got a voice like hot syrup over French toast, and them snaggles to boot, Reb thought. He said, "I'd right like to pass some of that time alone with you in a booth, Hollis, boy. I got a good notion for you."

"Well, all right, then," the young man said with a kinky wink. He pinched one of Honey Lee Merry's green-covered nipples, and he and Reb took their drinks and went to a dark booth, with Tom Waits whispering something among strings and rumbles.

Reb Klayville settled his obstinate leather-holstered .44 revolver and hunched over his whisky in the amber shadows.

"Got a foxy thing," he said, feeling hot all over.

"What thing?"

"You know Annie Mae? Huh?"

Hollis Younger nodded and took a sip.

Reb decided to blurt it out. "I got a proposition, Hollis, boy. Annie Mae's neat nookie, an' I want you to come to my place an' fuck her so I can watch." He covered it fast. "Now, don't get me wrong, now. Annie Mae's got a steam up for you, an' she'd like to play party with you, with me there so she'd feel right. How about that?"

"With you right there?"

"Me right there."

"I ain't never done nothing like 'at. Ain't my style."

"But you'd like to get Annie Mae on her back."

"Well, yeah—now you come out with it."

"Then what's to hamper you?"

"Well, it's kind of funny, like, you ask me."

"What's funny?"

"Funny-funny," Hollis Younger said.

David Bowie was on the box now.

"I can't see a funny thing about it," the sheriff said, feeling wild and shot to hell. "You just got to do this thing." His voice was tense and rising. "She's waiting for you, boy! What's the difference I want to watch, or not?"

Hollis shook his head dubiously.

"Well, will you, or won't you?"

"Now?"

"Right dead now. You know what kind of mouth she's got, an' tits an' ass an' legs and everything else. She'll show you a come-how time."

Hollis eyed the sheriff curiously, drank his drink, smacked the glass on the table. "Okay, then. I'm feeling kind of wild and hairy, anyways. Don't give a damn. You sure you ain't making no fillum?"

"I ain't making no fillum."

Hollis stood up. "Let's get at it, then."

"Next haul I make, I'll see you with some prime smack," Reb said, rising slowly, fatly.

"I only sniff some," Hollis said. "But thanks."

"Sniff or shoot, it'll be okay."

"You're turnin' into a randy candyman, Reb. How come all the favors?"

"I like circuses," the sheriff said, muttering.

• • •

Hollis Younger was in the bedroom, and Reb had Annie Mae in the living-room hall. His wife wore tight pale cut-off jeans and a loose white shirt over big perks. She had a mouth like a toilet and eyes like holes in an ash-heap, with bunches of straw-colored hair strewn around. She looked like a seething pit of sin.

Reb was whispering hoarsely, quickly. "You'll love it, Annie Mae. I done it jus' for you. What with them snaggles an' all. You know how you got a yen for Hollis. All you got to do is function."

She swallowed. "I don't think it's right, Reb."

He made a crazy face. "You got to! I'm allowing it, Annie Mae, for Christ's sake. You'll love it. I can't always allow it, but I am now."

"But it ain't right, somehow."

"What ain't right?"

"Me doin' that with him, like that."

"Listen"—he lowered his voice, still hoarse—"You do it an' love it, an' I'll sit right there an' watch. I'll take care nothing happens. You know I bet he's good, too."

"But—"

"It'll be good fuckin'," Reb said. "And with me right there—"

Annie Mae bridled sexily. She tongued her lips and squinched her dark eyes. "Jesus, you got me screaming hot, now, you bastard. An' you're gonna be there watchin'?"

"Watchin' an' then some," the sheriff said, his Stetson still cocked at a slant over one eye. "Lookee here, Annie Mae."

He took her hand and scrubbed it against his bulging fly.

"An' that's just the thinking about it!"

"Well, all right, Reb, honey. I admit, I do kind of like Hollis Younger. But it seems to me you're giving me a big squeeze of freedom, what with you my husband, and all."

"Annie Mae, I love you. That's how it is. I want you to be happy, hear?"

Her eyes snapped and she ran for the bedroom. Lusting, fantasizing, breathing heavily, Reb Klayville plodded after his wife.

• • •

"Why, they ain't no snaggles, at all!" Annie Mae said, gripping Hollis Younger's stiff cock in her right hand. "It's just like anybody else's, just like yours was when you carried me off, only maybe longer an' thicker."

"It's the longer that gets you," Reb said, sitting in a cane chair by the bed. He wanted to unzip his fly and take out his for a minute there; just the sight of his wife, with her pants off, and her shirt open, her heavy snatch, and Hollis' stiff curved whang did things to him. But his beloved prick had wilted again. He felt pained and abandoned.

Annie Mae glanced slyly at her husband, then sat on the edge of the bed, and pulled Hollis Younger over to her, and kissed his cock.

Immediately, Reb Klayville's prong thronged with blood, and he could not stand it. He unzipped his fly and hauled it out, thinking of how Deputy Cliff Waters was out to the high school, snooping on them dopers, or maybe trying to find him with captured cohorts of the pusher, or information, or something, and he felt a little guilty about that—but only for a second, because his prick felt so thrilly.

Annie Mae lipped Hollis Younger's cock and said thinly, "Reb tol' me you had snaggles on it, but you ain't. Didn't you tell me that, Reb?"

Hollis Younger said, "What snaggles? Where?"

"Snaggles on your c-cock," Annie Mae said. "So it'd feel so nice, an' all."

"I said, 'maybe he might,'" Reb said, shifting his huge bulk for a better view.

"Anyways, whatever," Annie Mae said, sliding her open-lipped red mouth down on Younger's cock, sucking him off.

Hollis Younger began to fuck Annie Mae in the face, with a kind of excruciating agony. He stood stark naked, with his rod like a polished bronze candlestick.

Reb began jacking his dong, staring boggle-eyed at the two of them. Then Annie Mae simply fell back on the bed with her thighs wide open, and Hollis bent to her and speared her tight, nailing her to the mattress, juice running out of her pussy and down her ripe ass.

"Ah, God, you're somethin' moony!" Annie Mae gasped.

Reb Klayville's cock was like a steel spike as he stared and stroked impatiently. But then something came into him, something he had not counted on. It was a shocked feeling of amazed jealousy and anger.

Hollis Younger had Annie Mae spread wide up on the bed, now, easing it into her with a lusty guff, pumping his cock into her luscious twat, sucking on a nipple. Annie Mae was moaning like she saw a horror film, saliva trickling down one side of her mouth, her eyes lidded with hot desperation.

"You stop," Reb Klayville muttered, standing up, still working at his stiff prick. "You got to stop now. I aim to have some of that right in the mouth, an' I want you out of here, boy." He frowned when they did not cease fucking and groaning, Younger's ass working like a big ship's piston. "You hear me?" Reb shouted, still massaging his long, hard whang. "I want you to stop it!" He stumbled heavily onto the bed with his knees, still holding his cock.

"Can't stop now," Hollis Younger said. "Annie Mae's got too much a grip to let it lay."

But something in Reb Klayville's voice got to Hollis Younger. The voice thundered, "You stop right now, you stinkin' sumbitch!" and Hollis Younger tumbled back off Annie Mae, his rod spurting sauce on her white thigh. He lay there, jerking and sputtering, and something went crazy wild in Sheriff Reb Klayville at the sight.

Reb grabbed his .44 revolver and yelled, "You reeking shit, that there's my wife!" and he shot Hollis Younger three times, shuddering explosions; once in the chest and twice in the frightened face.

The face flew apart.

Reb did not hear the pounding feet on the stairs, he only heard the mad music in his skull, under his slanted Stetson, and he was only conscious that he had a big fat hard-on.

"Get over here, girl," he mewled, "get over here an' blow this, right now!"

Annie Mae knelt on the bed, mouth gaping, staring at Reb Klayville as he moved lumberingly on his knees toward her. Hollis Younger lay in a swath of blood and facial bone across the white sheets, his tool still sticking up.

"Suck it! Damn you, now," Red gasped, as Deputy Cliff Waters lurched into the room.

"You got jealous, you fat slob," Annie Mae sputtered.

"What's going on in here?" Cliff Waters wanted to know, his red lantern jaw sticking out, eyes startled.

The sheriff had his revolver in one hand, and his prick in the other, forcing it toward Annie Mae's face.

"My God, you killed 'im!" Cliff Waters said, drawing his gun. "Reb, you drop that piece and stand back, now."

Sheriff Reb Klayville's prick began to sag as he half-turned toward his deputy. Cliff Waters frowned, meaning business.

Annie Mae yelled it. "Reb shot him. He killed poor Hollis." She was in shock. "He didn't even have no snaggles."

"He rape you?"

"Rape me? Wow! It was the best suckin' fuck I ever begun having, when this old fart shot him dead, just watchin' an jerkin'."

Reb Klayville turned until he faced Deputy Waters full on. The revolver fell with a plop on the bed. His prick was a limp noodle.

"Damn you, Cliff," the sheriff said, fat tears working down his freckled cheeks. "An' just when I was goin' to get my cream." He let go an enormous sob that shook his entire body.

Annie Mae began laughing hysterically.

Deputy Cliff Waters unhooked glinting handcuffs from his belt, cuffed Reb's hands behind him. Reb stood beside the bed with his fly open, his red weenie peeking through.

"You get that sumbitchin' doper?" Reb asked, weeping.

"No, Reb—I didn't find me no doper. But I nailed a whole barn full of kids shooting the Paris death rush with snake venom. Now, you best come with me, sheriff."

"Piss-ant!" Annie Mae said, her round knee slipping in Hollis Younger's youthful red blood.

The Invalid

early 1970s

I picked Helen up after work that Friday afternoon, just as usual. It was four-thirty, and she was standing at the curb in front of the Union Trust. She was a teller in the bank and I worked for an insurance company just down the street. She waved and I parked the Volvo.

"Hi, Gregg."

"Honey."

She had the door open, and slid in across the seat. Her powder blue skirt hiked up across round, nylon-covered knees. She tried to yank it down, looking at me from the corner of her eye, but it wasn't much help. It was a short skirt.

"Trouble?" I said.

"Oh, no."

She looked wonderful, just like always, and I thought, How the hell long is it going to take? I had a monstrous ache for her. I'd been waiting a long time. We loved each other, and planned marriage, but she always managed to hold her skirt down. All the argument in the world didn't seem to change that. Sometimes it drove me crazy, because Helen was choice, any way you looked at it. She was ripe all over, with thick black hair, and a soft voice that seemed to be made for the bedroom. Only I'd never seen the bedroom, not with her.

I drove away from the curb. Well, tonight we were going out. I would try again. It was getting to be a kind of contest. I kept trying to tell her we should sample it before we married, but she would bat those big blue eyes at me and tell me not to worry, and if I pressed, she'd say, "Now, Gregg!" And I would wait.

It wasn't that she didn't get excited. You could tell she did, because of how she breathed. But she held the fort, I'll sure say that for her. Sometimes I thought, Maybe something's wrong with her. But then I would look at her good, and there was certainly nothing wrong with her. There couldn't be.

We drove through traffic.

"How'd things go today?" she asked.

"Fine. You?"

"Oh, fine."

We drove a while. I would take her home, then I'd see her later. I didn't know where we'd go tonight, but I wished we could stay at her apartment, and make hay. I sighed. It wouldn't work, I knew. We'd take in a movie, and eat somewhere, and I'd run her home, and maybe stop in for a drink. I'd make a play for her, and she would up with the barricade, and I'd head for home. It was always like that. But the thing was, I couldn't stop. I wanted her. And I would marry her, too. It was a crock.

"There's something I haven't had a chance to tell you," she said.

"Oh?"

"My sister came in last night. She'll be staying with me for a while."

"You never mentioned your sister."

"Of course I did. Agnes. The one who's married. She lives in Jacksonville. Only something happened, I don't know what, exactly, except she had some sort of fight with her husband. She wants to stay with me, now."

"Well, that's nice, in a way, I suppose."

"It's not nice."

"No?"

"I can't see why he didn't leave *her*—long ago. She's a mess."

"How so?"

"She's just a mess. She's ill all the time. A regular invalid, Gregg. I don't know what's the matter with her. It's awful."

"How d'you mean?"

"Complaints, complaints. All the time. It's started here already. She hasn't changed. She was always the same. Headaches, stuff like that. The apartment turned into a hospital the minute she showed up. I don't know what to do. I suppose I'll have to put up with her. After all, she is my sister."

"An invalid?"

"Yes. That's all you can call it. She's such a baby. She never grew up. She's a child. She'll always be a child. She hasn't changed since she was twelve years old. Always whining, demanding things, making everybody wait on her. She's a mess, just a mess."

I thought how that was fine, all right. Agnes would be in the apartment, which meant that even if I did have a chance, I didn't have a chance.

"Can't you tell her there isn't room?"

"She's my sister, Gregg."

"I know, but after all . . ."

"No. I'll just have to put up with her. Lord knows how long she'll insist on staying. She spends most of her time in bed. An invalid, that's all."

"Maybe she's really ill."

"Oh, she's ill, all right. There's something the matter with her, but what? I certainly don't know."

"Tough," I said. "We won't be able to use the apartment."

"Were you planning something?"

"Well—"

She laughed softly. "We'll be married one day, Gregg."

"I know that." I reached out and put one hand on her knee. She let it rest there a moment, then lifted it off.

"None of that, now."

I tell you, I should have got mad, something. But I didn't. I wanted her so much I was sick with it. And I kept thinking, There'll come a time, and it'll be before we get married, too. She always had the promise in her eyes, too. Then I'd think, Maybe I'm a fool.

"She'll wear me out," Helen said.

"Huh?"

"Agnes."

"Here we are."

I drew in to the curb in front of her apartment building.

"I'm sorry you're stuck with her, Helen."

She sighed. "What can I do? An invalid."

I visualized this wan, peaked stick of a girl, lying in bed, moaning, sipping hot tea and eating dry toast.

"I'll be by about seven," I said.

"That's fine." She looked grim. "Well, now I'll go up and face it. She'll be lying there waiting for me to come home."

"Wish there was something I could do."

"Yeah." She touched my face with her fingertips, smiled, slid across the seat, and was gone. I watched her walk toward the door, her long legs, the way her behind swung. It was nice, I'll tell you. Yeah.

I went on home and ate from the refrigerator, drank a bottle of beer, then shaved and showered. I sat around a while thinking how tonight I would make a very intense play. Maybe I could overcome her. Maybe if I got brutal. Maybe that was the angle.

But it would have to be in the car, and that didn't help. We couldn't go to a motel. She wouldn't hear of it.

Agnes. Damn her, anyway. Why did she have to have a sister? And especially that kind of sister.

At twenty to seven, I was dressed and ready. I got the car out, and drove over to Helen's apartment. In the elevator I thought, Brutality. That's what it'll be. Right in the car. Drive to a lonely spot, and attack her. It's the only way. I've got to know. Cripes, maybe she's frigid. I didn't want to think that way, though.

And now that she had her sister in the house, maybe she wouldn't have as much time to spend with me. There was no telling. An invalid.

I pressed the buzzer. There was a long wait. I pressed it again.

"Just a sec!"

It wasn't Helen. Agnes, then.

I waited. Finally, I lit a cigarette, and smoked that about a third of the way when the door opened.

This little blonde minx in a black mini-dress and silver-buckled shoes, black lace stockings, smiled up at me. She was as pale as paper, with enormous brown eyes, and a very red mouth.

"Hi!" she said. "I'll bet you're Gregg."

She had a little girl voice. She sounded about fourteen.

"And you're—?"

"Agnes. Didn't Helen tell you about me?"

"She did mention you."

"Sure. Come on in."

I went inside. She just barely moved out of my way, watching me very closely.

"Sorry to keep you waiting, like that. But I had to throw on something. Wasn't sure who it was."

"I see. Where's Helen?"

"Out for groceries for the week-end. She said to tell you she'd be about an hour late."

"Oh."

She looked me up and down. "Say, you're real big, Gregg. Helen didn't tell me how big you were."

"She didn't?"

"Nope. She sure as hell didn't."

"Oh."

She moved across the room to the couch, and plunked down. She leaned back. She was very small, but she was sure put together, you could see that. She certainly didn't look like an invalid. She was very pale, but that was all.

"Guess I'll have to entertain you, Gregg."

"Oh, that's all right. I don't mind waiting."

"Sit down, Gregg."

I started for a chair.

"Gregg! No, over here. Beside me." She patted the couch with a small, plump hand, and smiled at me. She had tiny seed-like teeth between the crimson lips. "I want to see you up close, Gregg. After all, you're going to marry Helen, aren't you?"

I grinned.

"C'mon, now."

I sat beside her on the couch. She twisted around, and tucked one leg up underneath. The skirt was very high, and her legs were plump and round.

Up this close I saw that she had very large breasts. They stretched the fabric of her dress. The blonde hair was straight and shiny, hanging over her shoulders. She looked like a kitten, or something like that. She kept smiling at me. And she was sitting on her foot, and it must have been uncomfortable, because she kept moving around on it, thrusting forward slightly, then leaning back again, and all the time smiling at me.

"What you and Helen doing tonight?" she asked.

That little girlie voice was a surprise every time she spoke.

"Take in a show, I guess."

"Oh?" She tipped her lips with a pink tongue that flicked like a snake's. Suddenly she leaned forward toward me, and put one hand on my arm. "She tell you why I'm here, Gregg?"

"No. Not really."

She winked at me, moved her fingers tighter on my arm, then began to inch toward me. She finally stopped when her knee touched my leg. I looked at her. She was smiling, that way. She gripped my arm with her fingers very tightly.

"I didn't tell her the real reason," she said.

"Oh?"

"She wouldn't understand."

"Well, Helen's pretty understanding."

"Is she? Is she, really, Gregg?"

"Sure. I think so."

"She wouldn't understand me. Nobody does."

So, I thought. Starting to complain.

"Only men seem to understand me."

"Oh?"

She leaned toward me and I could smell an elusive perfume. It was something, for a fact. She was very close, her face thrust at me, like that, with those red lips, and the tiny teeth, and the enormous eyes. Her breast was against my arm. She pressed still closer.

"All men understand me except my husband. He doesn't understand me. He left me. Something I did."

"I see."

"Can you imagine what I did?"

"No."

"I won't tell you, either. You'll just have to imagine."

"I can't imagine."

She lifted her left hand and drew a wave of hair away from her left eye. The hand dropped to my shoulder, and the fingers twiddled.

"Gregg?"

"Yes?"

"You making it with Helen?"

"How d'you mean?"

"You sleeping with her?"

I cleared my throat.

"Just asking," Agnes said.

I cleared my throat again. Her fingers were on my neck now. I could hear her breathe through her teeth, and she kept watching me, very closely.

"You think I'm awful, Gregg?"

"Why should I think that?"

She squeezed still closer. Because she was still sitting on one foot, her thighs were spread apart, and when she moved this time, her dress slid up revealing bare thigh above the rims of her stockings. Her flesh was very pale, and for a moment I couldn't take my eyes off her legs.

She snickered.

"You like that?"

"What?"

"My legs."

I looked at her. She had this sly expression, and she was so close her breath touched my face. She lifted her behind, and took her leg out from under her. Then she got on her knees.

I sat there.

"Gregg?"

"What?"

"Will you hate me?"

"I don't think so."

"Well, I've got the hots, Gregg." She ran one hand up her leg, under her skirt, and began rubbing herself. Then she leaned toward me, her lips pouting.

"Kiss me, Gregg. Will you?"

I kissed her. Her tongue plunged into my mouth and she began to writhe against me. I'd never experienced anything like it. She was breathing hard through her nose, ramming her tongue around in my mouth, shoving herself against me. She was wild.

I took hold of her then. I couldn't help it. There was something about her that got me. She was so small, yet so fully developed. It was exciting as hell.

She leaned back. "Wait!"

Her hand snatched at the zipper on the front of her dress, and it zinged down, and the dress was wide open. She was naked underneath the dress, with just the stockings and a garter belt.

"Feel me up, Gregg. Hold me. Before I go crazy. I can't stand it!"

I held her. Her skin was soft, silken. I ran one hand up her thigh, and she grabbed my hand and jammed it between her legs. She had her legs spread wide apart, kneeling there on the couch. She worked her hips, and then suddenly broke free.

"Jesus," she said. "Hurry!"

She sprawled back on the couch, with her thighs wide apart, leering at me. I sort of fell over on the couch beside her. She squeezed against me, and her hand went to my zipper. She got hold of me, making all sorts of strange noises.

"Oh, boy!" she said. "Oh, boy-o-boy-boy!"

"Wait," I said.

"Get on me," she said. "Hurry up. We don't have a hell of a lot of time."

I was sure ready. I'd never been more ready at any time in my life. The room was a whirl. It was crazy, the whole thing. I couldn't help myself.

I knelt between her white thighs, and she lifted her buttocks, her mouth open, her tongue out, her eyes wild with it.

"Now," she said. "Nice and easy."

There was nothing easy about it. I got on her, like that, and we worked away like a couple of maniacs. Her breasts were huge, with the biggest nipples I'd ever seen. And she certainly knew how to make a friend.

She groaned and moaned and twisted her head from side to side, the whites of her eyes showing.

"Now, Gregg! *Now*," she yelled.

I was doing all I could.

"Marry me! Marry me! Marry me!" she yelled.

Everything was insane. She bucked and kicked and scratched and chewed my shoulder. Then it was over.

We lay there, me on top of her.

"I always say that. I don't know what gets into me. I always say, 'Marry me,' like that. It got me into trouble."

"I can imagine."

"Jesus. We better not lie here like this."

I climbed off her. She smiled up at me. Then she sat up, got to her feet, and ran for the bedroom. I sort of lumbered after her, still dazed. I wasn't certain what had happened. I was certain, but I wasn't certain. That's how I felt.

I went into the bedroom. She had her dress all the way off, now, and was taking off her shoes. Then she peeled off her stockings, and the garter belt. She tossed the clothes into a closet, ran across the room, and dove into bed.

"There," she said.

I stood looking at her.

"You'd better zip up, Gregg. Helen'll be back any minute."

"Oh. Yeah."

I zipped my pants. I was still trying to get my breath.

"I'm glad you're you," she said. "I'm really glad you're you."

"I'm glad you're you, too," I said.

She lay there with the covers up to her chin. Her yellow hair was fanned out around her head on the pillow, and she looked like a little fourteen-year-old girl.

"We'll be able to do it lots," she said. "Did you like it?"

I nodded.

"I could go some more, Gregg. Too bad there isn't time."

Just then I heard the apartment door open. I went into the living room. It was Helen. She had two large sacks of groceries. I took them from her, and she smiled, and I carried them into the kitchen.

She whispered. "Was Agnes any trouble?"

"No." I shook my head.

"I'll hurry," she said. She put the groceries away, then went quickly into the bedroom. "Be right with you, Gregg."

I waited in the living room.

"Are you all right, dear?" I heard her ask in the bedroom.

"I'm all right. You run along, Helen, darling."

"I'll try not to stay out too late," Helen said.

"Thanks," Agnes said.

Helen and I left the apartment. "It'll have to be a late show," she said.

"Guess it will."

"You talk with her?"

"A little."

Helen paused by the car door, and looked at me. "I'll have to wait on her hand and foot, Gregg. She's just an invalid, that's all."

I shook my head and mumbled something.

Helen watched me. "I know her better than she thinks I do. I know everything about her. I know exactly how she is, Gregg. Exactly."

"Yeah?" Her voice was funny.

She winked at me. Then she chuckled. "Yes," she said. "I really know my sister. And we're not a bit alike. Not a bit, Gregg."

She got into the car and we drove off. She didn't tell me what she meant, but I had a strange feeling.

Meet Me in Hades

early 1970s

"It's simple enough," Sam Dargon said, handing me a drink. "I want you to knock off my wife."

I took the drink, leaned against the huge fieldstone fireplace. Sam Dargon turned and slumped in a soggy leather chair.

"I don't get you," I said warily.

"Look, Kurt," he said. "You been here an hour. I'll be more explicit, don't worry. I can understand your need to know. We're old pals, right? But that isn't enough. We haven't seen each other, haven't even corresponded in six years. Sure, we'll get drunk, hash old times. But, hell, Kurt—first there's this job I want you to do."

He was so damned complacent.

"I think you'd better explain," I said.

He brooded a moment. A big man, he was actually swollen with bloat. He ate too much, drank too much, always had. The heavy face was a balloon, the pale hair thin scraggles across the reddish skull. The blue-and-white polka dot silk shirt was cut like a tent. Fat thighs strained cream slacks. He wore leather sandals. Money. Obviously. In Wisconsin, of all places, even though the lay-out was plush. Sunlight shimmered on lake waters outside, shot flickers through the big picture window, brightening his features.

"You don't react, Kurt," he said.

"I'm figuring you're just making mouth noises."

He laughed. It was like Sidney Greenstreet, his belly humping, wheezing in the throat.

He picked up his drink, took a sip, set it down, leaned forward, lifted a fat hand. "Okay, pal." He sucked a lip. "I know who you are, Kurt. You aren't just Kurt Standish, the happy-go-lucky son-of-a-bitch, anymore. You're Kurt Standish, hit man for Leonard Missouri. Since I seen you last, you're big time. I was told you're a conscienceless killer who does the job. Straight enough?"

"How did you—?"

"Listen, Kurt. I ain't been standing still. I'm peripheral, see? I make mine, and it's plenty, right off the top. But I don't eat the meat on the table. What I got is my own. I know the boys. I need a job done. I asked around, and they told me who. I got in touch with Missouri, and he loaned you out. To me."

"You have changed, Sam."

"Change, smange—I want you to hit my wife. My way, Kurt. I'll give the orders. Missouri said you'd do it, and I figured for old times' sake, you'd agree."

I took a long drink, draining the glass.

"Where is your wife?"

"She's out maybe whoring with a local. She'll be back soon enough."

"Why don't you just dump her?"

"Dump, smump—I want her dead!" He got a little purple around the eyes. A vein in his throat stood out, pumping, like a sick worm. "Dig it, Kurt. She got onto how I make mine. She got my books, she knows everything. It's too much. She can hang me, and she told me she would if I don't kiss her feet. Kurt, I kiss *nobody's* feet! Nobody's."

"I see."

"Maybe, maybe not. The point is, you do the job, and we maybe run over to the islands, blast off for the moon, like the old days. I got friends there. Good hash, great booze, beautiful broads. Good time. Okay?"

I turned and walked over by the picture window, and stared out at the lake. The house, here, was high above the water. A balcony thrust out to the rocky shore. Green pines, tall, spiky. Inlets. Hills and sunlight. The son-of-a-bitch had me by the curlies. Missouri had let me go for this, without a word. The deck was stacked, and I would have to do the job. You always had to do the job.

The years crowded in and I said, "How you asking me to do it?"

He spoke with a rumble from back there in the chair. "That's better, Kurt. Well, I want you to take her out in a rowboat, and drown her, see? No marks—just hold her under. You tip over the boat, and swim back. I watch through binoculars from the balcony, and I say how she stood up and the boat tipped, and she went in. You tried to save her. But she didn't make it."

"You watch."

"My word's good around these parts. I been coming here for years. They'll listen to me, and you'll be off the hook, clean. We'll both be clean. And no more Virginia."

"Virginia, huh?"

"Yeah. The crazy bitch. Eager ass, that's what. She had me fogged for a time. But no more—no damned more."

"Watch the blood pressure, Sam."

He was panting like a horse with the heaves.

"Where'd she come from?" I asked.

"Once wealthy Carolina family, all dead now. Been to the best schools. Bright, and a looker. She hooked me where I live."

"When you want the job done?"

"This afternoon. I figure, I'll tell them you just got here. Wanted to go out on the lake. Then it happens. Better that way, right off quick. What a shame for you, all that."

"This isn't my usual way, Sam."

"Usual, smusual—who the hell cares?"

"Here she is, I think."

"Good. I told her you were coming. Said you were an old pal. No lies, huh, Kurt?"

An E-type had just parked in the drive, to the right of the house, below the balcony. I could just see it. A blonde, wearing buff blue got out of the sports car, and vanished by some shrubbery.

"It'll be perfect," Sam said. "The highway police patrol up here. They go past the house, on that dirt road, about five o'clock. I'll get out there and flag them in—right on time."

"You've got it all figured."

"Sure. You and Virginia row out on the lake around four."

"I don't like it, Sam."

"What don't you like?"

It was his wife. She stood in a broad entranceway to the big, plush room. What I saw was a shock.

"Nothing," Sam said. "Where you been?"

"In town, shopping. Picked up some absolutely marve hot pants. Wait'll you see." She paused, then moved into the room. "So you're Kurt Standish?"

"Yes. Nice meeting you, Mrs. Dargon."

"Virginia, please?"

She paused, glanced at Sam, then at me again. She was something. Everything about her was sex, and it came at you like it was shot out of a gun. Long, straight blonde hair, and round pale blue eyes, and a broad, damp-lipped red mouth. The skin was a creamy tan. The skirt was tight, and thigh length, and her hips swelled from a wand waist. The skirt snicked in, shadowing the crotch. The pale blue blouse was open halfway to the waist, and you could see the thrusting swell of breasts. She just stood there, emanating, with a kind of wise, sly look. My libido pawed the dirt.

Sam cleared his throat. "I want you to help make Kurt feel at home, Ginny. Remember, he's an old, close pal."

She hurried over to me, took my hand. Her palm was dry and cool. "C'mon," she said. "I'll start by showing you my new hot pants."

I looked at Sam. He grinned. I glanced at the clock on the mantel. Two-thirty. An hour and a half to kill. I went along with her, down a hall, past three doors, into a large, frilled, blue room. There was a big bed, an elusive odor of jasmine.

She let go my hand. "I'm not modeling hot pants till I know you better. I just wanted to talk to you about Sam."

"I see." I stared at her breasts, then her mouth.

"Is there something wrong? You'd know. He's been acting very queer the past few days."

"Nothing's wrong. Just excitement, I think. We haven't seen each other in six years, Virginia."

She gave a little pout. "All right, then. You can go now, Kurt. I've got to shower and dress."

Sam's voice came from the hall. "Put on that flame-colored bikini, baby. Kurt wants a ride in the boat, on the lake. Says he hasn't been in a rowboat since he was fifteen. You can take him out. Okay?"

She eyed me lazily. "Sure, if you want."

"About four, say," Sam went on. "We'll have a couple drinks, first. Be ready, baby. And remember, nothing's too good for old Kurt."

I excused myself, checked with Sam where my room was. He showed me, winked as he closed the door. My cowhide bag was on the bed. I lifted it down, and stretched out, bunching a pillow under my head. I lit a cigarette, drew smoke deep, let it out slowly.

I felt randy after being close to that. It was funny, how she got to me so fast. I kept picturing her on her back, with her thighs wide apart. It took some doing to put her out of my mind. Even then, she was there, along the edges, tantalizing.

Lots of women did that to me, though. Sometimes I couldn't control myself. And all the time, down through the years, I'd kept searching for one that would do that and stick. And stick. That was the hooker. She didn't look so damned wise to me. But it was Sam's business, and I knew I'd have to do the job.

What a waste.

Missouri had loaned me out. Hell. Well, I should be used to it. I wasn't. At first it had been easy, mostly because I was high a lot, and the killing didn't mean much. I never knew them, as a rule. Somebody would finger, and I would hit. I made it a rule to hit perfect, every time. It wasn't long before I had a rep. And then it began getting to me. Not so much that I was killing them, but more that somebody asked me to. I wasn't my own boss. Somebody stood over me.

And, damn it—I had never killed a woman.

I lit another cigarette off the butt of the first.

I swung my feet to the floor. She was getting to me hard. Why try to deny it? I'd seen her for half a minute, and I couldn't control the meat. Was I cracking up?

Sometimes I had dreams. They would all line up, all the ones I'd hit. They would stand there in front of me, with holes in their heads, and chests, with staring eyes. Then they would slowly walk toward me, very slowly, with those eyes staring.

They kept saying my name. "Kurt Standish. Kurt Standish."

I spotted a bottle on a highboy across the room. There was ice and a glass. I drank two glasses, filled another, and came back to the bed, stretched out again.

Some of it eased off.

The fat slob. He wasn't the Sam Dargon I remembered. Ordering me around, too. The bastard. I had to kill for him. A favor to Missouri. There'd been no talk about money. Never when it was a favor.

. . . and I'd never killed a woman.

You think things.

Fat Sam Dargon. He'd come a long way.

The door opened a crack. "Kurt?"

It was Sam. "Yeah?"

"You got swimming shorts?"

"Yeah."

"Put 'em on. It looks better. Right?"

"Oh, check, right, right, Sam."

"You miffed?" He stuck his head around the door.

"Naw. I'll be on the spot."

The door closed.

I got up and went in and stripped and showered, which was crazy. I hardly knew what I was doing. I kept thinking of that Virginia. Christ.

I put on the swim trunks and went into the living room. Sam was in the leather chair, drinking. We didn't speak for a minute. He poured a drink for me. I took it and leaned against the fireplace again.

He began talking about the good life, painting word pictures. After a while, I saw he was a pig, too. A real pig. And the bastard had that Virginia to get in bed with. Would he miss it?

"Will you miss it, Sam?"

"Miss what?"

"Her. Virginia. Not easy to put off."

He laughed that wild belly laugh. "Wait'll we get to the islands, and you'll see why I don't give a shit, pal."

"It's nearly four." It was Virginia. She stood in the hallway entrance, watching me. "You ready? Sam said four o'clock."

I sucked a breath. I chewed the inside of my cheek. Flame-colored bikini. It hardly covered her. She knew it.

"Yes," I said. "Let's go."

I followed her out and down off the balcony, and onto the pier, watching that behind, the way it bunched, the scissoring movements of those thighs. I began to get ideas that wouldn't be put down. My hands. A woman. The first time.

"Have a ball," Sam said. He was standing up on the balcony, a pair of glasses swinging around his neck. He lifted the binoculars, peered out on the lake. "Beautiful day for it," he called.

A mountain, standing up there in a polka dot shirt, waiting for the pay-off.

"You going to row?" she asked.

"Wouldn't miss it."

I helped her into the boat, my heart rocking when I touched her. Her breast brushed my arm. I got in. I untied the boat, picked up the oars.

I started rowing.

There she was. Right smack in front of me, with her legs spread slightly apart, so I could see her crotch, and I could see a few tendrils of hair, too, curling along that soft thigh.

I looked back at the house, over her head. He was standing up there, watching. Sunlight flickered on the binoculars.

I rowed harder.

"How's it feel?" she asked.

"Nice. Real nice."

I stared directly between her legs, now. I didn't give a damn. And she didn't close those thighs, either. I looked into her eyes. She looked right back at me, with her lips faintly parted. I could see the shape of her nipples through the thin cloth of the bikini bra. Lush, she was. Smooth, she was. I studied her thighs, the insides, close up to her crotch. It was smooth flesh. There was a little pucker, in close.

"You're rather bold, aren't you?" she asked.

"Yeah. I'm bold."

"Don't you think Sam will notice?"

"I don't give a damn."

A touch of alarm came into her eyes. I was rowing hard. I'd already turned the boat, heading for an inlet. The hell with Sam Dargon. I knew what I wanted, and I was going to have it. I couldn't stop myself. I'd had it like this before. I knew I was out of control, but it didn't matter. Nothing mattered, just Virginia Dargon, that's all. The way she looked, the way she sat there—and the way I felt.

"What are you doing?"

"You're going to get screwed," I said.

She stared at me, not speaking. She started to come to her feet.

"Get up and I'll knock you down with an oar," I said.

She sat down again. She tried to bring her thighs together now. I didn't give a damn. I knew what was there, and I was going to have it. It was so compelling, it was all I could think. There was a fog on my brain. She was a swarm, and there was nothing I could do about it.

"What—what are you doing?"

I was already entering the inlet. Trees shrouded us from the house. The branches came close to the water. I drove the boat at the bank, and came to my feet, and fell on her.

"Stop—stop!" She screamed it.

I ripped the bra off, bending her back down from the seat. She lay on the bottom of the boat, now, her behind up on the seat. I sucked at her breasts, and made a grab for the bikini bottoms, ripped them up the side. I tore them off, and saw her curly blonde nest. She was struggling, and kicking, but it wouldn't do any good.

"Baby," I said. "I'm sorry. But I've got to get it in you. That's all there is to it."

I got my shorts off, holding her down, and knelt in the bottom of the boat. Her legs kicked at me. She was a picture, lying down there, fighting. I grabbed her by the knees, and spread her thighs. Then I reached down and slid a finger in, working it. She arched her back, and began to scream again. I slipped on my knees up between her thighs, and stuck it in. Her behind lifted right off the seat and she gave a sharp cry. I bent over her, looking her straight in the eye, and took hold of both breasts, and slowly gave her the business. I didn't hurry. I eased it to her. It was tight and wet and hot, like I knew it would be. She struggled, but the wriggling only made it better.

"You'll like it," I said. "So shut up. Just get with it, Ginny, baby. You'll like it, I tell you." And all the time I eased it into her, in and out.

She cursed me with a rain of obscenity. Then she began gasping. I increased the tempo a little, with long strokes. Deep. She began to get with it. She couldn't help herself.

Then she gasped, "Oh, God—give it—!"

Her bottom lifted now, urging against me. The thighs clamped my sides tightly, and her hands reached out, fingernails digging. Her mouth was open, her head flung back.

"Jesus—Jesus," she gasped. "What a—screw!"

I really got down to work. I couldn't help it. I pumped her like a fiend. She went crazy, gasping, and moaning, and wriggling.

I was ready, and I was blind to everything. I shot and she came at the same time. The boat was rocking, and splashing. Water frothed at the gunwales. She gave a throaty yell, and pumped her bottom, then sagged under me. I lay there on top of her.

"Christ," she said. "You raped me."

"How about that? You liked it, right?"

"Yes. God, yes." She put both arms around me, working her hips slowly, and stuck her lips against mine. Her tongue probed, and it was a proper kiss.

I knelt back, rubbing her thighs.

We began to talk. First about little things, things that didn't matter. Then she said, "Why are you really here?"

"Just friends—old friends. Getting together."

"Some friend you turned out to be."

"I couldn't help it."

"How'll I go back there? You ripped my bikini all to hell."

"We'll just go back, that's all."

Because I couldn't kill her. I knew that now.

Well, we talked some more. And she said how she liked me more than I might imagine, and what were we supposed to do about that?

"I don't know."

I got the oars and rowed the boat out into the lake. We started back toward the house. She was naked as a jay, sitting there. I looked up and he was still on the balcony with those glasses.

"Will you be able to face him?" I asked her.

"Sure. But we've got to figure something out, right?"

"Yeah."

We didn't talk then. I brought the boat in by the pier, and tied it up. We climbed onto the pier. I had on my swimming shorts, but she was nude. I followed her up the steps onto the balcony.

He stood there, holding the binoculars. She paraded straight past him, into the house. He said nothing, just looked. But that vein was pumping in his throat, and his eyes were purple around the edges.

I lingered. What the hell. He deserved something, even if it was just an explanation.

"She was too much, Sam."

He chewed his lower lip.

"I'm sorry, Sam. She was just too much. I couldn't do it." He was plenty hot. We stood there for long moments.

Abruptly, he walked into the living room. I followed. He turned sharply. "So you laid her. All right. That's out of your system. Now you're going to kill her. Get that straight. I bought you. You're going to kill her, and I don't give a damn how. Because if you don't, I'll have *you* cut down. And I can do it. I didn't tell you, but I'm a partner with Missouri. Dig? Does that tickle your kidney, Kurt? Never knew that, huh? Well, it's true, sweetheart. You don't kill her, you don't do exactly as I say—I'll set up a contract on you—"

"You'll do nothing," I said.

I knew he would, but I had to say something. I was trying to think, and there was suddenly no way out.

"Dig it, Kurt," Sam said. "That's all I'm saying."

We stood there like that, staring at each other. Virginia entered the room, wearing a yellow silk robe. I didn't really look at her till she spoke.

"Just don't move, either of you."

I looked then. She had this revolver pointed between us, and her eyes were quick. She was a touch pale now. But she looked plenty bold, and quite efficient.

"What's this?" Sam said.

"You'll find out, darling."

"Put that gun down—"

"So he was here to kill me, eh? Well, I'll tell you something. I've got it all on tape, darling. I didn't trust you, the way you've been acting. And the way he acted"—she indicated me with a thrust of her chin—"I knew something was up. You wanted him to kill me, and my charms worked the other way. Well, big daddy—how d'you like this—?"

She fired the gun four times, straight into that blue-and-white polka dot shirt. Sam grabbed his gut, and thundered to his knees, gasping. Slaver trickled from his lips. His eyes rolled in his head, as he tried to focus on Virginia.

She held the gun pointed at me, now. I did not move. There was a look in her eyes that wouldn't quit.

"I kind of liked it out there in the boat," she said. "But I can think of better ways."

"What you said about having us on tape. A joke?"

Sam groaned and fell on his face. Blood began to seep from under him, oozing on the thick rug. He kept groaning.

"No joke," she said. She glanced at the clock on the mantel. "When we came back, you and Sam were on the balcony. I suspected something, because of what happened. I ran a mike out here from my room, and taped."

"Real wise, huh?"

"Yes. Real wise." She lifted the gun and fired it at the ceiling until the hammer clicked on an empty chamber. Then she tossed it to the floor. It struck Sam on the behind, and bounced. He was making no more noise. I knew he was dead.

"That was a stupid move," I said.

"Sure," she said, and right then they came into the room. Two of them. State troopers, guns drawn, nasty looking. They were young and earnest. Abruptly, I recalled what Sam had said about the highway police patrolling this area about five o'clock. I checked the mantel. It was two minutes past five. She had known that, too. They had heard the shots from the dirt road behind the house.

Very neat.

"What's going on here?" one said.

The other knelt quickly by Sam, turned him over carefully. Sam's dead bulging eyes peered at the ceiling, his big belly humped like a camel's back.

I didn't say anything. What point?

Virginia said it, in a low, contained voice. "This is Kurt Standish. He came here to kill me, hired by my husband, Sam Dargon. I have it all on tape. My husband was in the rackets in a big way, and I suspect you'll find that Mr. Standish is with the syndicate in some manner. Mr. Standish raped me, which can easily be proved if you take me to a doctor immediately. And then he killed my husband. I have no idea why he did that, except that he's kind of crazy, and probably thought I would go away with him—"

"You'll both come with us," one of them said. "Get on the phone, Sherm."

I thought how she would come into a wad of money. Then I thought how it might have been really wild, with Sam on the islands. He probably knew the right people.

They would believe her.

With my record, I couldn't win. I looked at her. Bright, and a looker, Sam had said. He'd been right about both parts. Well, I had always known it would end eventually.

I remembered what had happened on the boat. Now I knew it hadn't been worth it.

Second sight. But someday I would catch first sight of her in hell.

Escape to Never

late 1970s

They jumped me in Battle Creek. I came out of the Quikie Supermarket, with chops and a six-pack of quarts, and there they were. Waiting. I looked at them and knew it was all over, the running, the fear. Now I wouldn't have to live at night, look over my shoulder at every strange voice.

"Hi, there, Steve."

It was Quirt Quilligan, low in the echelon, but still one of Dom Alechi's favorite boys. He stood beside the gleaming black Cadillac, slowly nodding. The blinking neon from a bar called Rue Paradis, across the lot, shone on his face, changing it from pink to green, green to pink.

The other one, a guy they called Fruit-Eyes, sat on the car seat, with the door open, watching me. He held a black automatic on his knee.

"Just step over here, Steve," Quilligan said. "Or we'll let you have it with your groceries."

Quilligan was big, almost as tall as myself, with broad shoulders, impeccable in a pin-stripe. They both were neat dressers. I used to be.

I moved over by the car, thinking mean thoughts, ways of escape. There was nothing. They would gun me down, I knew that.

"Well, Stevie—it's been over a month, hasn't it? And, shame—you never told Dom good-by. A pity you lost the bag, huh?"

I just looked at him, feeling sick with sudden memory. There was so much back there that could gnaw and hurt. I could never wholly forget, no matter how I tried. But having Quilligan mention any part of it, made the pain of what had been good so much worse.

Dom Alechi never gave up until all the ones who'd spit on him were dead. He could do it, too.

"Get in," Fruit-Eyes said.

They called him "Fruit-Eyes" because of those big wide open blue-gray spinning eyes, that were always smiling. They were all that smiled on that face.

"Forget the stuff," Quilligan said. He reached out viciously and knocked the chops and the six-pack from my hands.

I got into the car. Between the two of them. I wondered why they were waiting. "Why you holding back?"

"We got to talk with Dom. How's it been, Stevie?"

I didn't answer. I was trying to think, with all the memories swarming. They brought it all back, everything I wanted so hard to forget.

We headed through the southside of town, taking dark residential streets. There were saffron streetlights, playing through shadowy elms, and that didn't help, either. Long walks at night. The call of a bird.

Some of it seemed so long ago. But it was just yesterday. And it was the big part of my life, too. You don't forget the good parts of your life, when it's like a knife.

Darlene. Christ, right there in the car I got chills across my back.

She had been Alechi's woman, Darlene Jesus was her name. What he'd called, "My Mexican twist, making the big time, up from Jalisco." Then that nasty laugh. "I just finished shaking the dungdust off her. What you think? Say something!"

Darlene Jesus.

Her beauty made your heart ache. But that's all Alechi saw in her. He never knew the woman underneath. She was his bright new diamond stickpin, and nothing more. He treated her like a whore, as he treated all his women—and when he found out she went for me, he took it hard.

Darlene and I found something together, something I'd never known existed. Maybe you know; maybe you've had it like that. If you haven't, well, you'd better start praying.

But before Alechi wised up, I started skimming tills at five of his different clubs. Darlene and I needed some kind of stake. We planned on South America, together somewhere—out of it, where there was no more dirt. We had to have it, and I had to make it. I didn't care how I made it, because that was what she did to me. And it was all straight, how she felt, and how I felt.

So one night I got word Alechi knew about Darlene and me, and he'd been hipped how I was taking him. I made one last stab for a real haul and hit The Righteous Pussy in North Hollywood and killed one of Alechi's guards in the carpark. Just as I reached my car, they began shooting and I dropped the bag. I had quite a lot of moo stashed with Darlene, but the big bag was gone.

A mad chase through L.A. and over to Glendale, where Darlene was waiting. They let me get there. I thought I'd lost them. All I'd lost was my reason for living.

She was dead. They had scalped her, cut off her ears, dug her eyes out, sliced her nostrils. And other things. She was dead.

On the dressing table mirror one of them had written in oozing lipstick: *"You're next, Stevie."*

Yes, Alechi could do it.

He was big in the rackets. All the government boys needed was somebody to make like a bird. Only nobody would ever sing on Alechi, because if anybody ever did—it was his death-warrant. Even with Alechi out of the way, word would be passed, and the contract would be filled. You could count on that. There was no way out—none. Alechi's insurance was steelclad. Talk and die. Who would do that?

So I took the broads as they came, now. There would never be another Darlene.

I'd been dreaming, all right. There would be no more broads, no more anything. We'd been moving slowly through a dim street. Abruptly, we parked in front of a quiet-looking house.

"Out," Fruit-Eyes said.

I got out and we went inside the house. The first thing I saw was the girl, sitting under the light on a couch, painting her nails. She was something. She wore a tight pink fuzzy sweater over really wild breasts, and a short red skirt that was even shorter, the way she sat there with her lush legs crimped up. The face was a sexy blank, oval and smoothly tanned, quite attractive libido-wise. Jet hair, a big tumble of it, flowed over her shoulders.

"Get your funky ass out of here, pig," Fruit-Eyes said. He had learned from Alechi.

She just looked at him. I could tell she hated him to the ground, and I got a good feeling about that.

"You heard the man, pig," Quilligan said. "Pigs don't sit around like that. They root and they eat their swill, and they like it."

Still she said nothing. Just went on painting her nails. She held her hand out, fingers spread, glanced at me, frowned slightly, then blew on the nails.

Fruit-Eyes went over to her, grabbed her arm, and gave it a brutal yank. "You got to be asked twice?"

"I don't consider that you spoke to me," she said. Her voice was well-modulated, a touch rusty. "Let go, please."

"Ah, let the crazy bitch sit there," Quilligan said.

They were very tough. It was their play. And I knew what they earned was plenty. Alechi paid well.

Fruit-Eyes let go her arm, and took a handful of that thick black hair and twisted. He snapped her head back so she had to look up at him. He twisted hard on the hair, so the scalp lifted, and I could tell it hurt plenty. But her expression did not change.

"When you're through, let me know," she said softly.

He gave her a savage push, and let go.

"Sit over there," he said to me, pointing to a chair across from the girl.

I didn't move. He stepped up and gave me a shove. I sat down in the chair. "I thought your kind went out twenty years ago," I said.

Fruit-Eyes just watched me.

"I'd better check with Dom, then," Quilligan said. "Or you want to make the call?"

"You do it," Fruit-Eyes said. "And make it fast. We either hit him, or we take him to Dom. Find out which it is."

Quilligan stepped to a phone on a table by the door. I knew it would be death, either way. It was just whether Alechi wanted to toy with me, or not. It would depend on his mood. I saw a poor gee once, one that they toyed with. His tongue was cut out. He had no privates, and they'd cut a small hole, and strung his intestines out, and tied them to a tree. The guy had tried to run. It was on the evil side. All while he was alive.

Thinking that, I remembered Darlene . . .

I would do anything—anything. But they had me pat.

Fruit-Eyes went over by Quilligan, and Quilligan dialed, and they waited. I looked at the girl. She was staring directly at me, blowing on her nails. Then she lifted one foot, and began painting her toenails. She eyed me. She had her leg up, so the thigh bunched at her behind, and the other leg down. She spread her thighs a little, straight in front of me, and she wore no pants. Just the lovely little nest, peeking at me. She knew what she was doing, but why was she doing it? To tantalize? Christ. Even the way things were, I couldn't help reacting a little. She was something else.

The call still hadn't gone through. Then Quilligan spoke to somebody, and asked for Alechi. He was told to wait. Quilligan and Fruit-Eyes muttered something I couldn't catch, talking in whispers.

The girl finished her toenails, got up capping the bottle of polish, and left the room. Quilligan and Fruit-Eyes kept muttering. Fruit-Eyes had his back to me, and he was standing in front of Quilligan, who watched the floor, holding the receiver.

The girl came back. She moved over by me, and looked down at me, and handed me a .45 automatic. It was just like that.

I gave her a shove, and came to my feet, holding the gun steady. "Hang it up, Quilligan."

Fruit-Eyes wheeled and saw the gun. Quilligan saw it, too. They both froze.

"Hang up, I told you."

Quilligan replaced the receiver in its cradle.

"Now, get over there." I gestured with the gun to the other side of the room. They knew I would kill them. There was only that. I couldn't think of any other way. I didn't want to kill them.

Fruit-Eyes was the one with nerve. He came at me like a fast halfback, hunched low, aiming straight in. I brought the gun down, but he was on it before I squeezed off. He caught my wrist, and pushed down, and I clubbed the back of his neck. At the same instant, I lost the gun. It hit the floor.

Fruit-Eyes was still game. I was crazy. I put everything into a right cross, and nailed him on the temple. He fell like a sledged steer. But Quilligan was in it, then. He leaped over Fruit-Eyes, and came at me with everything. But, hell, they should have realized I was desperate. I was berserk. Nothing could stop me now that I saw another chance to run—a way out.

"Bastard!" Quilligan said.

I caught him in the gut, and he doubled, flailing.

"You're out of it," I whispered, and grabbed his head and brought it down with all my might as I lifted my knee. He bit his tongue, let me tell you. And he was out of it. He hit the floor like a flat board.

I dove for that .45 automatic. Got it. Whirled around and started for the door.

"I'm going with you!"

It was the girl.

"Not on your life, baby."

"I mean it." She ran at me, grabbed my arms, and hung on. "I've got to, don't you see?" She was wild with fear. "They'll beat me to death. Honest." She swallowed quickly, begging, looking into my eyes. "I've got to. Take me with you—please, please!"

She was telling it straight.

We headed for the Cadillac. I drove right on back to the Quikie Supermarket, picked up a six-pack of quarts, cold, and found my car. We took that, and left the Cad sitting with the lights on, doors open.

We drove fast out of Battle Creek, through the night, with her sitting curled up across the seat. We did not speak for some time. When we hit Jackson, I pulled into a Howard Johnson Motel, bought a room. We went to the room, and I opened a quart for each of us.

"Drink up," I said.

"Jesus," she said. "You're something, all right."

"What would you do?"

"I mean, you're all alone. I mean, before me, that is. And you keep trying to make it—trying to escape Alechi. Jesus."

"Drink your beer."

"You hit like a truck. Those two—they're out like lights."

"I boxed in the Army."

"Boxed? Hey, that wasn't boxing, man. That was hitting. Jesus."

"What's your name?"

"Puddin."

"What?"

"That's right. True name. Puddin Jones."

"Well, Puddin. You can stay here a while, but then you'll have to make it on your own. I can't be burdened. Too many bridges."

"Jesus." She set her beer down, and moved over to me. "I've got to kiss that," she said rustily.

"Huh?"

She wrapped herself around me, and put her mouth on mine. Her tongue probed snakily, and she moved her hips against me. I felt one of her bare feet pressing the top of my shoe. She laid her left thigh against me, spreading her legs, and worked it in. I began to get hot and randy. You couldn't help it. She was so much. And the way she moved, the way she acted. It was like she wanted to eat me up. She pulled her head back and leered up at me.

"They treated me awful, Steve. I been around with them for a long time." Her eyes were a little damp. "I didn't know how to get away. Till you came, and I saw my chance. They told me what they were going to do to me. They laughed about it. They kept telling me, and I couldn't get away. It's because I told Dom off to his face. He gave me to them. Like—like—"

"Where'd you come from?"

"I worked for Alechi, at one of his clubs."

"I never saw you."

"Go-Go—nude. You just didn't catch the right show, Steve. But Alechi got me one night, and I told him off, you see?"

She began working her crotch against mine. Her breasts poked my chest. I dropped the beer on a chair, and we tumbled across the bed. The .45 automatic fell to the floor.

"Oh, how I need it—from you," she whispered. "You've got to wash it all away for me. I need it, Steve."

I had her skirt up, and she was writhing around, kissing me, and trying to yank up her sweater with one hand. Her other hand was at my fly, unzipping, unfastening my pants. I got my pants down, and we were both breathing hard. Then she kissed my belly, and in a second she was on me with that hot mouth, working away. She was kind of desperate. She made a lot of noise. Mixed in with it, I was sorry for her. Maybe she was trying to prove something, I don't know. All I did know was that I couldn't hold out much longer, the way she was. The very most. Puddin.

She lifted her head, and said, "In—in—hurry!" She wriggled around, and lay on her back, and lifted her knees. Her skirt was wadded around her waist, and her sweater was up to her neck, with those big breasts thrust at the ceiling. The lush red lips hung slack as she eyed me between her knees. "For Jesus' sake, Steve—put it in!"

I crawled between her legs, and she grabbed me, and slipped it in with a little cry, like an eager cat. Her behind began humping, and she clung to me, and moaned, her eyes clenched tightly. I really banged her. She wanted to wash everything away. She wanted to forget Fruit-Eyes and Quilligan and Alechi. Hell, I could understand that. I drove it into her, and we both came together.

It was wild. I shot and she was coming at the same time, digging those nails into my back, kicking and working that beautiful behind. I had both cheeks clutched in my hands, and she could really squirm.

We lay there. I didn't move away.

"I love you, Steve," she said. "I know how it sounds. But in our game—well, you got to be true, and you got to make it quick sometimes. So I'm telling you. I love you. I've seen you before, even if you never noticed me. And I've heard a lot about you. I even know how you were taking Dom. Right?"

"Yeah."

"I envied Darlene, because I knew about that, too. But—I'm sorry for what happened. It must—" She shook her head, and put one finger across my lips. Then she spoke in a low whisper. "I used to dream of being in bed with you, what I'd do for you. You haven't seen the half of what I can do for you. And you know, just then, when I—when I went down? I never did that before—"

"Come *off* it, Puddin!"

"All right. Don't believe it. I don't blame you. But it's true. And I'll do a lot more—I'll do anything—anything at all. For you. Because, Steve, I love you."

I knew this turn of events would require some thought. There was so much of Darlene inside my mind, left there, hanging around. And I'd never for an instant expected another woman lived who could be for real. But when a girl like Puddin really meant it, you had something. And I knew I needed what she had. It meant she would always be with you, always be by you—and she would never let you down. When her kind gave—they gave everything. I couldn't believe what she'd said. She'd told other cats she loved them. Did she mean it this time?

I looked at her, lying there. She watched me silently. Suddenly I wanted to believe her. She was like a little kid, all mussed up, her skirt up to her waist, legs open, and she'd just been laid. Soft and satisfied. You could tell that by her face. A kitten.

I heard the car stop out front, and a door slammed. The cars parked in front of the rooms. There should be no reason for worry, but I was worried.

I jumped off the bed, yanked my pants up, and buckled my belt, and went for that automatic.

I never made it.

The door came open, and they stood there. It was Fruit-Eyes, with Quilligan right behind, and Fruit-Eyes had his gun right on my gut. Quilligan's mouth was swollen.

"Well, well," Fruit-Eyes said. "So it's Puddin and you, Stevie." He shook his head, the eyes smiling. "What you know. We made the call after you left, and Dom says it's a hit—so—"

I heard her move. Fruit-Eyes altered the direction of the gun, but he never got off a shot. She was on that automatic on the floor by the bed, where it had dropped. She came up squeezing, and Fruit-Eyes' face dissolved in smashed blood and bone.

"Here!" She yelled it and tossed me the automatic.

Quilligan leaped into the room over Fruit-Eyes' falling body, and started firing at me. I felt a brutal sock in the left shoulder, but I was squeezing at him by then. I put four slugs in his stomach. He dropped his gun, and looked at his belly. Then he held his belly with both hands, and screamed. The blood spurted out between his fingers. He knelt down just in front of Fruit-Eyes, and he kept staring at the blood. He was mumbling something, but I couldn't get what it was. Then with one hand, he tried to reach his gun on the floor. But when he reached, he toppled over. I just stood there, watching him, wondering.

"We'd better go," Puddin said.

"Yeah."

"Will you take me with you?"

I looked at her. She had her sweater pulled down again, and her skirt was neat. It was like it had never happened. But I knew it had. I thought of Darlene, again.

"It wouldn't be right," I told her.

"What's right?"

I took a long breath. "But I'll always be on the run, Puddin. They'll get me sometime, you know that. There's nothing to do now, but run. That's all there is left. Would you want that?"

"They're after me, too," she said. "They'll get me, just like they'll get you, Steve. You asked me, did I want a life like that? I want you."

"Christ. You mean that, don't you."

"Yes."

"You're game to run, with no way out—ever?"

"I always knew that's how it would be. But I never knew I'd have you, Steve. Hadn't we better go?"

I looked at Quilligan. He was still trying for that gun on the floor. He looked up at me, and he said, "Stevie—we got boys everywhere. Remember that."

Then he coughed lightly, and crimson flecked his lips, and his eyes went dead.

"Well?" she said.

There was nothing broken in my shoulder, but the pain was beginning. I took her arm. We stepped carefully across the bodies.

Outside, people were congregating, talking in frightened whispers. Two or three started slowly for our room. I pointed the gun at them. "Get back."

But I had this feeling. An edginess. A hopelessness.

We ran for the car.

We never made it. The two police cruisers came in off the street fast, swooping on us, and they had us in a big white spot. I had a brief urge—shoot it out. I didn't do it. I just dropped the gun and put my hands up high, signaling. Because I thought of Puddin, and somehow she didn't deserve to die yet.

They would kill us like animals.

"Come along," was all one of the cops said.

They took us to the Police Building, and we were separated. I gave them my right name. There was no use lying. It was just a question of time, after they printed me.

A young police medic fixed up my arm, gave me a tetanus shot. They held me for a while in a tiny room, and I could hear them talking in the hall, but not what they said. Then they locked me in a detention cell, incommunicado. I was there two days, when finally, two of them came in, and one offered me a cigarette. I took it and he lit it for me. He had a square, freckled face, with sandy hair, and I'll always remember him.

"It's like this, Harkness. Listen good. We know you, and we know about you. Everything. And we don't want you. We want Dominick Alechi."

I didn't say anything.

"All right," he said. "It's all arranged to grant you immunity, providing that you tell us what we need to nail Alechi. Is that putting it straight enough?"

"It's putting it straight enough," I said.

"We'd like a quick answer. Of course, we can wait. But we prefer—"

"You know what it would mean?"

"We know, Harkness. We know you'll never really be safe. We know there's no place to hide. We know we can't always protect you—but we'll do what we can."

"It would never be enough."

He lit a cigarette of his own, and looked at the other man who just stood there staring at me. He was tall, stringy, with a horse face, and eyes like an owl.

The tall, stringy one said, "Well?"

"What about the girl?"

"She'll only get a couple of years, Harkness. She didn't shoot anybody, did she?"

"No," I said. "But—she has to get the same chance I get. Otherwise—" I shrugged—"no dice." Because I'd already made up my mind. It was all mixed in with Darlene, and what they'd done to her. And Puddin, and what they had planned doing to her. And—everything Alechi stood for. I wanted to be rid of it all, forever.

Neither of them spoke. They went away, and left me for five hours. Then they came back.

The freckle-faced one said, "Miss Jones will receive immunity too. She'll possibly have things to add to what you can tell us. Right?"

"It's possible," I said.

She did, too. We both laid it down, about Alechi. I hadn't realized Puddin knew as much as she did. The freckle-faced one, whose name turned out to be Almondekker, couldn't keep his eyes off Puddin's legs, either.

We told them everything we could, and it was enough. They kept us well-guarded until after they picked up Alechi. It took one week.

Then they turned us loose.

We're in a little town in the northwest, now. Town of no name. We have a mortgaged house, and I work in a gas station at the four corners.

Who knows? Maybe I'll fill your tank someday.

But it's not likely.

We have a little time. But, you see, we're tired of running. And we both know it won't be long before somebody like Fruit-Eyes, or Quilligan, steps out from behind a hedge.

Then it will really be good-by.

Lion-Eyed Moon Girl

I saw this old wreck of a '59 Cad creeping along the road, but really didn't think much of it. It was going very slow, and that was all I really noticed.

Des and I were out on Route 68, about a mile south of town, planting signs for Abercrombie's Turkey Bar-B-Q. I paint them in my shop; sometimes I even do a big board, but mostly it's small stuff, and anyway I keep satisfied. Tim Murphy, dead shot with an air brush, that's me. What can't be painted in the way of signs, I paint. But, as I said, mostly it's just small stuff.

Rockville is a little mountain town, but I like it. Someday, maybe, I'll weaken and go back to L.A., but for the time being, it's stop-over hour, lazy days. And anyway, I haven't forgotten what Janie did to me. Janie is in L.A. I suppose she's still my wife.

"About here?" Des asked.

"Yeah, that's fine. Slant it a little to the right, so they'll be sure to see it."

He tilted the sign, and lifted the sledge. We had three more to put out. Des Crockett, short, stub-headed, was a beer-drinking friend who liked to help me put out signs. His family had left him a little money, and he was going through it slowly, as was his way.

I looked up and noticed the Cad had stopped in the middle of the road, and there was a lot of wild yelling coming from it. The engine would rev wildly, but the car didn't move. It just sat there, like an aged, decrepit monarch of a place you didn't want to really believe existed.

I was leaning against Des's bike, a big black Kawasaki, stripped for ass hauling. My Model A roadster was parked across the road, gleaming maroon in the noon sunlight.

"You bastard!"

It was a girl. She leaped from the idling Cad, and stood there looking back into the car. She slammed the door. Immediately, the door flung open and a little guy, no bigger around than a pencil, the way it looked, came flying out and stood glaring at her. He had wild hair, it stood up all over his pea-like skull.

"You cockeyed bitch!" he screamed.

"I won't stand for it," she said almost softly.

"You will! You'll stand for anything, you crazy-assed bitch! You do me again, I'll tear your eyes out. Get it through your head. Don't never say that again, neither."

She was tall, wearing a leather skirt halfway up her fine white thighs. She had long straight pale blonde hair that reached almost to her elbows, and she kept brushing it out of her eyes. Her face was quite pale, with a strange sort of curling mouth, the lips extremely red. She kept blinking, standing there, staring at the little guy as he shouted.

You could breathe him away. I mean, he was a wraith. He wore corduroy pants stuck into loppy black boots, and a shiny black leather jacket. His mouth was open all the time, spewing rot at the girl.

"I'll break your arms," he shouted in that thin voice, red-faced and ineffective, like a disrupt scarecrow in an empty cornfield. "I'll tear your tongue out, you crazy bitch. I'll cut your feet off, you hear me, do you?"

"Now, honey," the girl said. She said it as if she didn't give a damn what he did. They were just words, that's all. She kept looking at the guy called Honey, brushing the hair out of her eyes, one hip sloped off, lazy-like.

"You can go stale here!" he screamed. "You can stink and go stale, dig? Go to hell—go to hell!"

Suddenly he just turned and ran for the Cad, jumped in. The engine back-fired and roared, and the car sort of shook all over, like a tired tank, then took off, groaning and lurching. One door was open, flapping back and forth. It gathered speed, like a battered old locomotive, and vanished down the road.

The girl just stood there. She wore white boots. She stared at her feet, and kicked the macadam, and looked around, eyeing the wilderness, then glanced over at me and smiled.

Now, you've got to understand, I wasn't counting on anything. It just happened, that's all. I mean, the feeling I got. When she looked at me like that, standing there all forlorn and left with everything hanging out in the middle of the road at high noon, I just turned over inside. Now, I don't pick up freaks. Don't get me wrong. But there was something about her.

I looked at Des and he shook his head.

The girl just stood there. Actually, there was very little traffic on 68, and I'd told Abercrombie that, but he'd insisted on putting the signs out here.

"Des?"

"Yeah?"

"Can you handle the rest of them?"

"The signs?"

"Yeah."

"Sure. I'll do them. You go ahead, Tim."

I didn't exactly look him in the eye.

I started over toward the girl. She just stood there, like she was waiting on a corner for a bus, or as if she'd just ordered something at a stand-up juice emporium.

"Hi," I said.

She looked me over. I stand six-two, and weigh in at 200, and sometimes I frighten them because I don't smile much, but actually that's because of a shot nerve from a belt on the jaw when I used to fight in the Navy. The S.O.B. caught me right—but never mind that.

"You all right?" I asked her.

She just stood there. Then you could almost see the word coming, and as it came, I noticed her eyes. I mean, I'd never seen eyes like that, and she said, "I'm fine," and I kept looking at the eyes.

They were huge, first of all. And round, with heavy natural lashes. She kept them sort of wide open, staring, like. But that wasn't it. They were lion's eyes. All tawny and shot with little flecks of gold and light. And when she looked at you, it was hazy, and maybe a little predatory, even, but definitely sleepy. It was as if she cared, but didn't care, all at the same time. Wild eyes. Animal eyes. Lion's eyes.

"What you want?" she asked.

"I just wondered if you were all right."

She didn't move from that position, with one hip shot out, and she kept brushing her hair away from her right eye. It would fall back, and she would brush it.

Dreamy. Sleepy. Like she was from another planet. Maybe from the moon?

"Listen," I said. "Is he coming back?"

"No."

I sighed. "What happened?"

"Nothing happened."

"You want a lift back to town?"

"Sure. You got something to ride in?"

I took her arm, and she gave me a funny look, slantwise, and then she half smiled. It was a warm smile, all crazy with promise.

We reached the Model A. I had restored it myself. A perfect job. I loved this car.

She pulled at my arm. "What do I have to do for this lift?"

"Don't think things like that."

"But, I do. I'm that way. I always think things like that, you know?"

"Get in."

She got in and I slid under the wheel. I glanced over at Des. He was just lifting the sledge again. He winked, and swung at the sign, and missed, almost smashed his foot.

I started the engine, and we moved onto the road, made a U-turn, and headed back toward town.

"What kind of car is this?" she asked. She asked it as if she didn't really care, didn't give a damn, just to say something.

"A Model A Ford," I told her. "Before your time, love. But they were a great car, and I picked this up for a song. Only you should've seen it. Christ, no wheels, no top, no doors, and the rest like a broken chicken coop. I brought it all back, myself."

"How daring of you."

She was staring out the window, doing that with her hair over her right eye. Her skirt was high up and tight across those thighs. She wore a loose, big knit, scarlet sweater that hung down. But it didn't hang where her breasts were. They peaked it out beautifully, and you could almost see the nipples through the knit. Almost, not quite.

"What was the beef?" I asked.

She said nothing, just began to hum. She glanced at me, and brushed her hair back, and smiled hazily, blinking those eyes. Definitely from the moon. I don't believe she even heard me speak.

We came into town. Suddenly she turned to me, and said, "Where's your place?"

"Why?"

"I want to see it. I want to go there with you."

She was getting to me with her suddenness.

"Okay. I'll take you there."

We drove up Oak Street, and turned onto Elm, and I stopped the car in front of the place. Now, it wasn't much, really. But I loved it. A big old house, with the shop hanging out off the front porch, built into the front porch, so it joined the house. I'd built it myself. An enormous sign, the largest in Rockville, and the fanciest, read: MURPHY'S MODERNS. That was all. Everybody knew.

"How nice," she said, getting out of the car. "And you're Murphy?"

"Yeah. Tim. Who're you?"

"Goldilocks."

She started toward the house. I followed her. We came into the shop, and I showed her around, showing her my air brush, and some other signs I'd done, and some art work. I painted pictures on the side, but don't tell anybody.

"And you live here, too?"

"Yes. Inside, of course."

"Show me."

We went inside. It was big and airy, with some old furniture I'd picked up. Big and old and comfortable.

She plumped down on a couch in the front room, and said, "You got a drink?"

I fetched two glasses of corn whisky, and handed her one. "It's potent," I said. "So watch out."

"Everything's potent," she said, and drank half of it like water. "Got any grass?"

"Well," I said.

"You got it. Get it up, father."

"I'm not your father."

"Just an expression."

"I don't smoke myself," I said. "I just keep it for friends."

"I'm a friend, then."

I got her the marijuana, and she expertly rolled a joint, and fired it. She sank back on the couch, and eyed me, dragging at the joint, and sipping from the corn whisky.

"I dig you," she said. "Really."

"Honestly?"

"Yes." She butted the cigarette, and finished the whisky, and said, "Now I feel better."

"That little guy sure was nasty."

She ignored it. She stood up and said, "Where do we go—right here? Or the bedroom."

"The bedroom," I said, looking at her dreamy, predatory, animalistic eyes.

In the big bedroom, she eyed the huge four-poster as if it were a foreign-type piece of machinery, and peeled off her sweater. She was pale, but it was a healthy paleness, and the breasts were not too big, not too small, but with enormous nipples. I'd never seen anything like it. Huge, and they stuck right out at you.

"All right if I keep my boots on?"

"Sure."

I just stood there.

"Get undressed," she said. "C'mon, Tim."

She dropped her skirt, and she was nude underneath. She had the biggest crotch of hair I'd ever laid eyes on. Like a cat curled up between her legs, sleeping. Or maybe not sleeping. Jet black, and the curls looked oiled and frisky. She was built just like a moon-girl should be built, let me tell you.

I had my pants off, and then my shorts, and she stepped over to me, and leaned against me, and pushed her mouth against mine, and stuck her tongue halfway down my throat.

Now, up to that moment, I'd been reacting, but slowly. Then it came over me fast. She grabbed hold of me like a handle, and led me to the bed, trying to unbutton my shirt at the same time. We finally got my shirt off, and she was breathing kind of peculiar. I looked at her eyes, and they were halved, rolling up into her head.

"I'm so hot," she crooned. "Oh, hurry—I can hardly stand it." Her mouth sagged open, the lips parting, and she sat down on the bed, and pulled me to her, and I felt her hot moist mouth. She began working slowly, moaning in her throat. And all the time she kept brushing the hair out of her right eye. She was looking up at me, with those halved eyes that were rolled into her head. It was like she was nine-tenths shot on dope. It couldn't be that, though. Only one joint wouldn't do it, and the whisky wouldn't do it.

Wow. The way she went at it. I thrust at her and she never lost a stroke. Then she pulled her head away and rolled back on the bed.

"You're ready now," she said. "I thought you were going to fold on me, all those Model A's and paint brushes, and everything."

She lay back with her knees up, her thighs spread wide apart, and she began working her behind, staring half-eyed at the ceiling. Her mouth was open and wet. She began to caress herself. "Hurry up, Timothy, is that right?"

"Yeah."

I lay beside her and took her in my arms, because she had me going, for sure. We kissed again, and then I chewed on her left nipple, and she was moaning, kind of crooning a song. Then she began to say, "Hurry, hurry, hurry, hurry . . ." By that time I was down to her belly. I went lower, into the moist kitten, and she worked her behind slowly, grinding it at me. She kept up the moaning. Then I knew she was actually humming a song of some kind. Weird melody. Then she suddenly gave a little cry, and said, "Rod me, Jeff—rod me!"

I knelt and she put her legs on my shoulders, staring at me with those otherworldly eyes, and I put it in. She was a machine that worked slowly, with a set tempo. All the time humming the tune, and staring at me. Then she began to suck my chin. She took my chin in her mouth, sucking on it avidly.

I thrust still deeper. It was something, really. She was very special and I knew it. I had the feeling very few men had been where I was, and I couldn't figure it—but it got so good right then, I didn't give a damn about anything. I had a grip on her writhing behind, and she hummed and lifted herself right off the bed, arching her back, driving at me.

Then she came. It was very sudden, but like her in every way. She flung her head back, wet-lipped, eyes staring and rolling and began to yell bloody murder. Obscenities spewed from her mouth, and she began to curse. "Lemme have it. Oh God! Don't stop! Oh God! Screw me, you bastard! Don't stop!" Then she began to chatter like a monkey, her teeth rattling, and I shot, and she just lay there, staring at me.

Right then I heard this racket out front. Somebody pounding on the shop door.

"You better go see," she said, wriggling out from under me. "You're okay, Lochinvar."

"Sure. You too."

I pulled on my pants, and went out there. I opened the door, and that little guy she'd been with in the Cad came rushing at me. Head down. Hair wild. Eyes crazy. Claws out.

"Damn you—you lousy skunk!"

He shrieked it. I got my hand on top of his head and tried to hold him. He was wiry. He swung and swung, not hitting anything but air. He kicked and cursed and wriggled loose, and got inside, and caught me twice in the gut. It was like being hit with pieces of twine, with knots at the end. Really. I shoved him away.

"What the hell's the matter with you?" I said.

He leaped into the air, and kicked at my groin. I wasn't having any of that. He snarled and spat and came at me, never giving up. Kicking and snarling, and striking with clawed fingers. Yelling curses in that thin, high voice. He was fast, and desperate.

"What've you done with her?"

Holding him off, I somehow thought of Janie again. Twice in one day. Back in L.A. What was she doing? If she could see me now. Hell. My wife.

He caught me a swift kick in the shin. I flung him across the room, getting a little irked at him now, and he fell down by the work bench.

I glimpsed the girl standing in the doorway, dressed again, brushing her hair away from her right eye, and watching, her lips parted, the eyes lazy.

The skinny guy leaped up and ran at me like fire out of hell. He was screaming, and dancing with hate.

Hell. I was sick of it. I reached one from down deep, and swung, and caught him on the chin. It wasn't everything I had. That would have killed the little bugger. But it was heavy. He lifted off his feet, sailed through the air, and crashed into a painting of a waterfall that was half finished. He ruined it, and lay there, his head hanging.

"Damn you!" the girl shouted.

She ran over to the little guy, and knelt down.

Just then the door opened, and Des stepped inside, carrying the sledgehammer.

"This was hell on the bike," he said. Then he saw them over there, the girl holding the skinny guy's head, crooning softly, "Jeff. Jeff. Jeff. Darling, did he hurt you?"

The little guy was still out.

"What happened?" Des asked.

"Nothing. Just a misunderstanding."

She looked at me. "He's my husband. You have no right—damn you. You knocked him out. Can't you see he's my husband? Jeff, Jeff, darling!"

He began to come around then. All the fight was out of him, but the way his eyes looked he was still game. She kissed him on the forehead, and tried to smooth that tangle of hair. "He's my husband, you big bastard," she said.

They got up, and she held to him, and they left the shop. The Cad was out there. They got in and the engine roared and back-fired, and they drove slowly away.

Love, for Christ's sake. Love, yet. He was her husband.

"What the hell happened?" Des said.

I thought of Janie, out there in L.A. She had played around. That's what did it for me, back then. I couldn't take it. But look at those two. I thought about it fast, standing there. Then I turned to Des.

"Des," I said. "Damn it all, I think I'll—"

Candy

He was a huge man, with broad swinging shoulders, and a large, red face with a mouth that was incongruously small. The mouth was forever pursed, red-lipped, pouting, like a rose-bud. His eyes were small, round, black, bulging, as if he were always trying to see something he couldn't quite make out; as if he wanted something desperately. He did want something, and he knew what it was.

He wanted the little girl in the red coat.

He stood by the playground fence, watching her on the swing. She was about five years old. She was such a pretty little girl, with a piquant face, bright red lips, and large round brown eyes. Her chestnut-colored hair looked so soft.

Yes, he thought. And she's built just right, too.

He wiped his mouth with the back of his hand. He lived just down the block. He had a cellar room in the Mayside Apartments. He was the janitor.

If he could only . . .

He seemed to writhe under his bulky red sweater, and though it was snowing lightly this afternoon, and though there was a chilling wind, he was sweating.

He reached back to his hip pocket and adjusted the heavy gun that rested there. It was good, feeling the cold steel of the gun and his pursed lips twitched.

He watched the little girl in the red coat. He had been watching her for days.

He felt in his other pocket where the candy was. Certainly she would like candy.

If only . . .

A sturdy little boy, the same age as the girl, was pushing her on the swing. He wore a black jacket, and a leather cap with ear-flaps. They chattered together. There was only one other boy nearby, and suddenly he scampered away from the swings, running toward the slide.

The man swallowed, gripping the fence with club-like fingers. The gate was only a few feet away.

"Hey, there," he called.

The girl in the red coat went on swinging, the little boy pushing her.

"Hey, you, little girl!"

He called much louder this time.

Both the girl and the boy looked at him.

"Here a minute."

"Huh?"

"Come over here. I've got something—something for you."

The girl looked at the boy and they both giggled.

"Come on over," the man said, moving to the gate. "Something I want to tell you."

The little boy pushed the girl and she swung on the swing. They were both giggling, looking now and then toward the man.

The man's lips pursed and pursed.

Inside, he was cursing them. He drew the back of his hand across his mouth again, then turned his head and spit. Then he looked back at them.

"I've got some candy," he said. "Just for you, girlie. Come over here. I want to tell you something."

"You have candy?" the girl said.

The man nodded eagerly, looked around, and nervously drew the paper bag from his pocket. He held it out.

"See?"

The boy stared at the man, and stopped pushing the girl. The swing ceased swinging. They stood there.

"Don't be afraid. It's for you," the man said.

The boy and girl looked at each other. Then, suddenly, the girl ran over by the gate in the fence. The man thrust the gate open, and she walked through, facing him, smiling. The little boy abruptly ran over and stood beside the girl.

"It's for the little girl," the man said.

The boy did not move.

"If you got candy for me, then you got candy for Johnny, too."

"Of course, of course," the man said. His hand trembled holding the bag.

The boy and the girl eyed the paper bag.

The man probed in the bag, fished out two pieces of chocolate. He gave one to the girl. The boy snatched at the other. The man looked at him fiercely, but the boy didn't notice.

Damn the kid, the man thought. He'll foul me up.

He was trembling inside, and his bulging eyes were very bright, glistening. His mouth pursed in and out rapidly, his lips like red rubber.

He turned his head, searching the street both ways. Nobody was in sight. Inside the playground, other children whooped and shouted, running about.

The man took a deep breath. "Do you like kitty-cats?"

"I like 'em," the boy said.

"Yes," the girl said.

The man patted the girl's shoulder. "I want to show you where I live," he said, breathing rapidly. "It's nice and warm there, and what d'you think. There's a big kitty there, and that kitty wants to meet you."

"May I have another piece?" the girl asked.

He quickly handed her another piece of candy.

"Me, too," the boy said.

The man thrust a piece of candy at the boy.

"How do you know the kitty wants to meet us?" the boy asked.

"He wants to meet this little girl," the man said. "He didn't say anything about you. You better run along and play."

"If I come and meet the kitty, Johnny comes, too," the little girl said.

The man watched them munch the candy. He realized suddenly that he would never be able to get rid of the boy. He was breathing in short, choppy breaths, and his heart thudded violently. She would come, he knew it. She would come right now. He could hardly contain himself.

The hell with it. Let the boy come too. They were little kids. They wouldn't know anything about what he wanted to do. And they would never tell. He would fix it so they would never tell.

He was desperate.

"May I have another piece?" the girl asked.

"Not now," the man said. "We'll go to my place, and I'll show you the kitty, and then we'll all have some more candy. It's a bag full. See?" He held up the bag. It was certainly a big bag of candy.

"What's your name?" the little boy said.

"I'm Mr. Brown," the man said. "Call me Mr. Brown."

"Where d'you live?" the girl asked.

"You come with me. I'll show you."

He looked around warily, took their hands and, walking between them, hurried along the walk toward the Mayside Apartments.

"Does the kitty really talk?" the girl asked, running by his side.

"Yes, yes," Mr. Brown said. "Really talks."

"Is it much further?" the boy said.

"Just down here," Mr. Brown said, guiding them into an alley beside the apartment building. "We got to hurry," he said. "Hurry, now. That door over there."

"Can we have some candy, then?"

"You can have the whole bag."

They reached the door. He opened it, thrust them inside, followed them, and closed the door.

"Down there," he said, pointing into yellow-lit darkness. "Don't be afraid. My room's down there. I live down there. That's where the kitty is."

"All right," the boy said. "I'm not afraid."

They went down a flight of stairs into a cellar. It smelled of oil and old things, newspapers and dust. They approached a door. Mr. Brown opened the door.

"Inside," he said.

The little boy and the little girl entered the room. It was a rather bare room, fairly large, with a naked light bulb dangling from the ceiling. There was a big brass bedstead, a battered couch, and a paint-peeling bureau. A chair and a table stood at the far side of the room. Magazines littered the floor; they were everywhere.

"Where's the kitty?" the girl asked.

Mr. Brown was crooning peculiarly in his throat. He put both nervous hands on her shoulders, thrusting her over toward the bed.

"You come right over here," he said rapidly. "You sit on the bed, with me, and I'll tell you a story."

"How about a piece of candy?" the boy said.

"Here, here," Mr. Brown said. He put the bag of candy on the bed.

The boy rushed over and took a piece of candy. Then he began running around the room, looking under the table, by the bureau.

"I don't see any kitty."

"Now, just sit here with me, and take the heavy coat off," Mr. Brown said to the little girl. "You didn't tell me your name, little girl."

"Sherry."

"Well, Sherry, what a pretty name. And what a pretty little girl."

He helped her off with her red coat. She wore a dress of gold, very short, and red stockings. He sat beside her on the bed. He put one arm around her. He was sweating profusely now, and trembling all over, the whites of his eyes showing underneath.

"Where's the kitty?" the girl said.

"He'll be along. You just wait and see. You just sit here with me."

The boy was running around the room.

"I don't see any kitty!" the boy said. He seemed a little angry, now.

Mr. Brown cast him a vicious glance.

Then he patted the little girl's knee. "Well, Sherry. You're very pretty, you know that? And what a pretty dress!" He felt of the hem of the dress, pulling it back up her leg. Then, abruptly, he hitched on the bed, pulled the gun out of his hip pocket, and laid it on the bed. "That's better," he said. "That was sticking me in the rear. Uncomfortable. Now," he said. He lowered his head and kissed the girl on the cheek. She stared at him. He gripped her knee. "You and me, Sherry, we could have a lot of fun together. We could play."

"Play what?"

"Why—why—we could play doctor and patient."

"How you play that?"

"Well, I'd be the doctor, and you'd be my patient. And you'd undress, and I would examine you."

The boy, who had been running around the room, suddenly caught sight of the gun on the bed. He ran for it, grabbed it up.

"A gun! A gun!"

Mr. Brown was far too swept up with emotion and desperation to care about anything. Let the kid have the gun. Maybe it would keep him quiet. Anyway, he thought the safety was on.

"Maybe that would be fun," the little girl said to Mr. Brown. "Then I could be the doctor, and you'd undress, and I would examine you?"

"Yes, yes, yes, yes," Mr. Brown said, beside himself now. He crooned in his throat, and began rubbing her arms with his hands. He nuzzled close to her, the breath rushing in his throat. "Oh, how we'll have fun," Mr. Brown said. "We'll have a barrel of fun. Can't you just see?"

"Boom! Boom! *Bang!*" the little boy said. He rushed around the room with the gun. Abruptly, he turned and pointed the gun at Mr. Brown.

"You're the sweetest little girl I ever knew," Mr. Brown said.

"Bang!" the little boy said.

"I want to play doctor and patient," the little girl said.

"We will, right now. You undress, then," Mr. Brown said. "I'm Doctor Brown. I'm going to examine you."

The boy slipped his finger over the trigger, pointed the gun at Mr. Brown, squeezed. There was a loud explosion, and Mr. Brown felt a terrible shock in his chest. The damned kid had shot him! The safety hadn't been on. He sagged backward on the bed, clutching his chest.

"What's the matter, Mr. Brown?" the little girl said. "Aren't we going to play? Sit up, Mr. Brown."

Mr. Brown groaned. He tried to speak, but he couldn't. He just lay there. He felt dizzy, and pain was beginning to come in deep waves. He was bleeding.

"He's sick," the little boy said, running to the bed and looking at the man. "He's real sick. You can see. He can't even move."

"Oh," the little girl said. She slipped to the floor, and began putting on her coat. "He's a doctor, he ought to be able to take care of himself."

"He was only playing," the little boy said. He shook Mr. Brown's leg. "Mr. Brown, Mr. Brown, you all right?"

Mr. Brown did not answer. He saw the two children through a foggy haze that was growing thicker and thicker.

"We'd better go," the boy said. "Think I can take this gun? It's a beauty."

"No. You mustn't, Johnny. That's Mr. Brown's."

"We'll take the candy, then. He said we could have the whole bag."

"I guess that's all right," the little girl said.

"He must be awful sick," the boy said.

Mr. Brown was very sick. He lay there on the bed, watching them, watching most of all the little girl in the red coat. He sobbed deep inside, but it did not help.

"I bet there wasn't no kitty," the little boy said. "He lied, that's what."

"Well, he did give us some candy."

As they left the room a heavy veil settled over Mr. Brown's eyes. It was the veil of death.

Tweak

August 1977

Oh, man, look at that! A perfect beauty, and she's parking her car, too. If only the rest of her's like that head. The eyes, the cheekbones, the contours. But she's with somebody, damn. It's a girl, though, so it don't matter. She'll be alone eventually. . . .

His name was George Stebbins. Breathing hard. Tingles running up and down as he swung his Mazda wagon in beside the Pontiac Firebird, craning his neck and at the same time trying not to be obvious. He didn't want her to make him. Not that they ever did. They were somehow so very stupid. And he was having a reaction already, just knowing it would work again tonight. The thing was, too, he hadn't even cruised much. He'd just driven up here to Crossroads Shopping Mall on the off chance he might have some luck.

Of course, he couldn't be certain yet that she would be the one. But, from all indications, and the way he felt, things looked right. He judged his targets by emotional impact.

Now, play it cool. Get with it. He grabbed the black leather strap of the Polaroid camera case that did not contain a camera, but other implements, and hooked it over his neat right shoulder, keeping an eye on them. He did not stare, openly. He slanted his cold grey gaze, tilting his strong dimpled chin.

Where would the night lead him? He always wondered that. He never knew. It was an adventurous surprise. But the rising promise was strong this time. In like Flynn; the wicked, gallant movie actor was an idol of his, and Mother, and he wiled many an hour with old films on TV. Mother. But the thought did not dampen his spirits. He could hardly contain himself. And he was actually having an erection. Man, it felt good. Well, the shrink had said it was psychological, hadn't he? My God, what wasn't? Name me one thing. Dope.

He giggled. Idiot shrink. If he could see him now.

He dallied, lighting a cigarette, watching, patient.

The two girls got out of the Firebird and the blonde driver locked the car. She was the one he watched, and she was truly something, all right. Shiny black skin-tight shorts over a fabulous ass, and a paper-white blouse across tanned shoulders, a fat white purse, and all that glorious floating hair, just like Farrah, like it was alive. Built, my God. He'd seldom seen anything like it. Long-legged and slimly lush, with beautiful big ones—and the nips showed. And that broad quirky red mouth, with the glistening white teeth. Jesus.

For George Stebbins, they had to be complete; all of a piece.

The other girl, a phantom in his vision, was dark and wore yellow jeans. She barely registered, though he cursed her murmurously, because from experience he knew that if she weren't there, it might not take so long to organize the picture. But, there was nothing he could do about that.

Hey—they were walking toward the mall.

The way she moved—!

He was out of the car fast, slammed the door, and started after them, not caring much about distance for the time being. For all they knew he could be anybody.

He wasn't just *anybody* . . .

The camera case banged against his hip as he strode along, tall, slim, impeccable in a tropical sky-blue suit, with plump tan tie and gleaming shirt, shoes glinting like foxy mirrors. His fire-red curly hair was so thick and neatly parted, combed, it looked waxed. He walked with neat, clipped steps, the shoulders not moving at all, the pale, planed face with the chill grey eyes terribly determined.

His gaze was focused on the shiny black bunching shorts as the girl hurried on, gesticulating, talking fast with her friend. Other people were amorphous blobs, vari-colored nonsense at the edges of his vision.

They entered Crossroads Shopping Mall; colored lights, air-conditioning, rock music, Thin Lizzy—smells of mustard, hot-dogs, other simmering foods, blaring TV sets, the modulated murmur of strolling people, looking.

He was very excited over finding one so quickly, with Mother at the back of his mind, admonishing: "You must never do *that* with a girl, Georgie. You know what I told you I'd do if you did; if I found you out. I mean it, Georgie. We can be friends, or otherwise." Blinking redly, with the flickering razor blades behind his lids, the knives, the scissors, the meat cleaver—that was most awful. "I'll do it, Georgie."

He forced himself off that track. He concentrated on the black shorts, the fine legs. Of course, there was the chance it wouldn't pan out. But, he had to try. The chase itself was a big part of it—half of it. Well, maybe not *half*, he mused with a shadowed smile, but it was fun. The promise of what could come. Ah. The culmination and the intense, lingering aftermath of forever. Yes, then. A heavy night ahead . . .

Where was she!

He panicked, hurried along the waxed tile floor, past the theaters, a sweet-smelling candy shoppe, a stereo center wavering Sinatra with a sixties "Strangers in the Night" . . . he saw them, relief blooming around his heart. They stood at a pink-neoned lunch counter, ordering. The fearful tightness remained with him, however, and it was some moments before he breathed deeply again.

He lingered, staring nervously in the window of a pipe shop, jerking his dimpled chin around, trying to see them.

"*. . . yes, Georgie—you know what I'll do . . .*"

He had been eleven years old, then.

Maybe he should smoke a pipe. Men with pipes looked so easy in the mind, so at peace, unharried.

. . . Oh, please, God—no razor blades tonight . . .

Pipes in the window. The black shorts. Yes. The two girls left the lunch counter carrying cokes, talking. They seemed to be walking aimlessly. If they went to a movie, it would mean he'd have a long wait, because he had made up his mind that she was the one. A spectacular find.

He trailed after the two girls, eyes on the black shorts, the bouncing blonde hair, the thighs, the ankles. She wore tiny black slippers.

Somebody bumped him and immediately laughed, a throaty chuckle. "Hi, dude!"

It was a girl. Two girls. They stared boldly at him as he paused, abashed. They looked butch, both of them, dressed in ragged jeans and sweaty checkered shirts that looked slept in. Snarled brown hair and one with a freckled face—he hated freckles. Both girls were big, brown, tough looking, but grinning, bridling.

"Where ya goin', dude?"

"No place." His gaze jerked away to the black shorts which were just vanishing around the corner, past the ice cream parlor. He smiled self-consciously and took a step.

"Wait, man. We wanta talk with you, dude an' all."

"Gotta go."

A giggle, a sneer. "Don't know what you're missin', man."

"Sure."

"He says, 'sure,' the dude says *sure.* Listen, dude, ya want some wild head? Bet ya wash it with cold cream, huh?" The one with the freckles had hold of his arm. He felt the brush of desperation, damn them. "Or—is it you're scared? You scared, dude?" She stuck her tongue out and waggled her hips at him, still holding his arm. "S'pose I unzip your fly, right here? What'd ya do? Yell for mama? Uh, huh, dude?" The leering face, the terrible health, the shining eyes.

He tore away from the hand, from them. They called something after him as he ran, his solar-plexus snarled with anxiety . . . once a girl had tied him to a tree, taunting him, just like them, hitting him with a stick—it flashed in his mind. Cold cream. The bitch.

He'd lost sight of the blonde. He couldn't lose her. He mustn't—

He ran on, slid around the corner by the ice cream parlor, looking frantically, gulping guilt, saw them. They were along the mall, walking slowly, talking. They turned into a small record shop.

He stopped walking, patted the camera case.

O.K. He felt certain they weren't going to a movie, so they wouldn't be too long. And they weren't meeting anyone, or it would have taken place right away.

He turned abruptly and strode back the way he'd come.

"Hey, dude!"

Those two obnoxious females again. The bold freckles. They grinned at him, by a white cement bench, munching hot-dogs.

One made a motion with her fist.

He ignored them.

He heard them laugh and the one with freckles stamped her foot twice.

Blushing, he continued back along the mall to the exit, and went on outside into the humid cool of dusk. It would be dark soon, and this pleased him.

He kept trying to think of the blonde in the black shorts, but the freckled girl intervened and he cursed her in his throat, scowling. Always somebody like that, everywhere he went. Why didn't they stay home. Why didn't they go someplace else. He didn't want them, couldn't they see that?

He came along the rows of cars, found the Mazda, stood there a moment, surreptitiously looking around, then ambled over to the driver's side of the Firebird, in full control again. It was already dark now, with only the blue-white glare from the arc lights in the parking area. Between the cars were shadows.

He fished in his jacket pocket, came up with a bunch of keys, selected one, tried it in the Firebird door. It did not work. He tried another. No luck there, either. He glanced up at the sky, took a deep breath, and tried another.

Smooth as oil. He was inside in a moment, door closed and locked. He slid over the seat and down onto the floor in back, squinching against the panels in the narrow space. He flattened himself as much as possible, while at the same time trying to find the most comfortable position. Don't wait. Get set.

He established himself at last and grinned in the darkness. Then the grin went away, because he began to consider the wondrous finality.

The camera case was on his stomach. He drummed on it with his fingertips. He was breathing fast. It was always like this. Carried away with thinking about it. There was something about hiding in the car, too, all secret, like he was. Hiding from her. And she wouldn't know. They would return, and she would get behind the wheel and he could listen to them talk, hear her voice and be near her, and she wouldn't even know. Sometimes he touched them, touched their hair, reaching up from behind the seat, touched their shoulders, even, before they stopped and he got on with it. And they never even knew, never suspected. He'd bet he could sit right up on the back seat and they would never know, never turn around, never realize. But he wouldn't try that, not George Stebbins.

What would she be like?

Tingles wrung him and he held his breath.

He patted the camera case, thrilling.

There was not only anticipation for the event itself, the sharp, clean moment when it happened; there was the aftermath, the long moments of savoring the labeled deliciousness. It would last a lifetime. He could always recall these moments. He would remember the Firebird, the blonde hair, the black shorts, the thighs, everything. Crossroads Shopping Mall. Where would he be in ten years? Even then, he would remember, having the ever-present reminder. And so delicate, so cute, so marvelous. Sometimes he thought he could actually smell them afterwards, sniffing and remembering, lingering for hours, bathing in ecstasy. Oh, God—how could such wonderful things happen. And nobody knew. Were there others who did what he did? Or was he alone on this planet? And with the experience came the ultimate gratification which could occur no other way. The gods were kind to him; they allowed him a complete freedom and gave him surcease. Sometimes he thought he might go insane with it.

Better check things while there was time. Yes.

Pale white from the arc lights shone in the car window, slanting down to where he lay. He craned his neck, opened the camera case and checked the contents. Yes. Everything was there. He was ready.

He was nervous now.

Someday, when he was an old man, he would write a book about it all—a case history. He giggled silently. It would be so entertaining, he knew. And the shrinks would nod their heads. All right!

Sometimes they had to be what he termed elite. He would enter a cocktail lounge and wait, and finally come up a winner. But tonight had been different. He had wanted a bright young thing with no particular sophistication.

Funny. He was never afraid. Something carried him through; a kind of warm wind inside him that stirred him and blotted everything else out, only the one goal.

Damn it. He'd had a flash of that butch with the freckles. People were such clots, really. There were girls and girls. Some were simply shitty. Imagine.

He held his breath. Voices were approaching. Yes. She was here, and the key clicked in the door lock and the door opened, and he heard her shift in across the seat, and then the other door opened, the other girl got in.

Suppose they were sisters? An evil thought. He held his breath like that, hearing them talking, thinking that. But it couldn't be—it couldn't.

He began to breathe easier.

"I wanna see 'Love Story' again. It's on TV."

"Me, too."

"You can come over . . ."

He tightened when she said that. He was trying to tell which was the blonde, which voice. Anyway, they weren't sisters. But—it could still monkey-wrench things if . . .

"I can't come over tonight. Mom's fixing my hair."

"It's twenty to nine. We'll have to hurry."

That was the blonde, all right. She had a throaty way of speaking, husky and very young. Vital. Jesus. He lifted his hand as the car swung out into the street, and slowly raised it up to the top of the seat, then over, and he felt her hair. He let his hand lie there, feeling her hair. There was no particular thrill, just the knowledge that he could do it without her knowing. It was very fine hair, and this did give him a thrill. Fine hair, fine horse, the barber had told him. Yes. Well, it was true. He wondered frantically . . .

She tossed her head. Had she sensed something? No.

They continued talking. They discussed boys, and their last dates, and future dates, and rock stars, and "Love Story" and the sheerness of the stockings they had just purchased at Crossroads Mall. The dark-haired girl was flighty, but the blonde was serious, and her name was Jeanette. Serious and young and with fine hair.

They sped rapidly through the night.

George Stebbins lay there on the floor in the back seat and held the camera case on his stomach. Boy.

They drove for maybe ten minutes, then the car stopped.

"Thanks, Jeanette. See ya."

"You, too."

And they were alone in the car, traveling towards home base. Now he began to fidget, because the time was approaching when he would have to act. It was always like this. He still was not afraid of anything, but he got worked up inside. His breathing was shallow, little gasps, and he was perspiring. The cramped position was beginning to tell.

Then, a flash, Mother: *"You do, Georgie, and I'll cut off your weenie with the scissors or something . . ."*

And gradually, since that time so long ago, he'd begun to dream about razor blades. He would close his eyes and see them, cutting. Razor blades, and scissors and knives. He'd actually feel them in the palms of his hands, glinting against his lids.

No. No. He tried refusing the thought now, and it went away, like always at a time like this. Yes. Damn her, I'll kill her someday—a tiny voice . . .

He opened the camera case with trembling fingers, brought out a thick wad of cotton and a small bottle. He held the bottle in his left hand, the cotton in his right, craning his body up a little from the reclining position. Streetlights flickered past. Then the car slowed, turned into a shadowed drive, and braked. The engine cut off.

He was up in a flash, drenching chloroform onto the cotton until it streamed.

The girl was opening the door. She hadn't heard him. He reached around her neck with his left forearm, throttling her, pulling her head back, and smothered her nose and mouth with the swatch of chloroform-saturated cotton. He gripped her hard, holding her as she struggled and made throat noises.

"It's all right," he muttered nervously. "I won't hurt you, darling, Jeanette. Rest easy, now. Be over in a second."

She fought crazily, arching her back against the steering wheel, trying to catch hold of his arms. But she was already beginning to go limp. She had to breathe and what she breathed was putting her to sleep. Her eyes blinked rapidly, then closed, and she went quiet in the seat.

But George Stebbins took no chances. He held the cotton to her nose and mouth until he was completely satisfied. She was inert. He let go of her. Her head flopped and she slid down in the seat, lolling.

Looking toward the house, he clicked the door shut. Lights were in front windows, but nobody had come out on the porch.

Leaning over the seat, he began undressing the girl. He took off her blouse and marveled at her breasts. They were larger than he'd thought. She wore a black lace bra, and he took this off. Big nips, all right. Look at that. He tossed the blouse and bra on the floor, then turned her around till she lay on the seat, stretched out, with legs curled up. Then he unfastened her black shorts, and managed to strip them off, breathing fast and hard. He paused.

He picked up the bottle of chloroform and the cotton, and stuck them back in the camera case. Best not to forget that. Then he brought out a rolled condom. He took out his long, hard penis and methodically urged the rubber on, his eyes blinking rapidly. He crimped his erection back into his pants, and zipped the fly closed.

Then he looked at her again. Beautiful. He would always remember her. He reached down and ever so slowly stripped the flimsy white panties off her hips, down her thighs, and off her ankles. He dropped the panties. Then he took off her tiny black slippers and she was completely nude. He arranged the position of her body again, until he was satisfied, staring owlishly at the thick curls of shadowed pubic hair.

What a pussy . . .

He spread her thighs and she lay as if sleeping. She really was sleeping. She was the most perfect he'd had in a long time.

He took up his camera case and brought out a pair of tweezers and a tiny black plastic-lidded box half-filled with cotton. He set the box on the back of the seat, and from the case took a pen-flash, which he flicked on.

Leaning over the seat, he directed the beam of the small flashlight straight at her crotch. He was breathing at a terrible rate now, and he took the tweezers and carefully, meticulously selected one pubic hair and tweaked it out. As he did so, his hips slammed wrackingly against the seat and he groaned with a fearful ecstasy. He stood hunched like that for a moment, sweating and shaking, mouth wide, eyes staring. Then, fingers still trembling, he opened the tiny black box and deposited the single pubic hair on the cotton inside, closed the box and placed it in the camera case, along with the glinting tweezers. He closed the case.

This was the very best in a long, long time. It was a perfect specimen for his collection, and what had just happened at this moment could be repeated over and over for as long as he lived.

With lingering thrills, George Stebbins climbed over the seat, opened the door, and slipped out of the car.

He closed the door, moved along the drive to the street, then turned down the sidewalk, neat and clean, with a full moon riding above the trees.

It sure was a beautiful night.

Sometimes I Love You—Sometimes I Hate You

early 1970s

I mean, really, it was a wretched morning. I mean, it was lovely, but wretched, because I felt horrible, and my tongue was like a hot cement step, and all that sex with Barney, and everything, I told him, "That's what it's all about, darling." I was thinking of Gregg, you know, and was Gregg better than Barney? I mean, really, and I got to thinking about all the others, while there in bed beside Barney, especially Timothy, the way he would just, like a crazy man, insist I keep my shoes and stockings on all the time, and nothing else—my garter belt, it had to be black, and then I thought of Father, and what he had said to me.

"You all right?" Barney asked.

I looked at him, and I knew he was a fool, because really that's what it was all about, but I knew I would never, never get enough, and you'd think I was a nympho or something, but I wasn't, not at all.

"You're entirely wrong," I said.

"About what?"

"What you think of me."

He laughed and got that devilish look in his eyes, and it made me dizzy just to see it, knowing what it meant, especially the way he grabbed my leg, and I thought of how Gregg might be, would he grab my leg, would I ever really know? I had to know. I mean, really, there were no two ways about it, but Gregg was so stupid, and then I remembered the dinner engagement, and I had to meet Gregg this afternoon, and it was nearly eleven right now. I still wore my watch.

"Do you have a thing about them?" I asked him, and he looked at me with that long horse face, and I said, "Barney, tell me, do you have a thing about watches?"

"Oh, for Christ's sake, Gloria, cut out the shit."

"You didn't make me take it off."

He just kept looking at me that way, blinking those silly eyes, his hair all standing up, because, really, I wanted to know. I was desperate about things like that, but how do you explain that if they don't ask you to take off your watch, then they have a thing, and then I remembered the dinner again, and I knew I must look like a wet bird after all that gin, and those five joints, and all, and the sex, the sex, the sex. Sometimes I thought Father was right. I mean, it was a desperate situation, really it was. Really, he would say, "Now, Gloria, I know what you're doing, and if you just get married, it'll be okay, then, my sweet." He always called me "My sweet," like that, and he *was* sweet, only was *I* sweet? And sometimes when he spoke to me about it, I would just think hard as hell about What would become of me?

I leaned back, with Barney holding my leg, sort of massaging my thigh, only he didn't want to do anything about it, really, I mean, and I thought, you know, of What will become of me?

"What you giggling about?" he asked me.

It was just like him to ask something stupid, and I thought how I was supposed to meet Gregg at two, but why two o'clock in the afternoon for dinner, and would they have any grass? Of course not, it was dinner at his uncle's, his name was Everett, retired with gobs, and living in Nyack, a lepidopterist I think it is, I mean, really, and very prominent in philatelic circles, which was all right, but I don't dig butterflies, only I could lick the stamps for him, I really love to lick stamps, sometimes they flavor the glue, peppermint, wintergreen, only I remembered they have these hinges, well, I could lick his hinges. I had to shop for something to wear, I mean, just anything would do, but I had to have something fresh the way it smells from the shop, fresh-smelling, and the girl saying, "Do you like this?," and saying, "Charge it," because Father wanted me to dress well.

Father always said, "Wear something new, baby, it makes you feel new." I thought that was apropos, just now, I mean, truly, my tongue was covered with positively layers of silt, and then Barney reached out grinning and I said, "Oh, no, because you really don't want to."

He groaned something and said, "Look, does that look like I don't want to?" and I suppose it was because a doctor told me once, "It's nothing, you're just over-sexed, is all," but I made the doctor examine me anyway, and you know what that led to, right in the office, on the table, the edge, anyway, I mean, really, I couldn't help myself, thinking about Gregg, and I said, "Gregg, darling," and I could have killed myself.

"It's Barney," he said.

And it wasn't any good, I mean, it was good, but why couldn't he be like I hoped Gregg would be, or like Desmond, that night at his apartment with the Holland Gin and the bluebirds, what a cunning name, I mean, they say you shouldn't mix them, but, I mean, Barney was all covered with sweat, even with the air-conditioning, and it dropped in my eye, and he was laboring, just laboring, I mean, you know?

"It should be spontaneous," I told him, sliding off the bed. "I haven't even time for a shower."

"Where you going?"

I was half dressed already, he was so slow answering, and he just lay there with that horse face, covered with sweat, and I said, "I have an appointment. I mean, you know, I've got to go home, because Father—actually there's somewhere I absolutely must be at two."

"I thought we'd spend the day."

"Oscar," I said, I mean really, he was out there someplace, "you couldn't spend the day with me."

That hurt him. Well, I mean, I was dressed now, and I stood there looking at him, and then at my watch, and it was after eleven, and Father would be fit, I mean, you know, "See you, Barney," I said, and left, thinking about how would Gregg be, and my damned obnoxious tongue, but I hadn't really meant to hurt him, the way he looked when I said it, getting pale, you could see the blood leave his face, so I caught a cab and went home, and Father said he was worried.

"My sweet," he said, I mean really, he said, "My sweet, you shouldn't act this way." His face got all nasty, I mean positively wretched, and he bit his lip. "Don't think I'm hasty, Gloria, but you simply can't go on this way," we were in the kitchen, and he had on this polka-dot thing, oh, we had plenty of money, Mother, and all that, when she died, but he clung to it, he positively clung, "Why don't you get married, my sweet?"

"Yes, Father," I said, and went upstairs to my room, and it looked like a forgotten cave, really it did, you could just smell the loneliness, the distance, I mean, you know? I showered and wore that blue frock, and ran downtown, and found just what I wanted in a real short red one, I mean, maybe this red wasn't just exactly right for dinner, but Gregg liked red, so I bought it, and went home and gargled again, and I wore the shell bracelet and earrings Richard had given me that time on the lake when we had what he called "The Marathon" in the Chris-Craft, and thinking about boats brought Andy to mind, with his Cessna, and how we had that interim over Lake Champlain, diving, diving, and he would say, "It doesn't matter, Gloria, just you, is all," and I thought we'd crash, and I screamed, and I didn't really give a damn, we were that stoned on crystal, and how Andy could, I mean, really, and later he told me he thought the wings would tear off over the golf course, when we pulled out.

Gregg wore a dark jacket with a white scarf, and white slacks, and shoes, and he looked positively damned, I mean, really, so handsome, and how could he be so stupid? I mean, I loved him. I loved him so much it ached and hurt and my heart banged away, and I could just hardly talk, the way he looked, and he was so stupid. He was an ass, I mean, literally.

God how I loved him . . . lying awake nights with one of them beside me, or on me, thinking, Gregg, Gregg, darling, my darling, I love you, I love you, I mean, really, it was tedious, simply tedious.

"How are you, Gloria?"

I mean, really.

"We're not going to Uncle Everett's, we're going to my place."

"What?" I said, because I had never seen his home, but he was quiet and kind of nervous, so we rode to Valley Cottage in the Porsche, with Gregg driving like a wowser, but just sitting there, and every once in a while he would look at me and grin, he was so stupid, God damn him to hell, and I thought of what Father had said, how he told me, "Gregg is a fine young man, Gloria," and I hadn't even been to bed with him, the way he was so stupid.

"Uncle Everett will be there," Gregg said, and we drove in a long gravel drive, with trees and flowers, and the lawn so green, and got out and went into the house, there were two wings, I mean, and it was all summery and lace curtains and potted plants, with a grand piano smelling of lemon oil, and we went into the left wing, and I thought how Gregg was all alone, all he had was his Uncle Everett, and we came into a big room. "Over there," Gregg said.

We plowed across a thick carpet, and up to this old fellow in a wing-backed chair. He had eyes like cracked marbles, and a cream turtle-neck, with a gold medallion hanging on his chest, and Gregg cleared his throat, and said, "Uncle Everett, this is Gloria."

Just then a thin man in black came by with a tray and I took one. It was a martini, and I looked at Uncle Everett over the edge as I sipped, and it was good, and he said with a voice like wet newspaper, "This is marvelous, Gregory. And how are you, Gloria? You should have come long before this. We should have met, I've heard so much about you," and Gregg looked at me and grinned, and I loved him so, and the glass was empty, and I said, "I'm glad," and Uncle Everett said, "There are sandwiches on the table behind you. Is the martini to your liking, Gloria?"

I nodded, and Uncle Everett turned to Gregg and winked, I mean, and then he stood up, like a stick with clothes on it, and Gregg looked at his watch, flipping his wrist, he wore it on the inside of his right wrist, which seemed to me to be an affectation, I mean, really, but it couldn't matter less, and he said, "I've got to make a phone call upstairs," and his face got red, and he turned and rushed off across the room.

So I was going to say something about licking the stamps, or just anything, but the man in black came past me again with the tray, and I smiled and he smiled, he was really young, I mean, it was a shock, and I put the empty glass back and took another, and smiled at him, and then smiled at Gregg's uncle, and he said, "You don't have to stand there, my dear. Go have a sandwich." Then he said, "Anyway, I have to leave now." He lifted one hand with an effort, "Marvelous, meeting you," and he moved on out of the room, just like a stick, I mean, really, and I went over and stood by the table of sandwiches and salads and junk, and thought of Gregg, and the slim, handsome guy in black came up to me again, and I smiled, and gave him my empty and took another, and he said, "Would you like to help me mix the next batch?"

"Should I?" I said.

"It's up to you. I'm his valet."

"I didn't know they had them anymore, except in hotels. How come do you—?"

"I do everything," he said, and he stood there a long moment, fidgeting the way they do sometimes, I mean, you know, and then he glanced at his feet, and I knew he was embarrassed, so I nodded to him.

We crossed the room and went through a large dining room with lots of silver, and down some stairs, and through a butler's pantry into a big yellow kitchen, and I wondered what Gregg was doing on the phone? Through an archway in the kitchen wall, I could see what looked like a game room, all chintzy.

"You dig me, don't you?" he said.

"Not particularly."

"The drinks are all mixed," he said. And then he was very close, and I often wondered if there was something about me that looked that way, I mean, did my lip hang out, or something?

"I don't even want to know your name," he said.

"I wouldn't tell it to you, anyway."

"Come into the butler's pantry."

"What's in there?"

"I'll show you. C'mon."

We went into the butler's pantry, and I'm not kidding you, I could feel the martinis, and I'm not kidding you, the way he acted, I mean, the way *I* acted, I just couldn't do anything about it, I mean I had one hand in an open loaf of bread, squeezing the slices, and I thought, Gregg, Gregg, Gregg, for God's sake, Gregg, and we were both panting, and he had my skirt up, and then my pants off, and I rammed them into my purse, and bread fell on the floor, and I chewed his chin, and a bird was chirping somewhere, chirping and chirping, and then I knew it was a squeaky cupboard door I was leaning against, and he was saying, "Baby, you, baby, I just couldn't, baby," and I said, "I know how it is," and some more bread fell on the floor, and I thought, What if Gregg came? But it wouldn't matter now.

"Can I phone you?"

"No."

"But can't I see you again, somewhere?"

"No. Positively not, you fool."

I really socked it to him, I mean, I chilled him cold, and I had my pants on again, I felt secure, and in the kitchen I found the gin. I poured a glassful, and drank and drank, and somehow got it down, and then poured another glassful.

"You beat everything," he said.

"Go press a pair of pants," I told him.

He tightened his lips, I mean, he really did, and I could feel the gin, and Gregg came into the kitchen.

"I'm smashed," I said.

Gregg stood there. The other one left the room. Gregg looked so stupid, and I loved him so. It wasn't sentimental mush, it wasn't, I mean, I was so drunk, and I didn't care, I tell you, I did not care a damn, I just loved him to death, I needed him, and I wanted him, he would protect me, but he was so stupid. He stood there watching me, his eyes all gone with whatever it was inside him, soup, or something, I suppose. The dope. The absolute dope.

"Gloria?"

"Yes, Gregg?"

"Are you all right?"

"Of course, Gregg."

"Gloria, you look marvelous."

"Do I, really?"

"Yes." And he lifted one hand, and it was trembling, and he said, "There wasn't any phone call, Gloria, I don't know how to tell you, my God, I don't know how."

"Well—?"

He just stood there, and his eyes got all wild, or something, and I took a long drink of straight gin, it was like cool water, now, and I thought, Oh, Gregg.

"Gloria, come with me."

"Sure."

We went into the butler's pantry.

"Somebody spilled the bread."

He was in idiot.

He said, "No. Not there," and he tugged my arm, and we went back through the kitchen into the game room, or whatever it was, there was a dart board, anyway, and red and blue chintz, and cases of butterflies on the walls, and Gregg made a motion toward a long white couch. I sat down. Well, I mean, really, I fell down on the couch, and looked up at him, and he had his head held back and his mouth open, so I figured, well, he's sick. Something's happened to him, and he said, "Damn it, damn it, Gloria. I don't know how to say it. I just—" and he began to shout—"I want you, Gloria," he said this very loudly, and then he began to whisper, "I want you to marry me, will you, Gloria? I love you, I've loved you all the time, all these months, it's over a year." He was trembling all over, and he sprawled down beside me on the couch, close against me, and he was wild with it, the way he tried to kiss me, missing my mouth, and making a grab for one breast, and my gin spilled, and he said, "Will you marry me? Gloria? Will you? I can't stand it, really, I can't."

It was stupid, he was an ass, I mean, really.

"You love me?" I said.

"Yes," he said, nodding his stupid head.

"I love you, too," I told him, and he was so damned utterly stupid, but I did love him, and I wanted to cry, and then I did cry, and he held me, and he kissed my forehead.

"Does this mean yes?" he asked.

"Yes," I said. "Yes, yes, yes."

We would be married, because I did love Gregg, so much, so awfully much, I mean I had waited so long and now here it was. I knew we would be happy, positively.

Father would be happy too.

Mantis 36

It was happening again. In her mind's eye she could see the rigid, satiny cock. She was sucked irresistibly toward it, her cunt moist and palpably alive between her slimly plump thighs.

She did not know what she was, she only knew who she was and where she was, sitting behind the wheel of the scarlet Turbo Carrera, flashing across New Mexican desert in the late afternoon. She did not often think about what she hoped for; she didn't really have to consider the problem, because it always seemed to solve itself. She only came to clear realization during the sex act, not before.

She was Desi Aemes, guiltless, with thick scintillant blonde hair, patient pale blue eyes, a heart-shaped face with an upturned nose and a broad red mouth, smiling, revealing showgirl teeth, Vegas teeth, and a neck of beauty that deepened into swollen tits nippling a dark pullover under a Rocafort Canary Mandarin. The side slit in her black Ginza skirt revealed more provocativity, all of her a jarring sensuality that threatened the libido of every man she met.

She cruised at eighty, spat on cops, because sometimes she remembered that Shay had never worn a uniform; but not often did she remember. She bought cops. She bought everything and everybody.

Desi Aemes was well fixed, a prime-looking screw.

Where was Shay?

She experienced a sharp wrench of confusion at the thought and pressed the accelerator until she was reeling in the nineties. She drove carelessly but with stirring expertise, one long-fingered, diamond-ringed hand on the wheel, the other holding a smoldering cigarette.

The last thing she recalled was a motel in Amarillo, a scene tinged with red, but what had happened there was beyond her ken. It was as though she reached out and back, seeking for something, but never finding it; sometimes a wink of discernment fluttered her way and she thought she knew, fumbling at the white split of dream, but ever missing with a sigh.

Satiny cocks, wet mouths, faces, hands, bodies in the night. Masculinity. A grin. A detachment from the passing scene through the mirrored flux of the car's window. Fingers and threats and findings, all a conglomerate of sensation only, so that often her bunned ass writhed on the cushioned seat, wondering with a scowl that only enhanced the platinum beauty of her statued face.

She ate irregularly, when she felt really hungry. She slept the same—but nights were tortured, semiconscious arenas.

There were only those times when . . .

When what?

She rolled the window down and flipped the spent cigarette out into the windstream. She immediately lit another. She realized she was approaching a town, a sign read: TUCUMCARI. She slowed. It was a small, quiet, mostly deserted spot, dusty, unprepossessing. Nevertheless, she sensed a mood of disquiet in herself, a tightening and tensing of nerves, a ruffle in the solar-plexus, a warm blush in the throat and shoulders, quickened breathing.

She breezed through the main section of town and soon was on the outskirts, her cunt anticipatorily moist. She glimpsed a motel sign, flashing crimson: NEW MEXICAN INN. *Vacancy. Restaurant. Lounge.*

Really, now. Where'd they get off with a place like this, way out here in the middle of nowhere? All fresh 'dobe with facades of deep lavender glass and proudly landscaped with springy fir and green sod . . .

Shay . . . *you cocksucker!*

Where are you? Shay? Who was Shay . . . ?

I'll go to Seattle and see Mama . . .

She stopped the Porsche opposite the motel, in the highway. She sat there staring at the windshield, palpitant.

Mama will be happy. We'll have a gay time, a gala time.

A car swept up behind her, braking furiously, nearly nudging her rear bumper. It backed, swung to one side, and passed her with a cutting wailing blare of horn, a man brandishing his arm.

. . . never really knew Mama, Daddy, either. Never knew them, but this time I'll get to know Mama—we'll understand really who we are, together . . .

Another car careened past, a sheer of sound.

She nudged the shift and turned over toward the motel, across blue gravel, past evening sprinklers, up to the lavender windows of the dark-looking lounge; cool in there, refreshing.

She felt thirsty.

Then I'll drive straight on to Seattle, I can do it, she thought as she fished her big black leather purse from the opposite seat and swung the door open, climbing out, flash of thigh, damp snatch. The curved calves sheened nylon and her feet toed white pumps.

Seattle, yes, Mama . . . we'll truly get to know each other . . .

Shay . . . was he in there? Could he be?

Don't do this to me! I don't know who Shay is.

Nevertheless, there was a pale face before her, like a cloud mass betwixt and between and she hurried, now, across the scattering gravel to the smooth cement patio, then through the wing door into the lounge.

For a split instant she was blinded in the shadows, smelling beer and whisky and gin and hearing soft sound, music swelling, and seeing *blood.*

She recovered, walked to the bar and half sat, half stood, at a tall black leather-cushioned stool. The place was for passing tourists, but she didn't believe they did much business.

In the shadowed cool darkness an aproned man stood looking at her with a sparkling glass in one hand, a clean white towel in the other. He was a smooth man, with sleek dark hair and Mexicana eyes, the lips calm beneath a thin mustache.

He said nothing. The music was not loud and emanated from a swirl-colored jukebox, not rock, either, more Spanish, something . . .

Wasn't it always this way before . . . ?

Before what?

She knew somehow that this was not new, but put it down to the fact that she had entered many lounges, bars, alone, thirsty; stopped at myriads of motels . . . *then,* why?

"Scotch and water."

"Scotch and water." He had a soft accent. It was pleasant. They were alone in the room of liquid amber and shadowed crimson lights, of ebony and darkness, of a twinkle at the backbar.

Ice tinkled. The tiny silver spout sputtered orgasmically and he was libelous with the liquor into a relish of clean glass.

She tried to pull herself together, because she suddenly felt down, way down. She could not control the feathering sensation.

The barman was smiling gently.

"Thanks."

She drank, felt in her purse, dropped two bills, tens, on the bar. The whisky warmed its way down and at the same time, *Shay* . . . it was the procedure, she knew, the drinking act itself. *Shay.*

She clung to the feeling devilishly, finished the drink.

"I'll have another. I've been driving a long time, terribly thirsty. I've got to go straight on all night. Seattle. See my mother. You know how mothers are?"

"Oh, yes. The same?"

"Yes."

Who was Shay?

Abruptly, she trembled inside and sat up on the cushioned stool, shivering with something she knew nothing about. No reason, really. Why? Why?

"Mama."

"I call mine Mama, too."

"Aren't they something to contend with?"

"Truly, they are."

She watched him hold up a winking glass. The music swirled, a guitar, soft-stringed by the fingers and thumbs, palpings, no steel.

"Perhaps I could buy you one?"

At first, for that brief second, she thought the barman had spoken. But then she realized somebody was seated beside her. She jumped inside, a shock, and her heart danced in tachycardiac time. For that moment she could not control herself.

Shay. Shay.

Then she was all platinum again, beautiful, swinging around on the stool, with the chin and cheekbones, and the scooped shadows and the Vegas teeth and the eyes like glazed marbles you might mistakenly dive into and never come up again, out of.

The immaculate legs, crossed now, revealing hot promise; the fingers with diamonds, the white nails, tapered perfectly, white, white, and cream and red and pale blue and blonde, out of nowhere, from the impossible cover of some magazine. And canary-sheathed breasts, so pale, so clean, so pure.

Momentary panic. What am I doing here?

"I really prefer buying my own. But—what say I buy *you* one?"

She was looking at him, directly into his eyes, but seeing him entire.

She heard the whispered word. It came from the music, interjected along with the sound of strings, plucked, palped . . . *Shay*. The single word, like the music, swelled inside her, burning her throat.

What was *it?*

The music cut into silence.

She whirled on the stool, looked at the barman.

"Could we have that number again, please?—and some more like it? Could you arrange that?"

"Yes, miss—certainly."

She thrust a ten-dollar bill at him along the bar.

He ignored it, walked smoothly toward the jukebox. She watched him, ignoring Shay, thinking, *again, again, just this one time, dear Plattsburg and he's back from Philly so early, he's not fooling me . . .*

The music swirled around her again, the soft palping of strings.

"All right?"

"Thank you, ever so—"

She turned on the stool and looked at Shay.

"I don't have a room yet," she said.

For a moment the man said nothing. He just sat there, half on the stool, staring at her. He swallowed.

He's changed. He's altered his appearance.

"I'm Des Stewart," he said. "Are you from around here? Albuquerque, I'll bet—huh?"

"Guess again, you rascal."

"I'll have that drink, then."

"What'll it be?" the barman wanted to know.

"Bourbon over rocks."

"Oh," she said. "A he-man, huh?"

Shay. Shay.

Who was Shay?

She took a sip of her drink and the barman poured the bourbon on rocks and the man, Des Stewart, drank, too.

She looked at him again: tall, in charcoal, with a heavy blue tie and a white shirt, chin and brown and dark eyes and thick black hair. Lots of chin. She liked that.

Something screamed inside her and her hand trembled on the glass. She could not define the scream and she did not understand the feeling now. She understood nothing. She did not know who she was, only where she was. She did not know what she was.

Then, suddenly, "I'm Desi Aemes. What's your handle?"

Now, lie to me, like all the others.

He chuckled. "I've told you, honey. I'm Des Stewart. And you're Desi Aemes. It's a dizzy desi, right?"

"Two of a kind," she said.

Some people entered the bar, shadows, talking. They moved to a table. Three of them. Immediately, the door swung and four more people came in.

I'm mixed up. Shay . . .

There were three women altogether.

Look at them, then.

But he did not look at them.

He spoke softly. "You said you didn't have a room? Did I hear you right?"

"Yes. That's what I said."

"I'm passing through, staying the night. I have a room."

"Let's have another drink."

They ordered two more drinks and she insisted on paying. He let her with a smile.

He's smoother than usual.

She leaned close to him. There wasn't much time.

"I don't really care," she said. "I mean, you don't have to tell me anything."

"I don't understand."

Oh, God, Shay! You shit—you absolute shit!

I'll make you think about it. I'll make you think about what's between my legs, because that's what you always wanted, that only . . . Shay!

She turned on the stool, uncrossing her legs, leaning toward the man, her knee touching his, and she saw his prick move in his pants. "Then, shall we go to your room?"

He did not know what to do. He just sat there, staring at her, not exactly believing it, because of what she obviously wasn't. She was not a hooker. She was something very special.

"Did I hear what you said?" he whispered.

"Yes," she whispered, smiling with the teeth, the eyes, "of course, you did."

"Should we have another drink first?"

"Why?" she frowned. "Buy a bottle." She was already off the stool. "I'll be outside. It's best we don't leave together."

"Number two-ten," he told her.

She turned and left the lounge. She clicked along the walk to the stairs and up the stairs and around the railing and down the outside until she reached Number 210.

She tried the door. It was open. She entered and stood in the air-conditioned quiet, the stillness; and then she heard the music. It was piped into the rooms, better than Muzak. The softly palped strings.

On and on . . .

She went to the big bed, laid her purse on the nightstand, and began taking off her clothes. The Canary Mandarin jacket, the webby pullover, dropping them to the floor, cupping her tits, thumbing the nipples, the black Ginza skirt, and she was nude excepting for gartered smoky nylons and heels. She toed the shoes off. She fingered her cunt, sat on the bed, then lay on her side and watched the door.

Shay . . .

She began to weep. Then that ceased and she just lay there.

The door opened and he stood there, staring at her.

He held a bottle. He closed the door and came to the bed, staring at her pussy, then into her eyes. But he had changed. She had known he would change and she was not surprised.

"Shall we have a drink?" he asked, his voice slightly hoarse.

"Not now."

She stared straight at his crotch.

He placed the bottle on the floor and stood there. He seemed not to want to stare at her, as if he were alarmed or ashamed or something.

"Don't be like that," she said, showing him her tongue, fingering her moist slit.

He stripped fast, except for the shoes and socks. He looked at her and she looked at his feet. His cock was enormous, jerking up and down, the head flaming.

He quickly sat on the bed and took off his shoes and socks. He was muscular, flat-bellied.

"Don't you think we should have a drink?"

"You really want a drink?"

"No."

Shay . . . back from Philly so early . . .

What was . . . ?

He was reluctant, an idiot.

He stood, put one knee on the bed and looked down at her. She came up and took his prick in her hand, smiling up at him, and slowly inserted the plumlike glistening head into her mouth, feeling the smoothness between her lips. He gave a little groan as she sucked his cock, cupping his balls, brushing his belly with her hair. His hands found her head, forcing his penis deeper, but she pulled back wetly, slipping her circled hand slowly off the end of his dong, and lay back, watching him.

He anxiously stretched out beside her and she lifted her round knees, watching him.

"My God," he said. "You're beautiful."

"Beast."

"I don't understand—"

"What's to understand, Shay?"

"My name's Des."

"Ah, yes."

She still did not know what she was.

She gripped his slick cock and they sucked mouths, tongues, and she felt his hands on her body, his fingers slipping into her wet slit. He came to his knees, leering down at her, jacking his long whang as she spread her thighs, still smiling, watching him. Then he was on her, slipping that thick long cock into her cunt, burying it, and she felt his balls against her ass. He thrust and she wormed against him and she knew what she was, and opened her mouth to his gaze. He worked his prick in and out, close against her, whispering sad nothings, fondling her, feeling her cunt, her ass, her thighs.

He moaned and she moaned, too, just to comfort him, writhing, too, because now she knew who she was and she knew what she was, and this was Shay. Shay. Shay who had sliced her life in two, stolen her life, her happiness, wrung her secrets, killed her baby, robbed her of everything— yes, this was Shay!

And her hand felt for her purse on the nightstand as he drove a more frenzied rhythm, fucking her cunt with wild strokes, and she reached beneath the leather flap of the purse and came up with the long knife.

The blade winked and she gasped as she drove it into his back, gouging for the heart, practiced, feeling the heart wring and twist and shudder as he tried to scream and she smothered that with her mouth and the blood flowed and she scraped in there with the blade, cutting and cutting until he gave a long sigh. She rolled him off her and began jabbing his chest with the knife, repeatedly. He was quite dead and blood was everywhere. She was sheened with crimson, glazed like ham.

She stood beside the bed and stared down at Shay. He had taken everything and now he was dead. She did not care. She felt nothing. She was content.

She carefully wiped the knife on the blue spread and placed it across the black purse. She had never seen so much blood. Was there so much blood, truly, in a person?

"Shay," she said softly.

Music purled into the room, accompanying the sound of her voice— the gentle palping of strings.

She moved to the bathroom on padding feet, entered and showered. Returning, clean, pure, platinum again, and cool, she quickly dressed, put the knife back into the purse and left the room.

She walked directly to the Carrera.

Shay . . .

She would go to Seattle and see Mama. They would talk and understand each other. Mama could tell her about Daddy, because she had never understood Daddy, either. She had never known either of them, and a child should know his parents.

She did not know what she was; she only knew who she was and where she was, cruising America in a hot scarlet Carrera.

Something, a shadow, lay before her—what was it? *Shay? Shay . . . who was Shay?*

She lit a cigarette, flashing across the dark New Mexican desert.

Mantis: Praying Mantis. Large insect.
Female turns triangular head and devours
momentary mate during copulation, murdering
at the moment of ecstasy.
In re Desi: Shay + 35 = 36.

Summer's Lease

middle 1970s

She ran like a faun, reminding him often of that animal, but she was human and all too beautiful. Much time was spent by him, watching her with binoculars from the large northside studio window, as she lay on the railed terrace, or played in the field, or entered the woods. He painted her over and over, in different positions; running and seated, lying down—and he had even accomplished some portrait work of her. Of course this was purely imaginary, because he had never seen her up close. He would not want that, even. It was the dream. That's what it had become. Something at once secret and delicate and marvelous. He could not even describe it to himself, it was so tentative; like holding a drop of mercury in one's palm.

Martens had rented the large barn-like room in the country above the woods and the lake, as he rented some place each summer, to get away from the grueling city efforts put into commercial work. He would paint for himself.

This summer, it was the girl.

He hadn't expected her. She had taken over. And now she filled his thoughts, his daydreams and his nightdreams.

He didn't even know her name. He didn't want that, either. He wanted no tie at all. Just the delicate dream.

She lived not far down the road from him, and he knew theirs were the only places within several miles, aside from the small store and gas station down at the corners. But that, too, was nearly three miles away.

What did she do out there, all by herself?

If she was visited at all, it must be late at night.

Martens never tried to watch her at night. He was only conscious of lights at her windows. Nights he would sketch and paint her over and over, in a hundred different ways.

The barn that had been converted into an artist's studio was filled with these paintings. They were immensely precious to him. He worked hard on the canvases, trying to capture the girl's seeming wildness, the untamed way she had of moving. Mostly she wore tattered denim shorts, and some sort of colorful scarf about her breasts. She had pale blonde hair that flowed about her shoulders, and down her back. It was full and cloud-like, this hair.

Sometimes he laughed at himself, because he did no other work, just painted her. Sometimes he got very drunk, and lay on the couch, and dreamed.

It was truly another world, this summer's place.

Each morning he rose with wild anticipation, taking a place before the large northside window, waiting, watching. He worked in between. The lavenders of twilight always descended, bringing regret. This regret formed like a large black ball of wool inside him, and he knew then that he would have to wait for another day.

At first he had been tempted to go directly over to her place, talk with her, see her close up, but somehow he hadn't, and now he was glad for this. He would never know who she was. It was just a long, tender dream. Her lithe, white limbs flashing in the sunlight, her hair flowing, or what he imagined as the pale blue of her eyes, turned directly toward him, lips slightly parted.

Martens had rented the studio for two months. He had already been here nearly one month.

Wherever he looked in this room, now, there she was, in myriads of positions. He had painted her nude, too, lying on the terrace, sun-bathing. And he marveled. Somehow her skin never seemed to tan. It was always that pure, soft white, glowing.

Sometimes he thought of what it would be like, returning to New York, being without her. But then, he would always have her with him on canvas now.

He did not try to dissect the feeling. He only held it, tentatively, and as tenderly as possible.

Each afternoon at three o'clock, Martens walked down through the field into the woods. This was his only exercise. He liked the cool dark of the woods, the shadows. He watched the animals and slowly made his way on a path to the lakeside, where he would skip stones, or just sit on a rock, or a log, and think of the girl.

Sometimes he was conscious of her as an emotion. How could he ever paint an emotion? Pure. White. Curved. Tentative and touched with heart-numbing beauty. The days and nights were hypnotic with thoughts of the girl.

Now it was nearing three, and she had just crossed the terrace, entered her house through glass doors that glinted in the slanting sunlight.

Martens scrubbed some paint from his hands with turpentine, and went to the door. He crossed the field slowly, not looking once toward her home. He wondered what would happen if they ever met. How would he behave?

Martens was not the rough, outdoorsy type. He admired seclusion and liked being alone. He lived within his mind, so the mental life with the girl was not new to him, though such a thing had never happened before.

He reached the pathway in the woods, and headed toward the lake. Squirrels chattered. A rabbit leaped bounding through the leaves.

There were moments when he thought of the girl that were excruciating. But he was a small man, and entirely self-contained. The only thing was, this summer was something vital. He knew he would have it for the rest of his life.

He reached the lake and sat on a log, and mused. He watched the water. He wondered if she ever came here to swim. He would like to see that. See her hair streaming down her back, her eyes laughing. The lips would be always parted across pearly teeth.

She lived alone, he knew that much. Often he wondered if she were a painter like himself. Or an actress, getting away from it all. A writer? A poet? He dreamed and questioned himself incessantly.

Almost before he realized, dusk had settled, and he knew he should start back toward the studio. He rose, tossed a pebble into the lake, then made for the pathway.

Coming through the woods, a cool summery wind drew overhead, roofing the early darkness. He came to the field and crossed it slowly, glancing toward her place. Lights were lit behind draperies. He wondered what she was doing. How could such a girl be alone? Maybe she liked being by herself, as he did. Maybe she dreamed, too. What were her dreams.

Martens smiled to himself as he neared the studio. The huge north window was still and dark. He had left no light. He entered at the somewhat rustic door and strode through to the kitchen area, where he switched on a light. He felt a touch hungry, but thoughts of the girl still lingered, as always. He put on the coffee pot, then wandered into the studio proper.

Abruptly, lights glared, and there stood the girl.

She was laughing. She held one hand over her mouth and there was near hysteria behind the sound. She was not alone.

A red-shirted, dark-haired young man stood nearby, staring at the painting on the easel. He wore heavy brown boots with gleaming brass buckles below flared tan pants. He cocked his head and looked at Martens.

"Well, you're back, I see," he said. The tone was a bit wild.

"What are you doing?" Martens asked. He looked quickly at the girl.

She took her hand from her mouth and he saw that she was as beautiful as he had supposed. She more than just resembled the portraits he had done of her from his imagination. She was a dream come to life. Only now she wore a red peignoir, and she was barefoot, her toenails gleaming. She spread her arms, looking at Martens, and said, "What *is* all this?" Then she laughed. "Aren't you going to explain?"

"You know damned well what it is," the young man said sharply. At the same instant, he grabbed the painting from the easel. It was one Martens was especially proud of, revealing the girl running down across the field. It was one he had been dreaming upon.

The young man hurled the painting to the floor, and slashed at it with his cutting heels. Then the two of them, the girl and the young man, seemed to become demons. They ran about the room as Martens stood there, watching, and they snatched paintings and tore at them, and flung them to the floor, and stomped on them. He could hear them breathing hard, panting.

The young man cursed and muttered to himself.

Martens heard the word "Pervert!" repeated over and over. "Artists are all queers—*queers*!" he said. He shouted it again.

The girl sidled up to Martens, and looked at him. Her eyes were the palest blue, with tiny spokes in them, and as he regarded her, those eyes seemed to spin.

He heard her speak. "What've you been doing, painting me, like this? What is it?"

"Using binoculars," the young man shouted from across the room. He slammed them to the floor.

Then the two young people became hysterical again, and soon the neat studio was a shambles of torn canvases, spilled paint, turpentine, linseed oil. Tubes of paint were squashed and oozing on the boards. The young man scuffed the multicolored paint across the floor, smeared the paint on the rugs.

Martens had not moved. It was as if his entire throat and stomach had turned to ice. His head was blocked. He could not think. He stared at the girl. She laughed at him, and her teeth were as white as he had imagined, only smaller, seed-like, and intricately even.

Then a rage came into him. It overpowered him. But the rage expressed itself in tears. They had entered his dream, and stomped it, ruined it, destroyed it. He stood alone amidst the wreckage. He wept without shame. But the rage did not subside. He trembled and his heart hammered; heat flushed his face and shoulders, and he heard himself gasp.

"He's bawling—bawling like a woman," the young man shouted.

All Martens could think was that she had been visited at night by this young man. They were animals. He knew her, and he knew the young man. He had seen them like this in the city. He was a part of the destruction.

The girl came close to him and touched his arm. "Don't feel too bad," she whispered, laughing quietly up into his face.

The young man snarled something, grabbed her wrist, and yanked her away. "C'mon, we're getting out of here, now." He turned a red, twisted face toward Martens. "And you're getting out, too." He paused, then said, "Or we'll do worse. See that you're gone tomorrow—you, and all this, too!"

"Johnny's jealous," the girl whispered quickly. "He's a monster, and he's terrible jealous, even if I look at anybody else."

"Shut up!" the young man said.

"He just can't control himself," the girl said. "We knew you were doing something, and when he saw those paintings, he went crazy—"

"Wait," the young man said. "Maybe he's got some booze." He ran to the kitchen area, and flung open the refrigerator, then slammed it shut. He opened cupboards, and came up with a bottle of bourbon. He came running back across the room, tearing through the oozing paints, and ripped canvases, the dreams. He uncapped the bottle and drank deeply, some of the liquor streaming down his chin. Martens watched his throat work. Then the young man handed the bottle to the girl.

She looked at Martens, then drank. She gasped as she lowered the bottle.

"Don't you see?" she whispered in that strident voice. "It's jealousy!"

"I told you to shut up."

Then they were gone.

Martens stood there for some time, unmoving, after they left. Then he turned out all the lights, and went to a chair. He took the chair to the window, and sat, and stared at her house. It looked so peaceful out there in the night. The saffron windows of her house revealed nothing. Jealousy had done this. Sitting there, he wept again, realizing just how precious this dream had truly been. Now it was shattered. Reality cloaked him like the Iron Maiden.

The young man did not know what he had done. It was more than destruction. It was like setting fire to his soul, watching it burn, laughing as the crisping embers floated away.

But now Martens was in another dream. He found himself at the trunk in the corner of the room. He withdrew the oil-silk wrapped package and took out something heavy, bound in an oily cloth. Moments later he stood there with the German Luger in his hand. Why he always carried it with him, he did not know. He had told himself it was for protection. He often oiled it and kept it in perfect working order.

Then he left the studio and walked along the side of the road toward the girl's house. He saw the car parked in the copse of pine. That would be Johnny's car. Jealousy. The young man had been berserk.

He approached the house stealthily, treading on damp turfy grass, the Luger clutched in his right hand, the smell of oil and night in his nostrils.

It seemed as if all the lights in the house were on. Paths of gleaming yellow trailed out across the grass. He reached the door and tried the knob. It was open. He entered. He closed the door and stood quietly inside, conscious of them talking from somewhere. The young man was still raging.

"The God damned son-of-a-bitch!" the young man shouted. "I should've killed him. Should've burned the God damned place! Shall I burn it, go back there? Shall I?"

Then Martens heard the girl. "What's the use? You've done all there is to do. Couldn't you tell by the look on his face? He was crying. It must have meant plenty to him. Calm down."

"God damned pervert!"

There would have been a time when the girl's words might have touched Martens' heart. Now they only edged the steel of his desire.

Yellow draperies covered all the windows.

He moved on down a hall and turned to the right. He saw them and said, "Don't move."

It was a large room, with a gray fieldstone fireplace at the far end. The fireplace reached to a beamed ceiling.

The young man stared at Martens. The girl began to giggle. The Luger was very steady and the young man's gazed turned to it.

"I'll kill you if you move," Martens said. He knew he meant it.

To the left, draperies covered the glass doors that led out onto the terrace where she had lain nude, so many times.

He acted fast, then, and he was in a dream—but it was a different dream.

"Get the drapery cords," he said to the girl. "Tear them down."

At first she objected, scowling, but when he stepped toward her, brandishing the gun, she ran to the draperies, and began loosening the cords. Soon she stood there, staring, with the cords dangling in her hands.

Martens brought a straight chair from the nearby dining area, into the living room, and placed it in front of a long, broad couch. The couch was covered with a leopard skin rug.

"What the hell are you trying to do?" the young man wanted to know. His voice was strained. His face was red again, eyes wild.

"Sit in the chair," Martens said quietly.

"I won't sit in any damned chair!"

"Yes, you will," Martens said. "You will, or you'll die. Do you want to die?"

The young man watched him for a moment, then went over and sat in the chair.

"Now," Martens said to the girl. "Tie his hands behind him to the chair, bind him to the chair. I'm watching. I want a perfect job—tightly."

He made her labor over it. He had her get more cord from other draperies, and he wasn't satisfied until Johnny was secure in the straight-backed dining room chair. Muscles beneath the red silk shirt bulged. The young man's face was pale now. His dark eyes glittered. He mumbled to himself continuously, but the words were unintelligible. Then he spoke loudly. "You don't have to do what he says. He won't shoot. He's afraid. Can't you tell? Can't you see it in his eyes?"

"I'm not afraid," Martens said. "And you know it."

He was surprised at the tone of his own voice. He tested the cords that bound the man. Young Johnny was secure. He could not even move.

"So, you were jealous," Martens said to Johnny. "You had a hard time of it for a while, didn't you."

The young man did not look at Martens.

"Now," Martens said to the girl. "Come over here." He stepped over by the long couch. "Take off your clothes and lie down."

The girl stared at him.

"Do as I say," he said, ramming her stomach with the black muzzle of the Luger. For the first time, he saw fear in her eyes, in those pale, beautiful eyes. And then the crimson peignoir dropped to the floor. She was nude underneath and her body was a ripe flower.

"Now," he said. "Lie down on the couch."

He glanced once across at the young man who was seated only four feet away, staring with bugged, half-frightened eyes, beginning to curse wildly, then, writhing against his bonds.

The girl searched the room frantically with those pale eyes, but then she stretched out on the couch, watching, waiting.

Martens looked down at her. He held the gun out and began to fumble with the zipper on his pants. These two would never really understand. They had destroyed him. They had violated his dream; a dream he realized now had been more precious than he'd believed possible. It had been a secret. People should not trifle with others' secrets.

Martens knelt on the couch, looking down at the girl. Her breasts were firm and pointed. Pubic hair glistened.

He shouted it: "You were animals. Understand? Animals!"

And as he sprawled on the girl, he thought, I'm an animal, too. And he would be, utterly savage—untame.

The young man, Johnny, was shouting, pleading. He could not look away. He could only watch, now, and there was no cessation.

Encore

early 1970s

He was no longer able to concentrate, now that he'd come up with the answer. His problem was a long-standing one. The solution was three days old, and he knew exactly how he would carry it off. Either that or rot inside. He had died sometime about a year ago and hadn't realized it until he understood that she was what was eating at him. His wife. Angela. And as far as he was concerned there was only one way out.

Fingers around her neck, a tight squeeze prolonged for a minute or more, and he would no longer be troubled. He would be stifling beauty, true, and he worshipped beauty, but the summation of the case was simple: Angela was wearing him out utterly with her damnable rituals of sameness.

She no longer surprised him. Small talk, which he could put up with to an extent in a fresh piece, had, with Angela, become a religion. He was tired of her thick black hair, the way it covered her shoulders. Her complete inevitability bored him sick.

Why didn't she reveal some imagination about herself?

No matter. He yearned for the old freedom. Divorce, because of her faith, because of her intense background, was patently out.

He sometimes almost wept when he entered the apartment these days. She would face him, her mouth would move, revealing those fine white teeth, the pink tip of her tongue. Her dark eyes would search him. To him it meant nothing.

He could not stand it. He could not.

In his paneled law office, he glanced across at his secretary. She was new, a ripe young flame-haired urn of promise. Anticipation touched him pleasantly. Soon he would have all the wild young things again, free to do as he might and would.

Sex was a big thing with him; the breasts, the smooth thighs, the piquant red lips, the snarled hair, the bedeviled eyes. These things were his. He had to have them.

Angela was a mistake. Mrs. Mistake.

Tonight, while his secretary was out to dinner, he would check that mistake, wipe it off the slate. He would go to the apartment, do the deed, and return, all quickly and in good order. It would take not more than three quarters of an hour. He would be in the office awaiting his secretary's return, and they would continue preparing the brief until midnight. Long enough. A perfect alibi. A cab on the other side of the block, entry from the rear of the apartment, it was all so simple, so final.

He deserved freedom. Angela was robbing him of his youth.

"You'd better run along and eat," he said. "I'll keep working. Then when you return, we'll really get down to business."

"I'm not so hungry, really. I can skip eating."

"Wouldn't hear of it."

"Really."

"Run along, now."

He regarded the swift scissoring of her legs, the slight toss of her head. The door closed.

He placed his hands flat on the desk top. Goodbye, Angela.

He left the office. In a cab, speeding through the streets of early night, he thought, Will I be strong enough? Physically? In films it always looked so easy. But thoughts of news stories reassured him. All he needed was his hands. It was accomplished every day.

Christ. She was a burden. A sore on his chin.

His heart thumped, and he swallowed dryly. This wasn't a little thing. But the hate that consumed him was very real. And the pink promise of freedom was sudden fire in his loins. It was like entering a foreign land, with luscious shapes on every corner, in every bistro, poised attentively, patiently waiting just for him. That's what he wanted, new ones, fresh ones, pink and palpable.

He would leave the door of the apartment open, make it look as if some intruder had caught her unaware.

God. To think. No more thick black hair.

No more Angela.

Why had he married her? What had he seen in her? She was always so strong for him. He had liked that. He liked them to have it in their eyes, in their unconscious movements, in the distracted touch of their fingers.

He took out his key, probed for the hole.

"Put a little hair around it," Angela sometimes said.

The door opened. A path of pink light showed from the open bedroom door, across the tufted gold carpet.

He breathed deeply, walked directly into the bedroom. He stopped sharply two paces inside. He stared. A girl with long blonde hair, wearing a black peignoir, black mules with silver puffs, was seated at the dressing table. She turned and looked at him, wide-eyed. She smiled.

"Gray," she said. "You're home."

He continued to stare. She rose, and moved toward him, the pink rounded flesh showing through the black lace.

Abruptly, she put one silver-tipped hand to her mouth, laughed softly.

"You like?"

"What?"

"My hair, silly. I had it dyed. I thought we both needed a change."

She moved very close to him. There was something about her, something at once fresh and terribly disturbing. Nothing about her was the same. Even her movements were new, vital. The curve of her red mouth was somehow altered.

"Well?" she said.

You little minx, he thought. You crazy little minx. Suspicion? Anticipation? Relinquishment?

She touched his arm. His hands found her inadvertently, without volition. Their mouths were together, and only lace was between him and that pink wealth of promise. Dazedly he wondered: had he been mad?

In moments they were on the bed. The lace came away. She didn't even seem surprised, just delightfully eager. And he dismissed his own disturbance in the violence of a new moment.

He was in a foreign land.

Daylight Dynasty

May 1976

Heaving a deep sigh, he closed the entrance door, which gleamed with gold filigree and silver leaf, then turned and strolled through the large foyer down the gleaming black steps, and into the immense living room of the sprawling apartment. He had the whole day before him, and it was planned well. There would be enormous sex, and a necessary death.

He paused, a huge man, clothed in purple silk.

The thought of the necessary death had stilled him. It brought a sense of suspenseful turbulence, of creeping fear, into him; it grew from his thudding heart and spread like spilling blood to every nerve in his big body.

But what was there to fear? Nothing. Nothing at all. It had to be done, and he had to do it. Why worry?

There was the golden wine, the crimson wine, the smoldering beakers of absinthe. Yes. He would feed the absinthe to Judith and she would submit to his embrace.

Ah, what a lovely day!

He strode to the near wall, the ebony panel of gleaming pearl buttons that controlled various mechanisms in the apartment. He pressed one and soft music swelled, a capriccio.

Damn! There was much too much sunlight, slanting through the ceiling-high windows overlooking Central Park. He nudged another button with a plump forefinger and sable draperies silently closed away the day, bringing morning night. Another button and wavering rose light suffused the apartment, apparently emanating from nowhere.

Perfect, then. Suitable for the errant mood.

And he was alone now, as he preferred. He was *homo multarum literarum*, as well as a man of pleasure—myriad pleasures, ready and able to feast, unrefuted.

But the killing . . . He should not consider that at the moment.

He slowly crossed the gold-and-purple rug, the thick extravagance of the nap hissing beneath the slippery soles of his glistening patent-leather slippers. He drank in the immense beauty that surrounded him, the costly paintings, a Dalí, a huge Pollack, a series of Miller watercolors above an ebony desk, Miró, the mind-jarring, ever-captivating Klee—his last piece, too, with the Death Angel in pale lavender, waiting—three startlingly ambitious, chirological Picassos like a blue of double vision; others, too, aswarm with mixtures of blatant or subtle color.

The hedonist. Ah! It was perfect.

But—the death . . .

Necessary, necessary. But a palestric task which he would attack *pugnis et calcibus*.

But, as the saying went, *cosa ben fatta è fatta due volte*: it was better to wear out than to rust out.

Ah, ha! A glass, then, before the pleasures of the day commenced. Amusement, amusement—eternal amusement.

He could not shake the fear. It was strong in his solar plexus, the sciatic nerves tingling with it, his thick neck stiff.

Not drink, then—snow. Yes. The true pleasure for the moment, the restoration.

Oh, Judith, he thought. Spread wide, encompass me.

He picked his way past gleaming furnishings, kicking aside multi-hued pillows, and selected the Ethiopian lounge chair with the small teak table at the right hand.

He lowered himself with a sigh, then was attentive to the rich dull silver bowl, containing the pyramid of white powder. He picked up the tiny silver spoon, ladened it, spirited it up each nostril—ah, snow. The fine tax of lovely warmth, excitement, touched him, lurking in his arteries. The precious cocaine; expensive, but worth every crystal.

He wished for Varese, for the sirens and the varied rhythms, but was too much in momentary repose to exert himself. He had a remote, but had left it lying on the blue-tapestried couch by the marble fireplace.

When Judith came he would turn up the air-conditioning and light a log. They would recline on the polar bear rug and lisp lovely lyrics.

After the death of that queer, Lloyd Butler, who was professing love for Judith, who was escorting her everywhere, he could rest.

Well, then—after today it would be different. He had planned well. There would be a carnival of satisfaction, a fantastical bite of satisfaction.

He must bestir himself, he knew. It was early, only eight-thirty in the morning. He would play the giddy goat, ignore the worm in his heart.

Another sniggling sniff, then. He suited the action to the thought, and erupted from the lounge chair. He would not even change clothing for this bit of labor; he would go immediately to Lloyd Butler's apartment and take care of the need. *Tête montée.*

But even with the cocaine, the fear was still there, perhaps even magnified, because he knew he was going to kill a man. He kept telling himself it was a necessity, but the fear would not recede. Well, he must make a virtue of necessity.

It was not the fear of killing; he could well do that; he could slaughter, in fact. But if somebody found out—if he were chased, caught.

Ah, God. He stood there for a moment, huge and filled with wonder and the terrible drive in his being which was sexual for Judith. She was a rage, a madness. His passion was unendurable. And this jelled with the awesome fear, everything excited by the coke.

He must endure.

Sometimes he vomited, thinking of them together, and of how Judith looked at the slimy bastard, clinging to his arm. He had seen them from the elevator, twice, leaving the building for a night of what? Of pleasure? Unspeakable.

Lloyd Butler, the queer, had to die.

Police, knocking at the door, then . . .

"Are you?"

"I am."

Disgusting faces and uniforms and sweat. Horrible.

"We must read you your rights."

"I don't understand."

"You're guilty and you know it."

"Of what?"

"Murder. We're from homicide. Now, then . . ."

He had an erection. Ah, God. Ah, God. Her white flesh, her breasts, her thighs, the snuggling fur of her . . .

Ah, the power!

Her fantastic ass, her lovely ass. Her mouth, leaning, leaning, damp-lipped. vulnerable, wanton.

Whore! Whore! I love you!

He could just barely contain himself. But he mustn't do *that*. He must save it for Judith, all the ripe, piercing power. *I have so much love to give, take, take . . .*

He was in the hall, thumping along to the elevator, the long-bladed knife in his sleeve. It had to be a knife, because he must see the blood flow, must commit mayhem, violent surgery on Lloyd Butler.

And he knew they were both home today. Afterward, he would call Judith on the phone and order her to his apartment. She would appear— ah, god, naked, naked, the submissive flesh. The flesh.

What if she wouldn't come?

She would, she would—he would command her. No. It must be endearing.

"I'm like a fence post. Hurry."

She was the genotype of Babylon.

"I want you to—"

Ah, the word from her lips, her mouth.

"I'll—"

His door. Lloyd Butler's door. Well, he'd had the key made weeks ago, fashioned at the locksmith's for a quarter. A quarter, mind you. And now this was the culmination.

Where would the queer be? What would he say?

Now he was afraid.

What if the chain was on? Nevertheless, he inserted the key, turned it, thrust against the door with his protruding belly. It opened softly, slowly.

He stepped inside.

The apartment of a base person, a peasant; threadbare, harsh to the gaze, brittle and angled and smelly.

There was Butler, coming toward him from the hall.

"It's you. What d'you want? How'd you get in?"

"Nevermind how I got in."

Butler.

Laisser aller.

He still did not reveal the knife. Moderation. Restraint.

"I've come to you about Judith." A damnable quaver was in his voice, along with capped excitement. A volcano was inside him, ready to erupt.

Butler laughed, a tall fellow whom women would call beautiful; ivory skin, wide, slanted eyes of pale blue, taunting eyes, bold as brass, the shit. Curly hair of yellow, all curling down his neck, ruffling over the collar of his cream shirt, a blade for a nose, with flaring nostrils, a perfectly shaped mouth with pink lips, a jutting jaw with a dimple; queer, queer!

Butler said, "You queer. Get the hell out of here, however you got in. Judith and I're getting married. Fishmouth. Go home and play with yourself. You think you're kidding anybody? Talk about Judith." And he laughed again, throwing his head back so his Adam's apple bobbled. The veritable shit.

Scandalum magnatum! Infamy, dishonor, shame.

He gurgled and leaped at Butler, drawing the knife from his sleeve, and the other man stepped back in alarm, lips parted.

"What's this?"

"I am a name to conjure with!"

Butler wouldn't even know what he meant. They were breathing in each other's faces. He could smell the cologne. Butler swung his arm up but at the same moment, the knife sunk hilt-deep into his gut.

He gloried in it. *Rara avis!* He was savage, headlong now.

"What have you done?"

"I'm killing you."

He was a fire eater, brave, valorous.

He sank the blade deeply again and the cream shirt oozed crimson. He withdrew the blade and slashed Butler's face. Butler was screaming. He cut at that mouth, slicing the cheek to one ear so the side teeth were bared and bloody, the flesh hanging open like a fresh steak. He swung the blade with all his might for the throat. Butler was still standing, spurting blood, trying to speak. His hand was at his cheek, terror in those eyes.

The blade cut in at the Adam's apple, and he tugged, ripping the cartilage and the flesh. He had severed an artery. Blood pumped, spurting out and terrible sounds came from Butler's throat.

"Who's a queer?"

Lloyd Butler crumpled and sprawled headlong, rolled over on his back and lay there, bleeding, pools of blood forming on the worn carpet.

"You dunghill! Judith is mine."

Butler's eyes rolled whitely in his head. And then he was dead.

But he knelt down, lithely now, and began plunging the knife into the body. She'd said it was like cheese. She was right. In, in—cut the dirty flesh. The queer.

He opened Butler's fly and sawed at the genitals until they hung by a string only, covered with blood.

"Never again. Did you, ever?"

There was no answer from the dead man.

He lunged erect, dropped the sticky knife on the carpet, surveying his deed.

Bell the cat. He was Lancelot, *sans reproche.*

Ah, God. It was done.

He plunged out of the door into the hall, slammed the door behind him, strode for the elevator and pushed the button for the penthouse. He was breathing heavily, gasping.

"We will read you your rights, now."

Milksop.

He had done it. Lloyd Butler was dead, a gone goose.

Fear. Fear. It was a snake in his gullet, a knife in his heart, the cup of denigration. Speed.

In his apartment he showered lustily, attending the golden plumbing, the black marble stall, the glass. He would burn incense for her, stand the tapers in the sand bowl, Three Roses, pungent and of the chapel, secure in contempt. So erect, throbbing—don't touch it—save it for Judith on the polar bear rug.

Out, the towel, the thrust of warm heat, and then he dressed in crimson and gold, doused himself with perfume, drenching his penis, lusting.

Out, light the tapers. Up with the air-conditioning. Fire the log. Pine, perfumed. A hickory to last and blend. An oak for time's immorality.

The ivory-and-gold French phone.

"Judith? Come up at once. I'm waiting."

"What?"

She couldn't have a flaw—her mouth was against the instrument, breathing, breathing.

"I can't wait," he said. "I can't wait. You're the only one who ever aroused me like this. I'm being truthful, you see? Not another woman, ever. I think of you constantly. You should see me now. Just knowing you're there. Come up, come up."

She gave a little laugh, sexy, lovely. He loved her. He adored her.

"What d'you mean?" she asked.

Courage, poltroon!

"It's you. I can't talk on the phone. Come, come immediately."

"Well, I *could* come—for a while."

Ah, God . . .

"Don't wear any pants."

"You fool!"

"Please? For me?"

He knew he was gasping at the phone. He pulled his mouth away, trying to restrain himself in the rose light, smelling the incense, the blazing pine.

She said, "Do you really want to?"

"Come. Now."

He cradled the phone and waited in the Ethiopian chair. He took a tiny ladle of snow. It was excruciating, this wondrous exaltation.

Look at it. God. Throbbing, throbbing. Take it out, show it to her at the door, flaming. Like a poker, stick it out at her, in her. Ah.

Her mouth was always so red.

He was dead.

He sat there in the chair, staring up across the foyer to the door. What if they . . .

His stomach rumbled. Hurlothrombo. Fear, fear. Why must he be afraid, so afraid? His clothing. Blood-spattered?

He hurled himself up and raced to the shower-room, found the pile of clothing. Yes, yes. Blood. The tell-tale heart.

He thumped and stumbled to the kitchen, found the lighter fluid under the sink, returned to the shower-room. He tossed the clothing into the tub, doused it with lighter fluid, struck it with a gold lighter, watched it burn. He set the exhaust fan going. There was no smell. But, anyway he doused the room with cologne.

The door buzzer sounded.

He was still erect, like a pile driver, hanging out.

He flung the door open.

"Judith!"

She stood there in the Scotch plaid skirt, green, red and yellow. The Bobby sox, the saddle shoes, her hair in a pageboy, and the brown eyes round and hot with it, the mouth partly open, waiting.

She stared down at him.

"Oh, boy—me too!"

She was inside, in his arms. She had hold of him. They struggled, kissing, mouthing to the polar bear rug, all white and furred before the blaze from the marble fireplace.

"I adore you, Judith. Quickly, now."

On the rug, up with her skirt. But she was leaning to it with her rosy lips, the wanton whore. Ah, God!

Lust, lust. More love than a man . . .

Coquette, love, mouth, in, thighs, wide open.

"Oh, you're wonderful."

"Judith, Judith. I've waited so long. I'll never get enough of you. Do it, do it—yes, yes. Ah, Jesus. Judith. I'm . . ."

It was a wild blur of violence such as he had never known, sensation was his bed.

"I must go."

"Yes, yes. I understand. It's all right. Then, tomorrow, Judith, darling?"

"Yes. Of course. Any time. But it's late now. It's nearly five. I've got to run."

"Five? Already?"

"Yes. Look."

And she was gone and he sat slumped in the Ethiopian lounge chair.

Strange how it was always over so quickly. Hardly begun, when . . . and now the trepidation, the horror. Judith had blotted it all out, but now he remembered crystally, the blood, the Adam's apple. *Fishmouth.*

He sat there, his belly moving.

Oh, dear God, I am sorry.

Please forgive me. Please. Please.

"We must read you your rights."

He began to weep with fear, trembling inside with a fear such as he had never known.

The charter of thy worth gives thee releasing.

He could only see the books, the walls of books.

The door-buzzer sounded, the door opened.

He thrust back in the chair, witless.

• • •

"Oh, son—what have you done? Not that again."

"Mummy. I couldn't help, I couldn't!"

"I come home from work and you've been sitting here all day, haven't you?"

She was a short, gray woman, carrying a purse over one arm, with worn shoes. She stood in the dusty, small apartment, shades drawn against the waning sunlight, her mouth pursed with something between sorrow and prayer.

"You've dirtied yourself. It's filthy, filthy. Here, I'll clean you up. Then you'll have to take a bath. Oh, son, son."

She wiped at him. Her face was wrinkled and gray.

Where was the incense . . . ?

"Mummy—Mummy . . ."

A brave note came into her voice, a note of reparation. "I just seen that pretty Judith Ankers and Lloyd Butler down in the lobby. They were going out and they looked so brisk, so clean, so healthy. Yes, Judith asked after you."

"But—Mummy!"

He sat there, an enormous lump of white flesh, his mouth sagging.

His mother sighed, slowly shook her head, looked around the near bare apartment. Her glance was wistful, her voice soft.

"Whatever will I do with you?"

He watched her, weeping and shuddering inside.

He thought, The torturing hour calls us to penance.

Ah, God—to atone.

Lover (I)

1960s

He couldn't explain it to anybody. They would never understand about Gert. The hell of it was, he didn't really understand it himself anymore.

"Honey," Alice said. "What you thinking about?"

"Nothing. Nothing at all."

"Then pay attention."

He rolled over in the bed and held her in his arms. He loved her. He loved everything about her. As soon as they were old enough, he wanted to marry her. It was lucky the way they could use Alice's mother's bedroom while she was at work. Afternoons, after school, it was always like this. Hot. Alice was really hot. She never got enough. He liked that, because he never got enough, either.

And she was so damned beautiful. Everything about her was in capitals.

"Love you, baby—really love you," he whispered, his lips against her ear, her soft dark hair tickling his nose. She twisted against him, murmuring. They lay on the bed, exhausted, but only for the moment.

"Roger?"

"Yeah?"

"What's with Gert Lammery? I mean, she follows you around like a cow. Looks like a cow, too. I mean, Roger—she's awful, the way she follows you around."

"Nothing. She's just nuts."

Alice was quiet for a time. She rolled onto her back and they lay there looking up at the mottled ceiling of the apartment bedroom. And he thought, Christ, I've got to do something.

Everywhere he went. Everything he said. Gert Lammery was sure to show. Inadvertently he clutched his hands across his face. It was driving him crazy. He'd flip, sure as hell, if she didn't stop.

In her thin tight black skirt, with all the gobs of huge fat bulging. Wiggling like she did, and that purple sweater stretched across her elephantine breasts, and the egg stains down the front. God, he had to do something. Her fat wet purple-painted lips, and her black eyes, and that thick greasy black hair, like maybe she smeared it with lard, or something. Sticking her tongue out, right in front of everybody—*just anybody*—and wiggling it. Scowling, too—always scowling, only he knew what that scowl meant, and he knew the only thing that would erase it.

That damned fool witch was pursued.

What had he seen in Gert?

Oh, man, that had been an error. He remembered what it had been, though. It was the way she showed her legs under her skirt: the enormous milk-white expanse of flesh bulging over the stretched and raveled stockings. There was something so obscene in it that he'd had to get to her.

And she'd known it.

Sly.

Well, so he had. And now look.

"Roger?"

He rolled off the bed, stood up, and began dressing, watching her. Alice was lovely, in every way. Just touching her sent him wild. Touching anything she wore. Seeing her walking toward him from the distance, with that fine little swing she had, and her smile, and the way her eyes were secret, and just for him.

"Roger?"

Not crazy and bold and obscene, like Gert's.

"Roger. What you doing!"

"Listen," he said. "I remembered something. Something I had to get at the store for Mom. I'd better move out. See you later. Wait right here for me, huh?"

She had come to a half-sitting position. Now she lay back, smiling up at him, one hand caressing her smooth flesh. Her body was slim and lush at the same time. And it was all for him.

"I might go see Ginnie," she said. "We got a swamp of algebra for tomorrow. I'm trying to keep my marks up." She gave a little giggle.

He finished dressing, notched his belt. He leaned quickly, low over the bed and kissed her. He almost didn't leave, then, the way she acted. Only he had to get out of here, be alone, and think.

He ran down the stairs, turned into the hall, walking swiftly through the shadows.

"Rog, baby?"

He stopped so hard he skidded.

It was Gert.

She stood just around under the stairs, holding her skirt up, eyeing him, scowling that way.

"God damn you!" he hissed. "You quit it, hear?"

"Quit what, darling? You been upstairs sleeping with little hot pants?"

He stepped over to her and lashed his hand across her face. She dropped her skirt and rubbed her cheek.

"How about coming over to the place?" she said.

"Don't you call her hot pants," he snapped.

"Well, she is, ain't she?"

"No!"

Gert chuckled throatily, and her breasts jounced. She held her bulging middle, and her hips shook, her heavy thighs jiggling under the tight black skirt. Her jetty eyebrows drew tight together, frowning.

"Rog, darling," she whispered. "I know it bothers you, the way I follow you around. So, I got a solution. You come over to the place with me once in a while, and I'll leave you alone."

He started to say something, then ceased. The "place" was an outfield building of the *Miner Lumber Company.* There were two loose boards at the rear of the building, and inside was a mattress. The nook was out-of-reach, between fifty-foot stacks of sweet-smelling pine planks. Any time after eight in the evening, Gert could be found lying in there on the mattress, waiting for whoever might chance past. Roger had seen a line of seventeen waiting behind the building once. Gert would show at around seven, just in case any of the lumbermill workers were interested.

He didn't know why. But Gert had something. She had a lot of meat. Maybe that was it. And it was free. Anything free was all good business.

"Well?" Gert said. "It's not much."

She moved her huge body up against him, and jiggled herself. She was breathing fast, and he smelled chocolate candy heavy on her breath.

"Nobody does any good for me," she said. "I try and try. But you're the only one's any good for me. I'd marry you, Roger. I'd be a good wife to you. I'd do anything for you. I'm crazy for you—I dream of you. I want you all the time. . . ."

"Stop it!"

"I mean it," she said, clutching at his waist, holding him to her. "Can't you understand? I love you, Roger." Tears stood like rimmed oil in her eyes and her plump lips trembled. "What can she do for you, I can't? Little hot pants. That's all. You used to tell me *you loved me*, Roger! You said you liked me big and fat, the way I am. You couldn't get enough of me." She grabbed at him desperately, jamming herself against him. "I can't get enough of you—*I want you!*"

He fought free, disgusted, thrusting her away.

"You think you're so much," Gert snapped. "I could tell you."

"What—tell me what?"

Her eyes lidded. "You come to the place for a while, right now, and maybe I'll tell you."

"You're lying. The hell with you."

Her face went mean, the flesh bunching, the eyes slits in the puffy flesh. "You don't come with me right now, I'll haunt you! You hear me? Everyplace you go, I'll be in front of you. I'll fix you proper."

There was a light pattering of feet on the stairs.

Roger bulled the huge mass of flesh under the stairs, pressing her against the wall. Gert took advantage of the situation as much as she could, and he felt her hot moist palms. She was crazy. He was scared of her.

The footsteps reached the shadows of the downstairs hall, and he saw Alice turn toward the front entrance, humming softly to herself. She carried a book.

"Come on," Gert whispered. "I'll make you love it."

Alice vanished.

Gert's voice was a moan. "I'll leave you alone. I promise. If you'll just do it once in a while. I'll leave you with little hot pants."

"Jeez, who's talking?"

He tried to keep the venom out of his voice, trying hard to laugh along with her. Because when he'd seen Alice just then, he knew for a fact that he had to do something.

"Will you?"

"Okay. I'll meet you there around seven-thirty. I'll come early, so I won't run into a mob."

"There wouldn't be no mob if you'd stick with me."

"I'm with you. Ain't that enough?"

"Oh, baby—you'll never forget this. Not tonight."

• • •

Somehow he escaped her. He left her there, panting under the stairs, and reeled out into the chilly twilight.

He knew what he had to do.

He hadn't been over to the lumber company ever since he'd met Alice. Alice was all he could handle. And he never wanted to go there again. But he would—one more time. Tonight. That would be the last.

Because he knew damned well Gert didn't mean a word of what she said. She lied like mad. She was a mad woman. After tonight she'd go right on fouling everything up. He couldn't take it anymore.

Time after time she came right to his home. Standing there, the way she was, with it sticking out all over her, egg stains and all. Not even for money. Give it away.

He could hardly see, he was that angered.

She'd show up at parties, that way. Everybody in the neighborhood knew her and what she was doing. Her mother knew it, but she'd given up. The teachers at school knew. His parents knew. All the kids knew. Everybody. And they could see the way she was after him, like a swollen bitch in heat.

So.

He calmed a little.

He would kill her.

It was that simple.

Because nothing would stop Dirty Gert except maybe if they tossed her behind bars. Nobody would do that. Not for years yet.

He would kill her.

It frightened him. The thought was no longer buried and unavoidable deep inside. It scared him, but at the same time he seemed to light up and feel really good, because it was the one answer. And right away he thought of all the ins and outs, and how easy he could pull it off.

They'd find her lying there dead. And everybody knew what she was. Why, hell—a wino could have her, even. So some guy had got to her; some damned pervert, or something, and he'd given it to her—right in the throat.

He quit thinking about it. It made him plenty nervous, because he knew he was going to do it.

It had been a hard thing, keeping it all from Alice. Maybe she even knew. But she loved him too much to say anything. She knew how much he loved her. And he did. In a way, he was doing this for her, too. Actually. For them. So that crazy Gert wouldn't foul everything up.

He went on home and ate supper, and excused himself, and got the switchblade that he kept taped behind his dresser. He left the house and stopped off at Alice's. Alice was still over at Ginnie's, her mother said. Her mother was slightly stinko on muscatel. Roger smelled it and spotted the look in her eyes, lazy and cool.

"Okay, Mrs. Donnegan. I'll be by later."

"You do that, young man." She grinned slyly. "You and my Alice getting pretty cuddly, ain't you?"

"I don't exactly understand what you mean, Mrs. Donnegan."

The woman laughed, flung a strand of pale blonde hair back in place, and fingered the tight belt on her red dress. She leaned forward, giving Roger an open view of ample breasts, exhaling sickly wine.

"I can tell when a bed's been slept in, junior." She quickly brandished a red-nailed hand as Roger assumed a shocked expression, his eyes puzzled. "It's okay, honey. You and Alice'll get married, n'everything—right soon."

"Sure. I got to run along, Mrs. Donnegan."

She patted his shoulder rather heavily, and winked.

"You be nice to my little Alice," she said. "I can tell a bed's slept in, a mile off."

He left, fast.

Man. She was something, for a fact. He was soaked with sweat. The way it looked, he might've even been able to take *her* into the bedroom, right then. Funny, you never knew how they'd take a thing. Yeah.

Only she might think different when she sobered up.

It was beyond dusk. Buildings bleakly hunched above the streets. It was nearly seven-thirty, and the alleys were dark and cold. He hurried along, keeping his mind a tight blank now.

He crossed the tracks, cut over through the vacant lots where they were going to build the hospital, and skinned over the fence behind the *Miner Lumber Company*.

Moving through weedy undergrowth toward the back shed, he thought he saw movement at the corner. He paused, tensing, staring directly at the spot.

Suppose somebody tipped Alice and she caught him with Gert. God, what a thought. He guessed he'd been wrong. There was nobody there.

He felt worried, though, and ran toward the shed before it could gather him up. He cursed Gert, thinking of all the things she'd done to him. She could ruin everything with Alice, if she half tried.

He opened the switchblade knife, went through the loose boards into the warm, pine-fragrant darkness.

His toe touched the mattress. He saw the faint outline of white legs. A whisper reached him.

"Oh, daddy—hurry up. I'm really ready!"

"Yeah. You bet!"

He sprang down, striking hard and furiously with the knife, wild strength driving him. Her scream changed into a wet noise. He kept cutting, pursued by fear and contaminated with hate.

Something struck him from behind, heavily, and a voice yelled.

"Rog. Stop!"

It was Gert, pummeling him, yelling at him, speaking in a rapid and breathless scream.

"Wanted you to see the truth. Wanted to show you, not just tell you—you wouldn't believe. Alice's been doing it here for over a month, every night before she meets you." Her voice changed into a choked shriek. "Wanted to show you—not this—not . . . Alice, baby—Alice!"

Abruptly, her tone changed to a frightened whine. She turned and crashed leaping over loose boards, running heavily.

Roger leaped after her, the knife clutched tightly in his fist.

Lover (II)

early 1970s

Mark Dobson could no longer stand seeing them, as he did every night, without doing something about it. He could not bear the realization of their intimate ecstasies; the sight of luscious young girls with their skirts up, their pants off, seeing them writhe in sexual surrender beneath pumping young punks who rode them like rabbits.

Visions of their twisting heads, their crimson mouths, their swollen breasts and round behinds, filled him with crazed desire. He was no longer able to sleep, when returning home each night after cruising the three lovers' lanes in town, spying on them. He would undress and lie naked on his bed, unable to control himself, moaning with memories of bare white thighs, firm bellies, dark-nippled breasts, the thighs spread wide apart, the young mouths crooning obscene wishes.

Last night had been one of the worst. He had driven up Sand Canyon Road, left the car, and sneaked through the woods to where they parked.

There was only one car, a convertible Cadillac.

The man was older this time, but the girl was quite young, red-lipped, with flowing blonde hair. In the moonlight, he could see that she was very beautiful, with large round eyes. He knew the expression in those eyes was hot, lewd.

He hulked behind a tree and watched. They weren't ten feet away.

They kissed. The girl wore a black dress. Obviously they had gone out for the evening, but chosen this spot instead of a club or movie.

Dobson saw the man pull the dress down over the girl's round shoulder, baring white flesh.

"Let me unbutton," she said. "And I'll open the door. We need room, honey."

Dobson stared and the door swung open. As she unhooked the back of her dress, he saw the man pull her skirt up, revealing plump round thighs, the white skin showing above gartered black nylons.

"I didn't wear any pants," she said.

They clinched again, and he could hear them breathing, hear the rustle of silk. He saw the man's hand on her leg.

"Let's get in back."

"Better idea," the man said. "Outside."

She slipped out and stood beside the car. He climbed out, lifted the back seat, brought it around and laid it on the ground, not far from the tree where

Dobson stood watching. Only the placement of sparse shrubbery and the small tree hid him from sight.

"Oh, that's perfect," the girl said.

They stood, pressed tightly together. The man lifted her skirt, his hands worked on the round white buttocks. She moved her hips against him, then stepped back, reached down and unzipped his fly.

"Lie down," the man said.

"All right, honey."

She stripped off her dress and stood naked in the moonlight, then plumped down on the car seat.

"Hurry," she said.

The man dropped his pants, his shorts, and knelt beside her. He mouthed her breasts and she began to twist and wriggle.

"Now, Rog—now . . ."

She opened her thighs and rubbed herself, then pulled him over on top of her. They clung together, mumbling and gasping and muttering. He humped above her, eased himself down.

"Oh, does that feel good!" the girl cried.

From then on, for three quarters of an hour, they were at it, in every conceivable position. Their panting and groaning was wild. Dobson watched in a state of frenzied excitement, watched those long lush legs clamp around the man, watched her buttocks lift from the car seat, thrusting violently.

Dobson opened his own fly, thought better of it, and sneaked silently away, then ran for his car.

The following night, driving around, he knew what he would do.

He could no longer bear just watching. He had to have some of what he saw night after night. He felt that unless he did have some, he would go mad. Every hour of his life visions swam before his eyes; visions of bare flesh, of ripe curves. Every night was the same. He would sneak up on them, see unspeakable scenes that were driving him to madness.

Just meeting a girl, taking her out nights, waiting for the time when she might give in, wasn't for him. And whorehouses left him flat. He wanted something that struck back, but that was weaker than he was.

He drove to the same spot as last night. It was a lucky place and usually there was only one car there.

Jesus, he thought. If only the same girl as last night would appear. He yearned to caress those silken-clad thighs, feel that pumping bare flesh.

He stopped the car in the woods near the canyon parking area. He undressed to his shorts, smiled to himself, then stripped entirely naked. This part was necessary. He carried the revolver and the length of rope.

Anticipation had him ready. He hung the rope on himself, and laughed aloud. Then he started for where the lovers loved.

There was nobody there.

He felt let down, but forced himself to wait.

He waited for some twenty-five minutes, and he was entirely lax, now. It discouraged him. Suppose some patrolling cop discovered him? But that was unlikely.

He finally gave up in disgust. He would have to try one of the other spots. Just as he turned to leave, he heard the approaching sound of a car.

It came into view. It was the same Cadillac convertible as the night before.

He reacted immediately, strongly, feeling like a stallion.

The car's engine went silent. He looked around the tree. It was the same blonde girl, and man. He didn't care about the man. He would take care of him.

He would take care of the girl, too.

Tremors passed through his body.

They went right at it again, kissing and feeling each other impatiently. The man fondled her breasts; they were large, firm breasts.

Dobson abruptly ran around the car, shoved the revolver into the man's face.

"Get out of here," he said.

The girl gave a short yelp.

"Jesus Christ," the man said.

Dobson flung the door open. "Out!" he said.

The man turned and stepped from the car, his pants open.

Dobson gave a short laugh. "Turn around, put your hands behind you."

"Have a heart," the man said. "You'll never get away with this."

But he did as asked. Dobson bound the man's hands.

"Now, lie down."

The man groaned, but lay down on the ground beside the car. Dobson bound the man's feet. He jerked erect. The girl was making a run for it.

He came fast around the car and caught her. Her pliant, fleshy body thrust against him. He smelled rich perfume. Her breasts hung out of her dress. He gasped.

"What d'you want?" the girl said, frightened.

"You'll like it," Dobson whispered feverishly. "It's all saved just for you."

The man was shouting for help. This didn't faze Dobson; it was an isolated area.

She tried to scratch his face. He laughed, and caught hold of her dress, tore it down the front of her body, shredding it. He dropped the revolver, and flung her to the ground. He didn't care about anything, now, just having her. He was focused like a white beam of light, wild inside with crazed lust.

"Don't—" the girl pleaded. "Please—"

He felt her breasts, forced his mouth on hers. She writhed and twisted beneath him. He knelt, and took hold of her knees, and spread her thighs wide, putting his own knee between. She wore those black stockings and a garter belt. This, too, excited him. He ran his hands up and down her legs, moaning softly.

"You're crazy," she said.

"Yeah," he said. "Crazy for you."

He entered her and she gave a short cry.

"Kick him!" the man yelled from the other side of the car. "Kick him, Georgia."

"Ah, Georgia," the man said. "You're out of sight."

She moaned and twisted, but it only helped. He took her savagely, rested on top of her, kissing her, feeling her young body, then took her again.

"Haven't you got enough," the girl sobbed.

He said nothing, only drove into her still again.

Finally he was through. He stood up, looking down, breathing heavily. She lay, legs apart, watching him.

He chuckled. He retrieved the revolver, leaned down and patted her between the legs.

"You're terrific, Georgia," he said.

She just stared at him.

He hurried through the woods, running, and finally reached his car. Then he donned his uniform, put on his green peaked cap, holstered his revolver. He knew what he would be doing every night from now on, straight down the line.

A cop's life wasn't so bad, after all.

Caprice

early 1970s

Perruzi had been coldy considering it all through the early part of the afternoon. It was a terrible thing to think about, but he knew it was the only way. And when, just then, Angela came out of the bedroom into the living room where he was seated on the sofa, he suddenly knew for certain it was the right thing. He knew what he had to do. It was for Sesto, his son, that he would do it.

"Hello, Mr. Perruzi."

He shook the newspaper he was holding, glanced up at her, then down again. He could feel the blood surge into his throat, along his shoulders. He could not help it; she did that to him. That and other things, too.

"What're you doing, Mr. Perruzi?" she asked.

He wouldn't look at her, he wouldn't. Her voice was soft, throaty.

"I asked you," she said. "What're you doing?"

"I'm reading the paper."

"Oh."

He could see from the corner of his vision that she had moved closer to him. He could smell her now, too, the near elusive scent. She stood about three feet away.

"You like my dress, Mr. Perruzi?"

It was a pointed question, he had to look up, because it was bad manners not to. He looked at her.

"You like? Eh, Mr. Perruzi?"

She had slept all this time, since she and Sesto had returned home at three this morning. She had slept almost twelve hours. Now she was up. But there was still a hint of muzziness in her jet black eyes, with the startling whites, with the long darkly curled lashes.

He swallowed dryly. Inside, he writhed, and mentally he cursed her. His hands clenched on the newspaper, crushing it. Once looking at her, he couldn't move his gaze away. It was a kind of sacrifice, looking at her. He knew he had never in his life seen anything so beautiful, so exciting as Angela. And he knew he was looking at evil.

"It's a new dress," she said. "I've never had it on before. I put it on just for you, to show you how nice I can look."

Her lips were full and red, her face almost in the shape of a perfect heart, and her black hair foamed about her shoulders, catching vagrant flecks of light. Her skin was soft looking, and olive. She wasn't too tall, but there was something magnetic about her, something so sexually allusive it was startling.

The dress was gold colored, a mini-dress, with a gold chain at the waist. She wore black net stockings over her lushly curved legs, and square-toed black shoes, with gold buckles. She had an extremely narrow waist, with full curving hips, and the swell of her breasts drew the eye.

"You haven't said whether you like it, Mr. Perruzi."

He cleared his throat. "A new dress, eh?"

"Yes."

"I like it, all right. It's all right."

"See the back?"

She turned and looked at him over her shoulder. This threw one hip out suggestively.

Perruzi's lips felt dry.

She whirled and moved still closer to him. Her knees were almost touching his. She smiled down at him, her teeth like tiny white seeds.

"Sesto will like your dress," Perruzi said.

"M-mmmmmm."

"He'll be home at five, and you can show it to him." It was stupid, saying that. His tongue felt thick, his throat dry.

"Sesto's a good man," she said.

"He's my son," Perruzi said. "A good son."

"We'll probably be living here for a while, after we're married," Angela said, not moving, looking down at him. "Sesto doesn't make too much at the plant."

"You're only sixteen," Perruzi said.

She chuckled. "But I'm big enough. Don't you think I'm big enough, Mr. Perruzi?"

"Your mother and father should—"

"They said I could marry Sesto." She moved closer, and her right knee touched his left knee. She moved her knee back and forth. Perruzi sat there holding the paper. "Then, when we're married, I'll sleep in the bedroom all night, instead of out on the front porch till Sesto goes to work."

"My son needs his rest in a good bed," Perruzi said. "It's his bed. He should use it. Besides, there are street noises, trucks, cars . . ."

"Don't I know it."

She moved her knee back and forth, looking down at him.

"Say, Mr. Perruzi. Couldn't I call you Dominick? Or Dom. I know I've only been here a few days, but we're together all day long, and it seems crazy, calling you Mr. Perruzi. Can I call you Dom?"

It wouldn't matter, after tonight. "All right," he said. "Call me Dom, if you want."

Suddenly she moved over and plumped down on the sofa beside him. She curled one leg up underneath herself, the round knee almost touching his thigh. He was terribly conscious of her. She reached out and touched his arm.

"Dom?"

"Yes?"

"Y'know. Of course, I love Sesto, and all that, but I've got a secret."

The way she said it, leaning a little toward him, her eyes flashing, her voice throaty, he could feel the rocking of his heart.

During the past few days this is the way it had been going. She wormed her way into his confidence, and she wasn't fooling him, not at all.

"Want me to tell you my secret?" she asked.

He said nothing. He tried to look at the newspaper, but the black print swam before his eyes. He could smell her so. She was so near. The sound of her voice got to him in such a strange way. He tried to steel himself against her, but it was no help.

"I like older men," she said. "There. I've said it. It's our secret. Don't you dare tell Sesto."

"Sesto's only eighteen. You plan to marry him," Perruzi said.

"I wish he was like you, Dom. Dom, how old are you?"

What harm to talk to her? Tonight it would be finished. "I'm thirty-eight," he told her.

"A sexy thirty-eight," she said.

He stared at her. She patted his arm, and wriggled closer on the couch. Her knee touched him now. The hem of her gold dress was pulled far up in her lap, and he could see the plump bare flesh of her thigh where the black net stockings ended. They were fastened to black garters.

"You are," she said. "You're sexy as hell, Dom."

"You shouldn't say that," Perruzi said, hearing the hoarseness in his voice, trembling inside, unable to stop looking at her.

"It's true," Angela said. "You're so slim and trim and everything. Sesto's lots heavier than you."

He stared at her.

I'm going to kill you tonight, he thought.

Abruptly she was on her knees on the sofa, very close to him, eyeing him. She tipped her lips with her pink tongue.

"Are you as sexy as you look, Dom?"

"You shouldn't say—"

"I'm asking you," she said with that throaty way she had. Her eyes were bold.

He reached for her, unable to resist, held her in his arms, and kissed her. She was hungry for it. Her tongue was in his mouth. His hand slid down to the warm, satin-like softness of her thigh.

"Oh, Dom," she gasped. "I knew it would be like this today. *I knew it.* I didn't even wear any pants. See?"

He flung her backward on the sofa, wild with it, saying inside his head, I'm going to kill you tonight, I'm going to kill you tonight. To save my son. I can't help myself—God help me, I can't.

He had never in his life wanted anything so much as he wanted Angela.

Beneath him she thrust and writhed, moaning, gasping, panting in his ear, "Oh, Jesus, Dom, it's paradise, it's paradise—don't ever stop, don't ever stop."

It seemed as if it wouldn't stop. Even when it was over, he looked at her pink lust, and desire surged through him again. He took her again, brutally, savagely. He couldn't get enough of her. And she was full of it. He had never experienced anything like it.

They arranged their clothes and looked at each other.

"That's the best I ever had," she said. "You're better than your son, Dom. Believe it."

"Yes," he said, suddenly sick inside. "Now you can go away. You don't want to marry Sesto now."

She laughed. "I don't? Listen, I want to marry him more than ever, you dope! I'll be married, and we'll live here, and I'll have you. You still want me. I can tell. You're a real man."

He slumped on the sofa. He felt a terrible helplessness. She was wanton, evil, born of the Devil. She would ruin Sesto, wreck his life. He knew it now.

So he would go through with everything just as planned. There was nothing else to do.

"Oh, Dom," she said, standing close to him, thrusting against him, ruffling his hair. "You're really something else."

He cursed himself because he wanted to put his arms around her again, feel that pliant young body. He didn't. He leaned away from her.

"Guess I'll take a walk," she said. "I feel good now." She rubbed her arms, her eyes shining. "I just feel good all over."

She went out, across the front porch, and through the door.

Perruzi sat there, staring at nothing. He had done something awful. He hadn't been able to help himself. He had wanted her so desperately it had been a kind of hell. And he knew he still wanted her. He would always want her. Her beauty wrung his heart. But the evil in her did something else.

And there was Sesto. For Sesto, he would do as he had planned—he would kill her. It was the only way. Sesto meant more to him than anything in the world. His son had to have a good start with life. She would destroy him. She would break his heart. She would make of him something that he should never be.

This would not happen. Perruzi would see to that.

He hated her. He hated her and he wanted her, that ripe evil.

His feelings disgusted him. Sitting there, he said a short prayer. It did not help.

He loved his son. He wanted him to have the most he could give him. He could give him freedom from Angela.

Sesto would hate him if he knew what he planned. But his son would never know. He would wait until they were asleep, with Angela out on the cot on the porch. Then he would set the front door ajar, and take a knife, his long-bladed hunting knife . . .

They came in just then, Angela and Sesto. She had apparently met his son on the street. They were laughing, and their eyes shone with youth.

Perruzi felt abandoned, terribly alone. He felt he had betrayed himself for what he had done with the girl. But even now he caught himself looking at her covertly, at the swing and sway of her lush hips, at the red pout of her mouth, at the thick swelling of black hair. He forced himself to look away.

"Hey, what's for supper?" Sesto said.

"Nothing fixed yet," Perruzi said.

He looked at his strong, young, broad-shouldered son, blue-eyed, happy.

"Let's eat out," Angela said.

"Okay," Sesto said, grabbing the girl around the waist, swinging her off her feet. Holding her that way, he said to Perruzi, "Pop, we'll catch a bite somewhere, then we're going to an early show." He kissed Angela, nuzzling her throat. "We'll be back early."

"Yes," Perruzi said. "All right."

"Sure it's all right?"

Sesto was like that. He was thoughtful.

"It's fine," Perruzi said. "Go ahead, you kids."

Sesto went and showered and dressed, and Perruzi heard the two of them fooling around in the bedroom.

Then they left the house.

He did not eat. He just sat there on the sofa, thinking, wondering if he was doing the right thing, knowing it was the right thing, the only way.

He sat there numbly, but there was an eagerness inside him. He kept wishing they would return, go to bed, sleep. He wanted to get it over with.

He tried to read. He could not.

He turned on the TV, but the screen was a weird mélange of shapes that were meaningless.

Finally they returned.

Sesto told him about the film, as he always did, acting it out—it had been a war film—excited with the telling.

"You'd better go to bed," Perruzi said finally. "You need your sleep."

"Yeah. Okay, Pop."

Sesto and Angela hugged each other in front of him. He told them goodnight, and went to his room.

He undressed, put on pajamas, and lay on top of the bedspread, his heart beating, thudding. He stared at the dark. He breathed rapidly, he couldn't control his breathing, and there was a singing in his ears. A strange sensation, a kind of tingling, was in his chest.

He could hear them laughing, faintly. Then, finally, he heard Angela go out on the front porch, and it was quiet.

Occasionally the bleat of a car's horn reached him. And distantly, from somewhere, like a thin thread, came the sound of radio music.

He waited. He lay there, trying not to think, finding this not easy now. He thought of his son, of how much he loved him, of how good a son Sesto was, and he thought of what Angela and he had done that afternoon. Evil, he thought. Evil.

He waited two hours.

Then, silently, he went to the bureau, and opened the top drawer, and took out the sheathed hunting knife. It had a long, gleaming, heavy blade. Sesto had given it to him for Christmas three years before. There would be a kind of retribution in that. But his son would never know.

Just to kill her. To wipe her out. To banish her existence from this house, from his son's life, from his life—forever.

After it was done, he would hurry back to his room. And they would find her in the morning. He would have cleaned the knife. And it would look as if the deed were done by some killer from the streets. He would open the front door. Angela could never say she had checked it. He would say she had left it unlocked, forgotten.

He opened his bedroom door and passed quietly through the darkened house in his bare feet.

He entered the front porch. Metal louvres covered the screens, and they were nearly closed, so only the faintest of light penetrated. He could see her figure outlined beneath the covers on the bed.

Hate seized him now. Urgency took over. He breathed in short little gasps, and he was sweating.

He moved over beside the bed, his mouth open for more air, and he gave her a swift thought, remembering how it had been that afternoon, and that seemed to fire the hate inside him.

He swung the knife with all his might, aiming for where the heart would be, thinking, I will cut the heart. He struck brutally. The knife went in. She gave a short gasp. He felt the twist of the heart against the blade, and savagely cut at it. Then he withdrew the knife and slammed it in again, and again, and again, and he was mad with it, a silent voice screaming in his mind, I want you, I want you, I want you—I'm killing you.

There was no further struggle from the body in the bed.

Abruptly, the porch lights came on, glaring brightly.

He whirled, dropping the knife on the cot.

"What are you doing?"

It was Angela, standing naked in the porch doorway.

He stared at her.

She looked at the bed.

He reached down and tore the bedclothes back. Sesto lay there, bathed in blood.

Perruzi gasped, cried out. He took Sesto up in his arms, but his son was dead. The job had been well done. Perruzi suddenly wept.

"Dom!" the girl shouted. "What have you done?"

Perruzi dropped his son's body back on the bed.

"You were in the bedroom," he said.

"Sesto wanted me to have the best bed," she said, speaking rapidly, her eyes wide with fright. "He didn't want you to know. Dom—Dom—did you do this for me?"

Covered with Sesto's blood, he snatched up the knife. His face was sheened with tears, twisted with a terrible anguish.

Angela screamed and turned to run as Perruzi lunged toward her.

My Husband Wanted Evil Sex with Me

May 1976

We were just four people, out camping in the Smokies. Two couples who had been friends for over a year, with two tents set up, out for fun. That's what I thought. It didn't take long to discover what Al, my husband, really meant when he'd said:

"Ginny, it'll be the best vacation possible. Frank and Laura suggested it, and I'm going to really make you happy."

It was funny, actually, because Laura and I had shared our innermost secrets all the time. We'd even told each other how our husbands were in bed, how they acted and everything.

Only I'd held something back; something that troubled me terribly about Al. It was what he kept pressing me for, kept at me about, eating at me, eating at me with scalding words that bit and hurt and shamed me. I could never tell Laura those things.

But, really, I thought everything was fine on this trip. That is until the first night in the tent, in the dark.

Oh, it had been swell around the campfire, cooking hamburgers and singing, and looking up at the blue velvet heavens, freckled with starpoints. And Frank had got off on his favorite subject about endlessness and the nothingness of space, and where the universe ended, and if it did, what was beyond, all that. He was a great science-fiction reader. And Al had oiled the .45 automatic he'd insisted on bringing along. "Just for kicks. And maybe some plinking. What's a man without a gun?"

And Frank had agreed. "But I always pack my own gun," he'd said. I didn't know what he meant at the time. I just laughed along with Laura and Al.

Laura was so sweet and such a knock-out for looks, with that thick, rich auburn hair, and the heart-shaped face with the big baby brown eyes and the pouty mouth that was naturally pink-lipped. And that body of hers; I kidded her about it. She had a shape that wouldn't quit.

She was something different from me, all right. I had to work at it, work hard, with cosmetics. I'd even studied it at a special school, so I could look nice for Al. But I had to dye my hair blonde, and it never came out right. And it wouldn't hang straight, the way I wanted when I let it grow long, so I had to try to iron it—but that didn't even always work. And I didn't have much in the way of breasts, just "nubbins" as Al called them, and my thighs were too thin; oh, how I dreamed of plump thighs, wishing, wishing. And my hips were like a boy's.

But Al loved me. I knew that.

Just the same, I was forever being embarrassed. Like back at high-school, about my funny mouth. It was shaped like an O, and no matter what I did, that shape wouldn't go away. I kept it very red with lipstick, because I'd read somewhere that you should be bold about your worst feature, the feature that troubled you most.

So many times they'd said it, back at school. "Bet you didn't get that mouth sucking coke bottles."

So many nights I'd lain awake because of those words. Staring at the darkness, withering inside, my heart hammering, praying nobody would ever say it again, because I'd never done anything wrong—and I never would.

Shame would just thrust through me, and tears would come at the very thought of those words. I always drank out of a glass, never out of a bottle. I was afraid; scared to the bottom of my being.

All because of those words, and because of what Mother had said. It was hateful. I knew it was ridiculous, but I couldn't help it. I hurt inside.

And then I married Al and he started, and it wasn't just that big fear, either—it was another fear, too. The same other fear Mother had always told me about.

I could never forget. Never.

And it started all over again the first night in the tent, when Al came to my cot in the flowing darkness, and slowly, ever so slowly, took off my pajamas and began caressing my thighs and breasts and kissing me, and murmuring those wonderful things he could say.

"Tonight's going to be different, isn't it, Ginny? Tonight, and all the nights up here in the mountains. I can just feel it, honey."

"What d'you mean, 'different'?"

And it was then that he began kissing and tonguing my nipples. He pulled the covers away, and softly, gently moved his hand between my thighs, and then he leaned and kissed my belly. And I knew he was starting again.

"No, Al—no—"

And I tried to pull his head back up. But now, for some reason, he was different. He was breathing hard and abruptly he thrust his head down and put his mouth right there.

I writhed back, gasping, and slapped at his face.

"Stop—Al!"

He didn't stop. He grabbed me by the hips, and then spread my legs and I felt his tongue. I went crazy with it, scratching and fighting him.

"Please, Al! Stop! You've got to stop!"

And he stopped. The silence was so thick you could cut it. It was like a block of ice. Black ice, with just a shaft of moonlight spraying in the tent fly, bathing his naked body, and mine, all scrunched up on the cot, shaking with fear.

"You're a bitch," he said quietly. "You're a strait-laced, blue-nosed prude."

I grabbed the blanket and yanked it up over me, shamed, embarrassed, wanting to weep with what I felt.

"What—what do you want?" I said in a weak voice.

"What do I want?" he said in that soft voice, his words like cold blades. He leaned close and hissed it. "I want an all-the-way woman, a real wife. That's what I want. Want me to spell it out? That what you want, Ginny? I want oral sex, the way other men have it with their wives. I want to do it to you and I want you to do it to me. Understand? You're nothing but a frozen mannequin, that's what you are. A dead fish, stiff and frozen. On ice. You *allow* me to do it to you, Royal George—and you freeze up even then. It's a damned chore for you. I'm fed up, fed to the damned teeth. Understand? If you can't give me what I want, I'll get it someplace else!"

"Al—please . . ."

"Stow it, fish!"

With that, he got up and stalked out of the tent, stark naked. I heard him walk away, down toward the lake.

I lay there shivering and shaking, thinking of Mother, crying softly, uncontrollably.

"They'll want to do things to you there, with their mouths, Virginia. It's vile and evil. And they'll want you to do it to them with your mouth. There's nothing more evil in the world. It's not normal. And you're just the type they'll pick on, with that funny mouth of yours, and the way you act around boys. You've got to stand up and fight for what's right, Virginia—you must never, never allow that—never, d'you hear?"

How many times had she told me that? Over and over. I could still see her pale, wrung face, and the way her tongue licked her lips, and the wild way her eyes got when she was talking about it.

"Swear it, Virginia—swear to me you'll never, never allow it, never do it!"

"I swear."

And that terrible night when my father was drunk, and I looked into their bedroom and he was on his knees, holding her head and she was . . .

Every time I thought of that, it wrung me inside; wrung me till I was filled with pain, weeping for Mother. And the next morning, after that, she hadn't been able to meet my eyes. But that night she was at me worse than ever before and she made me swear on the Bible, never, never to do it, to allow it. *Never . . .*

So I read about it, sneaking looks at books in the library on the sex shelf, frightened to death somebody would see me, and only feeling worse then, feeling terrible, frightened, because of how I felt inside, deep down. And I would dream about it, and wake up bathed in sweat, crying and shaking, with the terrible dream almost a reality, and the awful siege of wuthering terror growing up out of me.

And the kids at school, saying that about my mouth.

It was like I wore a sign.

I lay there, crying quietly, wondering what I could say to Al, and a shadow darkened the fly of the tent.

"Oh, Al—Al—please, come here!"

He chuckled, then, and I knew it wasn't Al. It was Frank, hulking there, just inside the tent.

"Frank? Where's Laura?"

"Where d'you think?"

"I don't know."

He stepped in and came over by my cot, and the moonlight sprayed in on him, covering him with blue-white mist and I saw his erect manhood, sticking out of his pants.

"Ginny," he said. "I've been thinking about you, and I can't get you out of my head. It's that mouth of yours, Ginny—"

He knelt on the cot and stroked my hair. I was frozen. I couldn't move. I couldn't speak.

"You don't have to say anything. It's Al, isn't it. He's not much for sex, is he, now. Laura's told me what you've told her. Bound to. It's not letting secrets out. He's just not much, right? Well, I can make everything fine for you. I know what you want—Laura and I both know. How could a guy miss knowing?"

"What—What do you mean?" I managed that much, somehow, shrinking away from the terrible horror that protruded toward me, the moonlight revealing it like a white spear.

He chuckled again and whispered. "Hey, now—take hold of it, Ginny, baby—bet you never got that mouth sucking on coke bottles. Right?"

How could he say it? How could he stab at the terrible part of me, baring it like he did? How could he know where I was weakest?

"You terrible, filthy animal!"

"Filthy? It's normal, Ginny—completely normal. Ask any doctor. What's the matter with you. Don't tell me I got you wrong, you little—"

I gave a cry and slapped wildly at him and sprang up and ran out of the tent. All I knew was I had to find Al. We had to leave this awful place, these wretched people. It didn't matter that I was naked, running through the night—nothing mattered.

I ran down toward the lake. And the moonlight was bright now, and I saw them, lying there, side by side in the white moonlight, both of them naked, just lying there on their backs, talking, touching. And I knew what had happened. She had done it to him and he had done it to her.

And I screamed, and turned and ran back to the tent.

Frank stood there. "What the hell's the matter with you?" he said sharply and made a grab for me.

I kicked at him and thrust him wildly, and ran into the tent and found the .45 automatic and ran out.

"Ginny!" Frank yelled. "Come back here!"

I ran down to the lake.

They were standing there now, in their nakedness.

"I'll kill her—I'll kill her," I screamed, running at them.

I heard Frank coming behind me, and Al was running up toward me.

"Ginny! Ginny, stop—you don't understand!"

I began firing the gun wildly at Laura. I was sobbing hysterically, weeping blindly, and all I could see was my mother. I was killing my mother, and I knew it. Awful sobs wracked me as I pulled and pulled the trigger of the bucking automatic and loud booms echoed across the wooded slopes of the lake and Frank had hold of me, fighting for the gun. I was killing Mother. I had to kill her. Because she'd lied to me, and she'd made my life a hell and destroyed my marriage, my entire life was gone because of her.

Then I was just lying on the ground in a huddle, with Al's arms around me. Frank had pulled the gun from my hand. He flung it down, now.

Laura ran over to him and they held hands.

"C'mon, baby," Frank said to her. "We're getting out of here—as far as possible from these two crackpots. Hope we never see you again, Ginny— and if we do, it'll be too damned soon."

Then they were gone.

There was just Al. Al and I, naked, lying there on the ground.

And Laura wasn't dead. Mother was dead. I knew she was dead, because right here, right now, something had gone out of me and I knew what it was. It had taken a purge of wild fright and fear, and it was all gone—all the horror.

I was trembling, but Al held me close.

"You'll be all right, honey. Don't worry. We were just lying there, talking. We didn't do anything. I was mad, but I'm not mad anymore. I understand, Ginny, honey. Honest, I do."

Something sweet and good came into me. I clung to him. "A thing happened, almost, with Frank, too," I said. "But it didn't happen. But you don't have to worry anymore, Al."

"What d'you mean, Ginny?"

I half-laughed, half-wept with the immense relief. The load of the world was gone from my back, and it had all happened in an instant.

"Mother's dead," I said.

"I don't understand, honey."

"You will, someday. I'll explain it all. But the way it is, Al—I'm not afraid anymore. And I'm going to prove it, right now."

He turned his head up the slope. "Look. They're taking down their tent."

"Let them." I began to laugh and hug my husband, experiencing a freedom for the first time in my life. It must have been something like that Primal Therapy everybody's talking about, digging down into the brain and setting free all the trauma of early life. "I love you, darling," I whispered. "I'm your wife, and from now on I'll do anything you ask."

He stared at me. He gave a little burp of a laugh.

"My God, Ginny. What's happened?"

"This has happened," I said, and suited the action to the word.

The Killer

early 1970s

Slowly, I opened the cabin door, not knowing what to expect this deep in the Colorado mountains. Sunlight followed me in, and I stopped short, drew a deep breath.

A voluptuous girl, completely nude, hung by her long black hair to a wooden stake in an overhead beam. For a long moment, I couldn't believe what I saw. I just stood there, staring.

Her lush white body, big breasted, long-legged, revolved back and forth, swinging on that glistening hair. The eyes were closed, the plump red lips faintly parted, the cupped hands dangling limply against her thighs. She was a beautiful girl, classic of feature, and my heart rocked.

Was she dead?

I snapped out of it, then, leaped across the sparsely furnished room, grabbed a chair. Standing on the chair, I circled the girl's hips with my arm, lifted her high, and with my other hand slipped the knotted hair from the wooden stake.

She fell across me, a dead weight. But I'd already felt the warmth of her body. If she was dead, it hadn't been long.

On the floor again, I glanced quickly about, spotted a big wooden bunk, tossed with tousled blankets. I carried her over there, and lay her down, stretched her out.

Quickly, I thrust my ear against her cushiony, big-nippled breasts, listening, my own heart hammering.

She was alive. I checked her pulse. It was like a rabbit's. Her scalp was okay, none of the thick, gorgeous jet hair had pulled out.

There was a sink and a pump. I found a basin, filled it with cool well water, snatched up a towel, and returned to the bunk. Laving water on her face and forehead, I tried not to look at that body. It was disturbing and difficult not to react, not to want, to think things. She was helpless, unconscious. I couldn't recall ever seeing such an exciting body. Even Jeanie hadn't had this much.

I swallowed, remembering. Jeanie was the reason I was here, alone, riding that Honda deep into the mountains, hoping. Inadvertently I tightened my shoulder muscles. Monda, his name was. He had taken my Jeanie, destroyed her—left her sitting in a bar over an empty whisky glass, her vacant eyes looking inward upon something she would not divulge, some unspeakable horror. She was broken, and finished, my Jeanie—a caricature of a once-beautiful woman.

I had followed Monda's trail all the way from El Paso, here and there gleaning bits and pieces of information about his evil career. I'd got a lead on him in Central City. An old whiskered miner said a man called Monda had come up this way three days before, hunting and camping.

"Oh—oh—" It was the girl.

She had just opened her eyes. She saw me, and immediately sprang backwards, hunching against the head of the bunk, her eyes wide now, with fright.

She looked as though she might scream.

"Hold it," I said. "I'm a friend."

But even those words didn't entirely calm her. She still regarded me through those wild eyes, the fear showing all through her. She clenched her hands at her breasts, just staring.

"Look. I found you strung up on a beam," I said. "Who did that trick?"

She slowly moved her head back and forth.

"How d'you feel?"

Still she did not answer. Just stared.

"Can't you believe me? Listen, my name's Mardy Blackwell. I'm up here looking for somebody. I saw the cabin, and felt tired. It's noon, and I've been riding a bike through the woods since six this morning. Thought I'd get some rest here. Nobody answered the door, but it was open. I came in—and there you were. Satisfied?"

For another moment nothing happened. Then she nodded quickly, flung herself forward, arms around my shoulders, and burst into choking sobs.

Her breasts pressed against me, and my hand was on her bare hip. The skin was smooth, silky, and warm. I let her sob for a while, then took her shoulders, held her away.

"What's your name?"

"Loraine—Loraine Desmond."

"What you doing up here?"

"He—he brought me here."

I frowned. "Who?"

"That terrible man. Monda, he calls himself. He's—"

I had her by both arms, tightly. "Did you say Monda?"

She nodded quickly. "I'm a painter. I was painting a landscape, Mr. Blackwell. Yesterday, that was. And he came by, and he's insane, I tell you. He dragged me up here, and stripped me. He just looks at me. He makes me pose for him, all sorts of vile stuff. All night it went on like that. Then, late this morning he said he wanted a better view, and he hung me up by my hair—"

"Where is he?"

"That's it. He'll be back any time now."

"Where'd he go?"

"Hunting—squirrels. To eat." She made a face. "But we've got to get out of here—"

"Call me Mardy."

"Hurry, I'll get dressed." She leaped off the bunk, and went to a pile of clothes on the floor. Quickly, she struggled into tight shorts, a pair of mocs. She picked up a thin white shirt, put one arm in the sleeve. "C'mon, Mardy," she said. "Don't just sit there."

"I'm not going anyplace," I said.

"What?"

"I'm trying to find Monda. I've found him. I'll wait for him."

She ran at me, leaned low. "You simply do not understand, Mardy. The man's insane. I mean it—he keeps laughing to himself, drinking all the time. He carries a revolver, holstered—and a shotgun. He's a giant, Mardy—huge—you never saw anything like it. And I'm not kidding, he's lost his head."

"Nevertheless—"

An explosion sounded from outside, and a load of buckshot struck the door, tearing a broad hole in it. Roaring laughter reached me, then a shouting savage voice.

"Who's in there? I'll kill you, whoever you are! This your bike?" I heard another explosion, and the sound of shot against metal.

"Quick," Loraine said. "The back door."

I was thinking perhaps she was right. I still wanted him. I was still torn inside. But I began to know I should wait for the right time.

We ran for the back entrance, and out into the narrow yard.

"The woods," I said. "Run for it."

Trees and thick undergrowth lay only a few yards away. We made it into the leafy branches, and started up a gentle slope. I could hear him back there, in the cabin.

"Wait," I said.

We paused, and I looked back through the latticework of jagged boughs. And then I saw him. Christ, she was right. He came running out the back door, carrying a shotgun, shouting, "I'll kill you both—!"

He was enormous, in a red-striped flannel shirt, and jeans and boots. He must have stood six-feet-seven. Shoulders like an ox. Chest that swelled into a barrel when he breathed. Legs like fence posts.

Now, I stand six-two, and weigh in at 210, but he had me there. I was always considered on the rugged side, but he had me there, too.

He started lumbering for the woods.

Loraine was already running again. I followed her. Her long, beautifully curved legs scissored in the patchy sunlight, and the shorts were skin tight across that grinding behind. The black hair flowed out over her shoulders and back.

The sound of the shotgun smashed the early afternoon, the echo rattling off into the surrounding hills. Shot raked leaves overhead.

I caught up to Loraine, and she paused. She was trembling as I held her.

"He'll kill us," she said. "I mean it, Mardy. He told me he was going to kill me. It's unbelievable, really—but true. He told me what he planned to do to me, and then he said he would bury me out by the well, to sweeten the water. It was awful!"

We jogged on up over the hill, and down the other side. There was a narrow gully, and the other side was thicker with trees. But we started up there.

It was heavy inside me. I couldn't let this chance get away. I wanted Monda, and I was going to get him—somehow.

We ran and waited and listened, ran and waited some more. Pretty soon, I could hear no sound from behind us.

"I'm exhausted," Loraine said.

There was a sloping declivity under a tall, thick, spreading pine. We slid down there on the slippery brown needles, and settled by the trunk of the tree.

"I think he quit," I told her.

"What are we going to do?"

"I'm going back there, after a bit. He's the man I'm looking for, Loraine."

"Are you crazy too?"

I grinned at her. She was half propped against the pine trunk, watching me. Tiny beads of sweat glistened on her upper lip and forehead. I looked into those eyes, noticing their color for the first time. A deep blue, with clear whites. They were exciting eyes. She was an exciting woman.

She rested one hand on my thigh, the fingers squeezing gently, and I watched her breasts rise and fall, the nipples perking against the thin shirt.

"He didn't really—do anything to you, then?"

"No," she said. "He was taking his time, see?"

The shorts were crimped at her crotch, and she had her thighs partially open. I could see the twin bulge, and something in me began to react against my will. I couldn't help myself.

She was watching me.

She whispered it. "I know what you're thinking, Mardy."

"Do you?"

"Yes."

"Christ, Loraine—I—"

She laid one finger across my lips, and said, "It's okay. I think I understand. I mean, I feel a little the same, I think. They say that when something bad happens, afterward, sometimes, you want sex more than ever."

"I've heard that, too."

Her hand moved to my fly, the fingers quick with the zipper, and in a second she had hold of me, working her hand.

"Feel good?"

I drew her to me, kissing her mouth. She plunged her tongue between my teeth, sucking. I dropped one hand between her thighs, then unfastened her shorts, and tried to strip them off. I was eager as hell. She arched her back, and I got her shorts off, and she lay back, her knees up, thighs wide open. The curly black hair on her crotch was thick, like moss, and glistening. She was breathing fast and hard. I opened her shirt, exposing those luscious breasts, and kissed them, chewing on a protruding nipple.

"That's all I can stand," she said. "You'd better do it to me now. I mean it—"

I was ready to explode. I fell on her, and slowly thrust it in. She gave a gasp, and arched her back, working her bottom. I had those plump pumping cheeks in my hands now, and we were trying to suck each other's tongue and screw and it was wild.

"Oh, baby," she groaned. "Give it to me—I mean, ride me down. Sock it!"

It was over with fast. We worked like fiends. I guess we both wanted appeasement, release, and once I thought of Jeanie, but that went away, because I was blind with this girl Loraine. She was something in every way.

She came with a series of wild moans and violent struggles and writhings, and we lay there, still together.

Then I began to know again what I had to do.

I rolled off, and pulled my pants up, fastened them. "I'm going back there," I said. "I've got to. You maybe won't understand, Loraine. But it's something I have to do."

"You're something, Mardy."

"So're you," I said. "But I've still got to go back."

"I'm coming too."

I shook my head. "You wait right here. I'll find you." I grinned at her. "Maybe—well, never mind."

"He'll kill you, Mardy."

"Yeah. Well, I've got to chance it."

I winked at her, and crawled up out of there, and stood up and started off through the woods, toward the cabin. There was no telling where Monda might be. He could be lurking anywhere between here and the cabin. He might jump me. I knew he was a woodsman.

But I had to go back. It drove at me. I had to do this for Jeanie. She deserved this much. She deserved plenty, but all I could give her was this.

I moved rapidly along, and there was no sign of him. One thing, I wanted to stay on this side of the cabin, if I could. The other side was a steep cliff that fell off for over three hundred feet, with a rock-strewn bottom. I couldn't run that way, if I had to run. And Monda had the firepower.

I reached the clearing.

Everything was quiet. There was no sign of him. Something thrust me on. I ran across the clearing to the rear of the cabin. Still nothing. I snaked along the side, and came around toward the front.

"Ah! There!"

He just suddenly appeared at the corner, the shotgun pointed straight at me. There was nothing to do. He looked like a mountain. I ran at him with everything I had, and dove. I caught the shotgun barrel with my right hand, and shoved just as he fired. The explosion deafened me.

"I'll kill you!" He shouted it, tearing the shotgun from my grasp. He swung it over his head, and I saw it come down. I rolled aside. If he'd hit me with that, I'd have been gone.

I didn't wait, but scrambled at him, and grabbed his legs. He beat at my back with the shotgun. I caught the barrel, and twisted with all my might. It tore from his grasp. I hurled it away, and came at him again. He kicked me in the shoulder, and I saw him snatching at the holster on his right side. He came up with a revolver, and he came firing. Two slugs puffed the dirt. He was a lousy shot. I caught his wrist, and we were face to face now, me on my knees, him glaring down, laughing at me.

"I'll kill you," he grunted. "Who are you?"

We were static like that, struggling, and I said, "I'm Jeanie's friend— from El Paso. Remember Jeanie?"

"Ah. You!"

He kicked again. But I dodged and hung onto that wrist, so he couldn't aim the revolver. I lurched to my feet and, still holding the wrist, went at him with my head butting into his gut. He fell back two steps, grunting like an animal.

I got hold of the barrel of the revolver, turned sharply, and brought his arm over my right shoulder. I came down with everything on that arm, hunching my back, and wrenched violently at his wrist. The revolver spun to the ground, and he cursed violently.

We faced each other again. I dove into him, head first, and he slammed my head away. I snagged his arm, and swung him around, and we began staggering, slugging at each other down past the cabin, and across the front yard among sparse trees.

I swung a heavy one from deep down. He had no guard. It caught him on the nose, and blood spurted. I'd felt the bone go, like chicken in wet paper. He lost his balance, the blood gushing into his mouth, and reeled backward.

I realized we were almost to the cliff.

Then he came at me like a bull.

But I was ready. He had his head down, and his arms out, and I place-kicked him in the face. For a second he was dazed. But he was thundering curses, too—clutching his head. I came at him, smashing at his shielded face. He reached out and caught hold of me and lifted me straight off the ground, whirling around, and running toward the cliffside.

He planned to dump me over.

I got my thumb in his ear, jabbed as deep as I could, and just dug at him. He screamed, and let go. We were on flat rock at the very edge of the cliff. I lay with one arm over the ledge, looking up at him.

I knew it was all over. He caught my feet, and lifted, and I slid toward that abyss. I saw the tops of pines, like black needle points, far below. And jagged rocks. He was sliding me over the edge, and there was nothing I could do.

The thunder of the explosion shattered the sound of his grunts and curses. He flung both hands up, grabbing at his side. Again the shotgun fired. Half his head went away in a spatter of bone and blood.

He took two staggering steps over me, and lurched, and fell sprawling out and down over the cliff edge. He was still alive. He screamed. But it did no good.

I lay there a minute, staring down, and I saw him strike and bounce and hit the rocks, spread-eagled.

Loraine came running up, still gripping the shotgun. "Are you all right? I had to do it. I had to. I didn't want to lose you, Mardy."

I got to my knees, and looked up at her. I looked at her, but I was seeing Jeanie. I'd done what I could. It was all right now. Then I could see Loraine again. I stood up and said, "Thanks."

"That was terrible, Mardy."

"Yeah."

She dropped the shotgun. "What do we do now?"

I didn't speak. We walked back by the cabin. He had wrecked the bike, shooting the tank full of buckshot.

"Hadn't we better report it?" she asked.

"Hell," I said. "He fell off a cliff. Some hunter accidentally shot him, and he fell. It's more than he deserves."

"Whatever you say."

I looked at her.

"Mardy?"

"Yeah?"

"Where are you going now?"

"Away. We'll have to hike it back to Central City. Then I'll just go away."

"Mardy?"

"Yeah?"

"Can I come with you?"

The way she said it, in that little voice, I knew she meant it. And it was then I knew I wanted her with me. I'd done what I came to do.

"Okay," I said. "Shall we wash up at the cabin?"

"We'll do better than that," she said.

It was good to shed the old life. There was always new life ahead. You had to meet it more than halfway.

Die Once—Die Twice

Mrs. Loretta Brady called me on the intercom. Her voice was brisk.

"William, forget about washing the cars. I want to see you immediately. It's important. Come to the house, please."

"Right."

As Loretta Brady's chauffeur, I couldn't say nay.

I swung my feet off the studio couch in the garage apartment, and stood up, stretching. I'd been going to put off washing the cars till tomorrow, anyway. Penny Brady and I had a date. And that was something I would not put off. If her mother only knew.

It was heavy, with Penny and me. How we were going to circumvent familial attitudes, I had no idea. But one thing for certain, Penny was making me forget a lot of evil, and remember that there was life to live.

I brushed my hair at the mirror above the bureau. Pure wire. The hell with it. I tucked in my shirt, and headed for the stairs; she wanted me right now, no point dressing in the damned uniform.

I crossed the stepping stones under the rose arbor, and headed for the back door. It was a big place, all gleaming white stucco, and glinting windows, turfy green lawns reaching to the Gulf sands, royal palms gesticulant in errant sunlight.

I went inside, along a glittering mahogany hall, reached the front room on the right, and cleared my throat, all the time thinking about Penny and tonight.

She would sneak out to the garage, you see?

"William?"

"Yes. You wanted something?"

"Come in and sit down, William."

I entered the long, broad room. Dim yellow sunlight shafted between heavily brocaded drapes, touching expensive furniture, thick rugs, glinting on an actual Picasso.

She was on the leather couch in front of the fieldstone fireplace. I took a chair opposite, and looked at her, and thought the usual things.

For a moment she didn't speak. Just sat there, staring at me, with those heavy eyes. In her early forties, she looked ten or more years younger. The auburn hair was thickly tumbled, the rather pale face as earnest as ever. She wore creamy hot pants, and a powder-blue sweater that was as thin as cigarette smoke. The legs were crossed, and they were slimly plump. Mrs.

Loretta Brady was a wad of sex that wouldn't quit. But, then, she couldn't come up to her daughter, Penny.

"You're not going to like me," she said. She spoke like Bette Davis, with similar inflections. The mouth that looked as if it had just tasted something bad, only enhanced the sexuality.

I didn't say anything.

"I mean it, William. I found this, the other day." She held out a flimsy-looking piece of paper. "Take it, William."

I reached across and took the paper. It was a newspaper clipping, all about how William Dexter, of L.A., private investigator, had broken a murder case the cops had shelved. I sighed. It was the one I always carried with me, the one that reminded me how I'd lost Norma. Norma had been my wife. A police car had accidentally run her down and killed her. I crumpled the clipping in my hand and stared at Loretta Brady.

"You don't have to explain it," she said. "I'm sorry about your wife. It told everything there. But, the thing is, I checked. I searched your rooms. I know all about you. Men shouldn't keep diaries."

I'd had a lot of practice about not revealing emotion. I used it now. What point blowing up? It would change nothing. I had kept the diary, it was really a journal of thoughts, in an effort to register some balance of feeling. I could read back, see how I'd felt a week ago; was I getting better? Forgetting Norma hadn't been easy. The way she died.

"Why did you quit?" Her tone was sharp.

"I'd had enough," I said. "I realized nobody gave a damn. Before that, I'd always thought people cared a little. They don't."

"You're bitter."

I sighed. "Mrs. Brady. You want me to leave, okay. But don't rub my face in it."

"I don't want you to leave, William. And please don't be so coarse. I want your services."

"I thought you had that."

"I mean, in your real work. As an investigator."

Something crowded my heart. It was a feeling of surmountable anxiety I hadn't had in some time.

"I need your help, desperately. I know you're good. Somebody plans to kidnap Penny."

I sat there. She looked at me sharply, rose suddenly and surged off across the room to a waxy-looking secretary desk. She opened the leaf, reached in, came up with something, and returned to me. The hot pants were so tight at the crotch, you could see the twin bulge. It made you want to reach out and fiddle. She stood beside me, handed me some small sheets of paper.

"Read them."

Letters clipped from newspaper print, pasted to the paper: YOUR DAUGHTER IS NOT SAFE. WE WILL TAKE HER UNLESS YOU PAY $500,000. WE WILL CONTACT YOU.

"That was the first," she said.

"Did they contact you?"

"By phone, yes. It was obviously a recording, played at a slow speed to disguise the voice. I had already contacted the police. They told me not to pay anything, agree to nothing. They said it was only a threat—"

I broke in, "That if it was real, whoever it is, they would have kidnapped Penny first?"

"That's right. So I told them when they called that I would not pay."

"But it didn't end it?"

"No. And the police do nothing. They claim they can do nothing until something actually happens."

"Why didn't you hire a regular investigator?"

"I learned about you. I know you're good. Read the others."

There were two more notes. Both promised Penny would be taken, and that after that she would be killed, unless the money was paid according to plan.

"This is all?"

"Isn't it enough?"

"Yeah. It's enough. Have you told Penny?"

"No. I didn't want to worry her."

I looked up at her, then came to my feet. "Mrs. Brady, how are your finances?"

She gave a short laugh, but the prim mouth did not change. "Beautiful, of course. You know that."

"Where's Penny?"

"In her room." She frowned, turned and took two swaying steps away, then whirled and looked at me again. "The fact is, my daughter hasn't been acting just right lately. I know something's wrong. You think they could have gotten to her, and she's not telling me?"

"No. She isn't really your daughter, is she." I made it a statement.

Her eyes widened, and she really looked hot for a moment. But she got hold of herself, as I knew she would. "Well, actually she was my second husband's child. But legally—"

"Yes," I said. "I know."

"Will you help?"

"I'll help." I had also done a thing that up to now I could not account for. Nobody knew it, but I was bonded, and my license was good in the state of Florida. Even though I hadn't intended to ever use it again. There it was. Habit. "I'd like to keep these notes. Didn't the police want them?"

"They had them. I asked for them back, when I learned of you. Wanted you to see them."

"Let me know if you hear from them again. Meanwhile, I'll continue as usual. Being a chauffeur is good cover."

"William, I am so frightened."

"You have every right to be. The cops are wrong. This thing is straight, I think. They're going to try. I've seen it before, and there's a good head behind It. I'm telling you this so you'll be careful with Penny."

The throaty voice came from the archway leading into the room. "Careful of what?"

It was Penny. Gregg Paulson was with her, very sporty looking in a white jacket and crimson slacks, flares, above gleaming boots. Neat curly blond hair, and a chin like Hairbreadth Harry's. Paulson was Loretta Brady's latest committee on the welfare of lonely widows.

"I was just telling William to drive more carefully, when you were with him. And, for goodness' sakes, he said *I* should be more careful with you, darling. It's all rather involved. Hello, Gregg."

Penny was smiling gently at me. I put the notes away, watching her. She wore skin tight denims, and a white blouse hanging out. The wealth of black hair folded around her tawny throat. Swelling, marvelous breasts thrust at that thin blouse, and I could see the hint of nipple. I glanced at her hips, and thought how I'd been there, and would be there again, and it was all worth it because Penny was for real. Just the way she looked at me, made me react.

"Well, William," Paulson said. "How's every little thing?"

"The little things are great," I said. "It's the big things that confuse."

He frowned, ignored me, and went over to Loretta Brady. He took her hand. "Drinks at the club? Right now?"

I started for the door. Penny stood in my way, looking extremely bold and sexy. She shot it at me in a whisper. "Fifteen minutes."

I winked and went out and down the hall, and back to the garage. I'd no sooner slouched on the studio couch, to re-check the notes, when there was a knock on the door, and Gregg Paulson opened it, and entered.

"Loretta tells me she's enlisted your aid in this awful matter, William."

"Yes."

He brought out a flashing gold cigarette case, selected a Turkish oval, and lit up. The smoke was acrid. "I hope you can be of help. You're not washed up, are you?"

"Washed up?"

"Because of losing your wife, like that, and all. I mean, it can affect a man. I wouldn't want somebody pretending to help Loretta, if they actually can do nothing."

I let it ride. What the hell. Maybe Loretta had the flag up. But I watched him, looking him over, re-evaluating. Maybe twenty-eight, give or take. young and very eager. Living high, too. You could tell that. But why Loretta Brady? He was one of these cream-tanned specimens that can walk off with your girl by nodding once.

"Maybe you can answer a question," I said.

He sneered, actually.

"How long have you known Loretta Brady?"

"What *is* this?"

"I need some information. If you haven't known her long, then you probably won't have it."

"Oh. I see."

"How long?"

"Over two years."

"When did Walter Brady die?"

"Two years ago."

"How?"

"Well, he'd been drinking heavily for months. Nobody knew why. He got stoned and drove off a causeway, into the bay."

"Did he drink much before—I mean before these 'months.'"

"No. He didn't. As a matter of fact, he was too bloody sober."

"And you knew Loretta then?"

"Well, we were friends."

"Now it's my turn to 'see.'"

"What d'you mean by that?"

"I'm busy, Paulson. So long."

He stood there a moment, his lips tight. I got up. He frowned, turned, and left. I had expected a big bunch of righteous fury. Nothing. A bit of a let-down.

I slumped on the studio couch again. Norma. It had all come back, and here I was, at it again. Norma had always said I'd never be anything but a detective. It was in my blood, she'd said.

I rubbed my face with one hand.

Trying not to remember. That night, that lousy night. I'd been on that case for two weeks, and she was worried because I wasn't home. She found a telephone note I'd made, phoned headquarters, and made them do a cross-reference. They did that because she was my wife, and I worked close with them. She came up with the address of this son-of-a-bitch who had killed my client. I was staked out there. I had just called the police, so I'd have back-up firepower in case. A mix-up. Norma came down there, worried, got out of the car, and started through a dark alley.

The police cruiser, traveling on orders, turned fast in and caught her dead center at the alley entrance. She was killed instantly, but badly mangled. They were awfully sorry, and paid for the funeral. Captain Larson sent masses of flowers. The cop driver, a country kid named Coy, from Butte, Montana, was later promoted to sergeant. Norma was dead.

It involved my work, the way I worked, never telling her anything, never letting her know where I was. I hadn't wanted her touched, you see. Ever. Sure. It's a nasty business, when you're hot, like I was in L.A. I had all the evil ones, it seemed, and this was a bad one. It was good-by.

I drank my way across the country, ended up in Miami, and started taking odd jobs. Louting it. One night I got lushed again, and drifted to the West Coast of Florida. I decided to pull myself together. Norma was still there; she would always be there. And I would never work at my job again. But I'd been feeling sick for months. I was tired of that, too. So I sobered up, landed the chauffeur spot with Loretta Brady.

And now there was Penny. Another mix-up.

I didn't have any family. Nobody. Once I'd had Norma. I couldn't get off it, sometimes.

But could I hope about Penny?

Only this lousy kidnap thing was for real. I knew that, all right. Well, get with it, Dexter, baby.

I reached for the phone, on a hunch, and called the First National Beach Bank. I knew where Loretta Brady kept her loaded stocking. I'd driven her there often enough.

"Hello, there. This is Acme Credit. Zachary Symons—have I talked with you before?"

"I'm Peggy Dedrek. I don't believe—"

"Maybe it was somebody else. We work with you so often, I can never be sure who it is. You should always answer." I gave her Loretta Brady's address and name. "I need a fast run-down on her savings and checking, both. Will you make that for me, sweet? I'd come in personally, but this is purely rush-rush."

"Acme, did you say?"

Was she going to be one of those?

"Yes, darling. Symons—Zachary."

Acme was well-known. She could make it easy, or difficult.

I put on a little squeeze. "This Loretta Brady thing is strictly hush, honey. But we've simply got to have it, and right now—this very minute."

"All right, Mr. Symons." She gave a tiny laugh. "A second."

I waited. I checked my watch. Penny was overdue. She'd said, "Fifteen minutes." If she walked in now, I'd have to cover.

She did. I'd no sooner thought it, than the door fell open, and there she was. She closed the door and came toward me in those skin-tight denims, unbuttoning the fly as she moved. She stood in front of me, and slowly unfastened the white blouse, slipped it off. She was nude underneath, and her big lush breasts stuck out at me, the nipples large, rosy, and erect. She ran her tongue across her lips, smiling, and opened the denims. More nakedness. She peeled them off, and I stared at her crotch, that unbelievable mass of shiny-looking black hair.

She knelt by my knees, reached across and unzipped my fly, then took hold of me. She looked up at me slyly, working her hand lazily, caressing, then she wriggled closer, her breasts pressing against my legs, and lowered her head, and kissed me. Then she was working with her hot moist mouth. There was nothing that would ever stop Penny. She had to prove she meant what she'd said about loving me. She was always trying to show me she meant it. I ran my fingers through that thick mass of black hair as she slowly, excruciatingly, worked away.

"Mr. Symons?'

"Yes?"

"Since it's Acme, we'll do it. On that account, savings. It's $14,000. Checking is $3,085. Will that help?"

"Immensely," I said, wanting to groan aloud, the way Penny was wriggling, and bent over me.

"Zachary Symons, you said?" She was making herself inviting, now.

"Yes."

"Well, don't forget, it's Peggy Dedrek, then."

I couldn't stand It. I muttered something, which was half a gasp, and hung up. $14,000 wasn't enough, not by one hell of a long shot. Loretta Brady was practically broke.

"I'm through," I said to Penny, and she lifted her head, and winked at me, her lips wetly parted.

I sprawled on the floor, and she crept around and went at it again. Her thighs were open, and I had to get it in. I thrust her head away, and leaned down and kissed her breasts, sucking on a nipple, one hand caressing her crotch. She began to moan, and arch her back. "Screw me, William—hurry!"

She lay that way, with her knees up, legs wide open. I climbed on, and she took hold of me, and I slipped it in. Everything went out of my head then. She began slowly working that plump behind, leering up at me. Then, suddenly, she gave a little cry, and said, "Do it fast! Harder! Please—" And I socked it to her. She didn't back up. She met every jab, grunting little grunts, and I had a tight grip on both cheeks, ramming it home.

She started to gasp again, giving little cries, working with her back arched right off the floor. She couldn't get enough. Her eyes were clenched tight, her mouth open, with just the tip of her tongue showing.

"Now!" she said fiercely. "Now!"

I gave her everything I had and came all the way down my backbone, from the back of my skull, like a streak of white fire, and into her. She came at the same time, and it was a wild moment.

"Oh, my God," she said, holding me tightly with her thighs and her arms. "I never, never had anything like that. Not even in high school."

"You're sort of special yourself," I told her.

We lay there, still locked. I didn't want to draw away, and I could still feel her move, squeezing every ounce of pleasure.

"Who was that on the phone?"

"I was ordering some shirts. All out. I mean, they're wearing out, you see?"

But right now, when I should have felt lazy, my brain was working fast. It was a hunch, a crazy hunch, but I had to get on the phone again. I didn't know what they could come up with after two years, but I was willing to bet about Paulson and Loretta.

"You're thinking," Penny said. "At a time like this."

I didn't say anything, just nuzzled her throat, thinking. It was so neat. So very neat. There was a lot of checking to do. And nothing to go on, absolutely nothing. Just a hunch.

"Penny?"

"Yes?"

"How well does Gregg Paulson know your mother? I want you to level with me. It's important."

She stared at me, still gripping me with her thighs.

"Well—"

"The truth, Penny."

"They do it all the time. Like a couple of fiends. I saw them twice, from the balcony. In her room. There's a picture window, and the drapes weren't drawn. It's been going on for some time."

"Does your mother like you?"

"She hates me, and she's always shown it. Till just lately."

"Did she love your father?"

Penny slowly moved her head from side to side. "No. She didn't. She wanted his money. He never knew it, till later on—then he began drinking. Only, only those last few days, he acted funny—as though it wasn't really the drinking. He had dizzy spells."

"He leave her a lot of money?"

"Enough, you know. But—she's spent it all, with Gregg. I don't know what she'll do. She's desperate, I can tell. He's the type needs money, you see? He's always at her. For trips to Europe, new cars, everything. She keeps him. I know about them. I've snuck up and listened to them. Daddy left me most of his money. It's a trust fund, but when I'm twenty-five, it's all mine. Over a million. I'm twenty-three now. Of course, if I ever died, it goes to Loretta—"

I came to my knees fast.

It was then the door opened again, and Gregg Paulson stepped into the room. He held a revolver in one hand. Loretta Brady was right behind him.

"So," he said. "Of course, we knew. And now you've had your last party. We were going to wait, you see. But I dig you, Dexter. We thought you were just a momentarily reformed lush, that it'd be simple. It will be simple, but you're trying to work the whole course, aren't you? That's why we had to act now."

"Riddles," I said. I slowly picked up my pants, and slipped them on.

"Get dressed, Penny," Loretta Brady said. She did not look in the least shocked.

Penny stared at her mother. But she dressed, and we both stood there, waiting.

"All right," Paulson said. "Downstairs. And don't think about looking for your gun, Dexter. This is your gun. Loretta picked it up when she searched your room."

We came slowly down the stairs. Paulson made us get into the Cadillac. Loretta Brady drove, looking quite austere. We whisked along Gulf Boulevard about ten miles, not speaking, and parked behind a duplex that was surrounded by thick green pines.

"Inside," Paulson said.

We went inside. I was beginning to catch on, but I didn't exactly know their next move. All I did know was that I'd been right in what I'd figured.

We were in a rumpled living room.

The gun was steady, Paulson's voice low. "This place is rented under your name, Dexter. You're all broken up because of your wife's death, how it happened. You're a drunk—please notice the booze?"

There were half empty bottles everywhere.

"Loretta will attest to the fact you were missing from the garage apartment for days at a time. She'll say she forgave you, because you seemed basically honest. Then she found the clipping from the L.A. paper, about your work, your wife's death. And these kidnap notes were coming to the house—"

"What kidnap notes?" It was Penny.

"Shut it, child," Paulson said grimly. "You'll know soon enough. Loretta will be believed. Since the police did nothing, she decided to employ you. Maybe *you* could get a line on whoever said they'd kidnap Penny."

Penny gasped, clung to my hand.

"The police won't check Loretta's bank account, like you did, Dexter. We caught you on an extension. You see, what we'll tell them is that it all blew up in your face. You had to act. You couldn't very well catch yourself in your own kidnaping. Yet, you couldn't refuse Loretta wanting to hire you. We saw you take Penny in the car, with this gun. We tried to stop you, but you stopped us. You brought us all here. You had lost out on everything, and you were desperate. You planned to kill us, because we knew."

"What'll we do?" Penny's voice was a whisper.

Paulson said, "Trouble is, during a tussle, when I jumped you— bravely—I got your gun and shot you."

"What about Penny?" My voice was hollow.

Paulson's grin was evil. He shrugged. "After all, Dexter—Penny has that trust fund which reverts to Loretta at her death. What else can we do?"

I just watched him.

"Sure, baby. But we've got to live right. And there's no love lost. Penny isn't Loretta's daughter. We were going to wait till tonight. But the way you moved on that bank, we knew you were for real. We had to act. You shoot Penny, and I get the gun, and kill you." He paused. "Dexter—the newspaper the kidnap notes were cut from, the scissors, the glue pot—they're all here. You planned to clean up, just leave us here, dead—but I didn't study judo for nothing."

He was ready. I could tell the way Loretta acted. She partially turned away, and he steadied the gun, face pale, now. I saw his finger squeeze.

Penny screamed my name, swung around in front of me, clung to me as Paulson fired. I felt her slump. Still trying to prove things.

Penny fell to the floor. I went at him headfirst, crazy inside. He fired again and something socked me in the right shoulder. It didn't stop me. I made a savage grab, caught the gun barrel, twisted it viciously.

Paulson muttered something, brought his knee up. I crouched and caught him around the thighs, lifting. I still gripped the gun barrel. I threw him heavily, twisting, and the gun tore from his hand.

He was fast. He struck on his side. I tried to take aim, never made it. He came at me on springs. All I could think sickeningly was Penny. From the corner of my eye, I glimpsed her lying on the floor. Loretta Brady just stood there.

Paulson leaped, struck me sideways with his whole body. He grabbed for my neck as we sprawled to the floor. I got my elbow in his groin. He backed away, rolling.

"The gun. Loretta! The gun!" He yelled it.

I half saw her scramble for the revolver. We had each other's upper arms, working to our feet, fighting every inch of the way. He was strong as hell.

"Gregg—out of the way!"

That was Loretta.

Paulson lurched violently aside. But I nailed his right wrist, whipped him back just as she fired over my shoulder.

She fired twice, missed me. The explosions blew my ears. With the second shot, I saw her. She was like stone, scared. The first slug caught Paulson in the face, just below the nose. It tore a bloody hole. The other shot went wild.

She stared at him as he crumpled. "Gregg," she whispered. "Oh—Gregg . . ."

I went over and took the gun from her hand.

Then I knelt beside Penny. She was still alive, but I could tell by the flutter of pulse in her throat that she wouldn't make it.

"William," she said weakly. "William, will we—?"

That was all.

She was gone. I let her head down slowly, closed her eyes.

I remembered how it had been with Norma. Now there were two deaths, because Penny, in her own way, had cared. We might have made something of that.

Two deaths on me.

"What are you going to do?" Loretta Brady asked.

Bette Davis again. Prepared to bargain.

There were no bargains in this life. Not ever. I went over to the phone, dialed the operator, and asked for the Police Building.

Pillow Face [incomplete]

late 1970s

The surviving manuscript of this story gives its length as approximately 1500 words, but the manuscript ends at the bottom of page six after 1012 words. Brewer, who was usually paid by the word for his stories, customarily overestimated their length, but not to such a degree. For example, there are two other stories in this collection whose manuscripts state that they are about 1500 words long: "Friendly Persuasion," which is actually 1399 words long, and "Lover (II)," which is actually 1452 words. It seems likely, therefore, that "Pillow Face" is missing at least two manuscript pages.

It was just too much, that was all.

Amelia was excellent in bed, and she had many other proclivities that were enhancing. His libido soared alarmingly at the very thought of her. He had been seeing a lot of her, dodging his wife Louisa. Lunches in out of the way places when he was supposed to be working overtime at Pitkins Plastics. But the fact remained that Louisa was suspicious. She revealed it in many different ways, regarding him with that peculiar scowl. Oh, she had alluded to nothing. It was that tiny look, the quiet look, the burnt toast, the lengthy silences, the perfunctory peck on the cheek and the frown as he left in the morning. And, worst of all, she had taken to covering her face with a pillow when they were performing calisthenics in bed.

Not that she reneged in bed. She was as eager as ever.

But that pillow. It was disconcerting.

James Armatage had a problem.

He did not want to give up Amelia, yet he knew he had to. It was only a matter of time when Louisa would surely catch on. Amelia wore an enchanting perfume called *Take Me*. And James Armatage had to spray himself with lighter fluid before he went home.

"You positively reek!"

"I spilled some lighter fluid."

"Well, can't you be careful?"

"I am careful. It just squirted out, that's all."

"Why don't you get one of these butane lighters?"

"That's an idea."

"I'll get you one."

"Well—I'm rather partial to the one you gave me."

"Throw it away, you fool. You spill everything."

It was that evening that he knew he had to rid himself of Amelia. True, she was in his blood, but that did not matter. In his way, he loved Louisa, and to top it off, she was pregnant. And this, in itself, made him a family man.

He dearly wanted to be a family man.

This evening, Louisa was seated in his chair, knitting booties.

"The girls are giving me a shower next Thursday."

"I thought you didn't have a shower till after the baby came."

"Well, it's not true. And the baby can come any time."

"Wow."

She regarded him above her knitting, her smile enigmatic.

"I have to make a phone call."

"Well, go ahead." Her needles clicked. "You have to ask me to make a phone call?"

"No."

"Well, then."

"I'll take it in the study."

"You might change your jacket. I can still smell that lighter fluid. Did you spill it again?"

"Yes. Couldn't help it. It simply squirts."

"I've got my bags all packed for the hospital."

"Fine."

He stood up and walked into the study, a small room, lined with books, a small desk. He locked the door. He picked up the phone.

"Amelia?"

"Yes."

"I've something to say."

"I just ache," she said. "I ache all over."

"Are you ill?"

"No, you foolish stud. I ache for you."

He hesitated. "Well, that's what I wanted to talk about."

"My aches?"

"In a way."

"Well, that's fine. When're you coming over."

"I'm not."

"You're not."

"No, Amelia. It's all finished. I won't be able to see you again. Something's come up. Oh, I may as well tell you. Louisa's going to have a baby. This puts a stop to our seeing each other. I couldn't possibly desert her now."

Silence.

Breathing on the other end.

Sudden laughter.

He said, "Why are you laughing?"

"It's funny, that's all. You and me. Together all this time. What we've got. Our plans."

"But that shouldn't make you laugh."

"It does, though."

"Don't you feel bad?"

"I'm pouting."

"Should I come over—see you—try to explain."

"No. You've explained enough already. I know your type. Fickle. You can't stand by your guns. But, James, I've got a surprise for you."

He knew enough that when a woman such as Amelia said she had a surprise for him it was time to watch out.

"What sort of surprise."

"That would be telling."

"Louisa's all packed for the hospital. Don't you see? It could happen any time."

"Is she big—I mean in the tummy."

"Not very. She doesn't show much. One of those."

"Oh."

"I'm sorry, Amelia. We've had it good."

"You telling me."

"I hate to say goodbye this way."

"I should think you would. Calling me so abruptly, and telling me such disturbing things. I thought you were going to get a divorce."

He bit his lip. "It just can't be. Don't you see. Can't we take this like a man and a woman, an intelligent man and woman?"

"I'm intelligent. Are you?"

"Are you mad?"

Silence again.

"I told you I had a surprise," she said.

"What is it. Come on, now."

"You'll find out." There was a click on the other end of the line, and she hung up.

He thought of calling her back, but decided against it.

He unlocked the study door, clanged into the living room, and saw that Louisa wasn't there. Her knitting lay on the chair.

She had gone to bed, he knew. She went to bed early these days.

He went into the kitchen and mixed himself a stiff bourbon, and drank it, leaning against the sink. Then he wandered into the living room, with another drink, and put on some records. He played them softly, listening in his armchair after placing the knitting things on the end table.

After about half an hour of that, he decided to go up to bed. Louisa would be asleep, he knew, and that's what he wanted. Amelia was too much on his mind.

He turned off the lights, locked the door, and slowly climbed the stairs to the master bedroom. He opened the door, and what met his eyes surprised him.

Louisa was lying stark naked on the king-sized bed, with a pillow over her face.

"That you?" she mumbled, her voice muffled by the pillow.

She was caressing herself.

"Hurry up," she said. "I can't wait. And the doctor said it's all right."